"I can't believe yo[u] nondisclosure just to avoid a lawsuit, Tony."

Undaunted, Kate went on. "That error was intentionally concealed. And not a single person has apologized."

Tony felt his temper begin to simmer. She couldn't be accusing him of unethical behavior, could she?

"I'm not trying to avoid a lawsuit and I resent that you're even suggesting I am. What I'm saying is that you're overstepping hospital boundaries...."

"I'm not laying blame here, Tony. All I'm saying is that when a mistake has been made an apology is in order."

The frustration he was feeling pushed him over the edge. "For God's sake, Kate, stop being a bleeding heart and get practical about your job or you'll lose it," he thundered.

She looked up at him with huge, wounded eyes. "Are you threatening me, Dr. O'Connor?"

"Of course I'm not," he growled. "We're simply having a discussion."

"No, we aren't. We're having a fight."

The pain in her voice made him ashamed of himself, but this had gone way too far for him to back down now. "I'm sorry, Kate, but the fact is I think you're wrong."

Dear Reader,

Families! We love them, but there are times they make us crazy. What always intrigues me about families is the myriad ways they force us to grow, to adapt, to reluctantly accept traits in them that we'd reject in acquaintances. Family members have the capacity to push all our buttons, to make us question our belief systems, reevaluate our boundaries. If life is a school, maybe they're our best teachers.

Always, I learn from each book I write. It's as if the people I create are actually *my* teachers, saying with a smile, "C'mon, Bobby, you've avoided looking at this part of your personality. It's time you took a peek, uncomfortable as it might be." This book taught me a lot about anger, and forgiveness, and the unlimited number of ways there are to live a life. I hope it makes you laugh—and maybe cry a little, the way it did me.

Thank you, readers, for trusting me enough to take you on another journey from beginning to end.

With my love and gratitude,

Bobby

The Family Doctor
Bobby Hutchinson

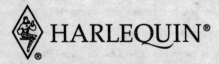

HARLEQUIN®

TORONTO • NEW YORK • LONDON
AMSTERDAM • PARIS • SYDNEY • HAMBURG
STOCKHOLM • ATHENS • TOKYO • MILAN • MADRID
PRAGUE • WARSAW • BUDAPEST • AUCKLAND

ISBN 0-373-71051-8

THE FAMILY DOCTOR

This book is for Patricia Gibson,
dear wise friend and mentor, who teaches by example
that for every problem there is a solution, and we get there
by giving up blame. For your constant encouragement
and assistance, I am humbly grateful.

Thank you to a charming young lady, McKensy Balch, for the use of her beautiful name.

CHAPTER ONE

Dr. Antony O'Connor's mother was making him crazy.

The shouting match they'd had before he left the house this morning was also making him late for the 7:00 a.m. meeting of the ethics committee, which was embarrassing because he was the one who'd insisted the committee convene at that early hour. Tony had only been chief of staff for four months, and punctuality was something he prided himself on.

The meeting was being held in the main boardroom at St. Joseph's Medical Center, just off the lobby. He jogged in from the parking lot, squinting irritably in the glare of the rising sun. He ignored the softness of the June morning, and he was oblivious to the slight breeze that carried the salt tang of the sea up from Vancouver's inner harbor. Shouldering his way through the revolving doors he hit the lobby at full, impatient stride.

"Morning, Doctor. Nice day, huh?"

The cheerful greeting came from his left, and he turned in mid stride to see who it was. The leather sole of his right loafer hit something slippery on the linoleum and he stumbled. Flailing wildly, he twisted to catch his balance, and felt his ankle turn painfully in the instant before he hit the floor. Instinct from years of playing rugby made him break the fall with his shoulder, but the wind was knocked out of him. For a dazed and breathless moment he lay prone, watching assorted feet rush toward him.

"Hey, Doc, you okay?" The news vendor from the lobby kiosk, in peacock blue trainers, was the first on the scene. Tony could hear exclamations of alarm from the elderly volunteers behind a nearby desk, and he sensed the beginnings of a general stampede.

To avoid it, he rolled to one side, got up on his knees, then pushed smoothly to his feet, ignoring the bolt of red-hot pain that shot from his ankle to his groin. On the floor was the foil candy wrapper he'd slipped on. He bent and picked it up, swearing under his breath, and shoved it into his jacket pocket.

"I'm fine, I'm fine," he assured two nurses and a clerk who'd joined the kiosk attendant. "Twisted my ankle a bit, nothing serious."

Before anyone could dispute that, he brushed off his trousers and straightened his jacket, and in spite of the pain that streaked through his leg and made him catch his breath, he headed down the corridor.

St. Joe's ER was having a memorable morning, and triage nurse Leslie Yates was doing her personal best to sort out sufferers in the order in which they needed treatment when the admitting clerk called, "Les, line three's for you. I think it's your mother."

She hurried to the desk and snatched the phone. "Hi, Mom, thanks for calling back. Listen, I won't be able to break off at noon to take you to your doctor's appointment. You'll have to call a cab. You wouldn't believe the scene down here this morning. Think Shriners convention and food poisoning. Yeah, I will. You, too. Talk to you later, Mom. Bye."

As Leslie hung up, she glanced around and shook her head in utter amazement. It was barely nine in the morning, and the place resembled a war zone. Stretchers were lined up, every cubicle and examining room was filled, and men with urgent, utter desperation etched on their faces stood in front of every bathroom.

Sounds of retching and moaning filled the air, and the putrid odors of feces and vomit hung over the area like a pall. Nurses trying to get the attention of overworked ER doctors raised their voices as they hurried from one bed to another, keeping a wary eye out for puddles on the floor.

"Bed four has a pacemaker and he's hyperventilating."

"Did you get the antiemetic into seven?"

"Where are the commodes we asked Geriatrics for? Marvin, get on to Housekeeping and tell them we're frantic down here, they have to send more staff to clean up this mess. Oh, and, Marvin, try the rehab ward again. They must have commodes we could use.''

Technicians drawing blood cultures and taking stool samples bumped into one another as they hurried from one sufferer to the next while doctors searched for veins and nurses hung more and more IVs of Ringer's Lactate.

As if elderly Shriners with gastroenteritis weren't enough, the ER *would* have to be short staffed. It was late June, and many of the medical staff were already on holiday, while others had succumbed to a particularly vicious strain of bronchial flu currently doing the rounds.

Leslie questioned still another suffering Shriner who'd attended the annual banquet the day before, filling in information as she listened carefully to the all-too-familiar recounting of symptoms. She slotted him in the lineup for treatment. It was days like this, she muttered under her breath, that reminded her she was fifty-three years old, twenty-two pounds overweight, and had bunions.

''Excuse me, nurse? Leslie? Leslie, I need an X ray on this ankle, and I need it immediately.''

The imperious and irritable male voice got Leslie's full attention because it belonged to Dr. Antony O'Connor, St. Joe's chief of staff.

Leslie usually saw his tall, vigorous figure striding down hallways, vanishing into some meeting room or another. She knew him well enough to exchange a polite good-morning, and she'd attended staff meetings where he was present, but she certainly wasn't on intimate terms with him.

Not that she and her friend Kate Lewis hadn't wickedly speculated about O'Connor and intimacy. Leslie surmised there wasn't a red-blooded heterosexual female at St. Joe's who hadn't had lascivious thoughts about Tony O'Connor. Physically, at least, he was a prime specimen.

This morning, however, he wasn't looking as hunky as usual. He was seated in a wheelchair in her admitting area, one hugely swollen bare ankle propped high on the chair's footrest, with a good six inches of well-shaped hairy calf peeking out from under the cuff of his gray trousers.

The volunteer pushing O'Connor was an elderly man named Harold, whom Leslie knew well. Harold rolled his rheumy eyes at the ceiling and made a face, warning Leslie that his passenger wasn't in the best of moods.

Maintaining the same tranquil expression she'd perfected from seventeen years of dealing with every variety of calamity the universe could devise, Leslie hurried over to the wheelchair, but her serenity was a facade. All the ER needed this morning to top the utter chaos was this—St. Joe's chief of staff requiring medical attention.

"What's happened to you, Tony?" She was

pleased that her voice didn't betray any of her inner tumult.

"Fractured ankle—I'd think that was pretty obvious," he snapped in a querulous tone, jabbing a finger in the direction of his swollen foot. "Call the radiologist. I need an X ray just to confirm that the damn thing's broken. And then get hold of Jensen—he'll deal with it from there."

Leslie's heart sank. She knew from long and painful experience that a doctor with an injury was like a bear with a sore tooth—unreasonable, irascible, impossible to deal with and ready to maul the first person in his path.

"First let's get you into an examining room." Which, Leslie knew, would take a miracle. All the examining rooms were overflowing with vomiting Shriners. But at that moment an orderly whisked a stretcher out of number three, and Leslie breathed a prayer of thanks and hurriedly wheeled O'Connor in. The room stank, so she located a can of air freshener and sprayed it around in liberal doses.

He made a disgusted sound, but she ignored it. In her books, freshener was preferable to the alternative.

"Now, what happened exactly?" Leslie put the can down and poised her pen above a clipboard. Usually this information was taken by a clerk, but she didn't have to glance in that direction to know that a long line of moaning Shriners and a few poor unfortunate walk-ins were waiting for the harassed clerks to get to them. It wouldn't do at all to send O'Connor over to sit in line and wait his turn.

"How did the accident occur, Tony?"

"Candy wrapper," O'Connor growled, his face flushing. "I slipped on the foil from a stupid roll of candies. Damn thing was on the floor in the lobby. What's with the cleaning staff, leaving junk like that lying around?"

"You slipped on a candy wrapper?" She was simply confirming information, but he glared at her from angry brown eyes as if she'd said something insulting.

"Yes, nurse, as ridiculous as it sounds, that's exactly what I did." His tone was not only sarcastic but strident. "And now I'd appreciate it if you'd call the radiologist immediately. I have another meeting, which I'm already late for."

Leslie struggled with the impulse, developed over her years as a triage nurse, to inform O'Connor that bullying would get him nowhere, and he was going to have to wait his turn. Good sense overcame impetuosity, however, as she reminded herself that this guy was the Big Kahuna, and she and her mother enjoyed living well on what Leslie earned at St. Joe's.

She knew that Antony O'Connor had been chief of staff for only four months. Leslie had seen him around before that, of course; he had a busy family practice and admitting privileges at St. Joe's.

During these last four months, however, he'd established a formidable reputation. The general consensus was that he was meticulous, impatient, critical of anything he deemed unnecessary, and willing to go to extreme lengths to correct whatever he saw as a waste of the medical center's time and money. It was rumored that his iron fist bore no sign of a velvet glove. He had energy to burn and had maintained a busy general practice after his appointment as chief, seeing his patients in the afternoon and spending his mornings at St. Joe's. Leslie knew he had a great rep as a GP. She didn't know him well enough to guess whether or not he had a sense of humor, though. She suspected not.

The wisest thing she could do, she decided, was to summon one of the doctors and let him or her deal with O'Connor.

After she finished this damned medical history. Pen poised over the clipboard, she began again.

"Have you been a patient here before, Tony?"

"Of course not." His tone was beyond edgy. "You know who I am, Leslie. Surely you'd know if I'd been seen in Emerg."

"Not necessarily." She didn't exactly spend twenty-four hours a day here. Although this morning it felt as if she had already, and she was only three hours into her shift.

"Age?"

"Forty-three."

"What medications are you on?"

"None. Well, I did take four Tylenol to ease the pain after I did this, but nothing on a regular basis."

"And what time did the accident occur?"

"Seven-fifteen. I was on my way to an early meeting."

It was now nine-thirty. The time lapse accounted for the extreme swelling evident in his ankle.

"So you walked on it right away?"

"Yeah, of course I did. It didn't get really painful and start swelling until afterward."

"You didn't try icing it?"

"There wasn't ice available."

Leslie thought that was a crock, but she didn't say so.

"Allergies?"

"Eggs. Look, is this really necessary? All this stuff is on record with the hospital already."

"In your personnel file, perhaps, but not here in Emerg." She kept her voice impersonal. "Next of kin?"

"Next of kin? I've got a broken ankle, not a broken neck. Damn it all, this is ridiculous." His brow furrowed and the flash of temper that darkened his thick-lashed eyes might have cowed a younger, less confident nurse. At her age, Leslie wasn't about to let him intimidate her. She'd seen it all, and she'd learned how best to deal with irate patients.

He glanced at her and recognized relentless determination. His tone took on a pleading note.

"Leslie, I've got a sore ankle, for cripes' sake. Next of kin isn't relevant. This is a total waste of time, in my opinion."

"I'm sorry you feel that way, but it's standard procedure." She wanted to remind him of his own insistence on procedure, but she bit her tongue and added, "We find this the fastest and most beneficial way to proceed. Now, next of kin would be…?"

His lips thinned and he scowled. "My mother, Dorothy O'Connor." In an exasperated tone he rhymed off address and phone number before she could ask, and as quickly as she could, Leslie finished the rest of the questions on the form.

"I'll send Alf right in."

She closed the examining room door gently behind her, took a deep breath before she remembered about the stench, and hurried over to Alf Jensen, who was treating a Shriner who'd gone into defib.

"We got trouble," she said in a low voice.

"You're telling me." Jensen applied the paddles and everyone stood back. When the monitor registered a heartbeat and the patient was stable, he sighed and turned to Leslie. "What's up?"

"Chief of staff's in three, suspected fracture of the ankle. He's mad as a hornet and wants an X ray stat."

"He'll have to wait his turn. There's only me and Sorenson and those new med students who don't know their ass from a hole in the ground." Jensen was noted for his colorful vocabulary. "And most of these Shriners are a hell of a lot worse off than somebody with a sore ankle.''

''I know, but he's the chief of staff, and he's not in a waiting mood. Can you go in and have a word with him? Please?''

With a short expletive, Jensen jogged over to three.

An aide pushing a gurney said, ''The patient rep is looking for you, Leslie. She's over there at admitting.''

Leslie saw Kate and waved a hand, conscious all of a sudden of the nasty stains on her green scrub suit and the fact that her hair was escaping from the clip on the back of her head. As always, Kate was perfectly groomed, her mass of auburn hair gleaming, a sky-blue summer shirtwaist skimming a slender but curvaceous body.

Kate's eyes, green as new summer leaves, took in the chaos. ''Wow, looks like you're having a busy morning down here.''

''Whatever gave you that idea?'' Leslie grinned. Despite the difference in their ages—Kate was a mere thirty-six—and the fact that Leslie would kill for such cheekbones and long legs, they'd become friends.

Six months before, Kate had been an enormous help with a problem Leslie had had with one of the ER staff, another nurse who Leslie was sure was drinking on the job. During the meetings that Kate had set up to resolve the difficulty, it became obvious that she was an expert at conflict resolution. Leslie had discovered that she and Kate had the same irreverent sense of humor. They were both divorced, though neither lived alone. Kate had her stepdaughter, Eliza, and Leslie had her mother, Galina.

"Phew, what a stench." Kate wrinkled her nose at the smell that no amount of air freshener could disguise. "I thought you might have time for coffee, Les, but it looks like you're swamped. Give me a call when it slows down and you can get away for a minute. I want to talk to you about a patient who was treated in Emerg last week."

"I'll buzz you when it happens. Right now we're up to our hips in alligators. Shriners with food poisoning and—" Leslie lowered her voice "—the chief in with what he insists is a fractured ankle. Slipped on a candy wrapper in the lobby, no less. Bet the cleaning staff are gonna get reamed out for that one."

"Tony O'Connor?" Kate's eyebrows arched, and her green eyes widened. Leslie knew that Kate had had her problems with O'Connor.

"The very one," Leslie confirmed.

Kate pursed her lips and gave a silent whistle as she glanced around at the loaded stretchers. "Lousy timing."

"You got that right."

"Did you get him to take his clothes off?" Kate asked in a whisper.

"Damn." Leslie snapped her fingers. "I knew I forgot something. What was I thinking?"

"You weren't thinking of me, that's for sure. The laughter dancing in Kate's eyes made Leslie smile. "How many times have I told you I'd like to know what's really under those Italian suits?"

"And how many times have I told *you* to just walk up to him and make a formal request?"

Kate grinned and shook her head. "Tempting, but I'm chicken."

"Rubbish. You're the bravest woman I know." Leslie wasn't joking about that. Where her job was concerned, Kate constantly and willingly put herself into the midst of conflicts that would have made Leslie run fast and far. "I've always thought you and Tony would make a striking couple."

Kate laughed. "I hope it wouldn't get to the striking stage, but you never know."

They were giggling when a clerk came hurrying over. "Leslie, paramedics are arriving with an MVA, ETA seven minutes."

"It's been such a quiet morning, it'll be nice to see some action for a change." Leslie rolled her eyes and waved a hand at Kate as she hurried off.

CHAPTER TWO

KATE LEFT EMERG AND HEADED back to her cub-
byhole of an office on the second floor, thinking
about Tony O'Connor and his injured ankle. She
hated to admit it, even to herself, but she found it
difficult to feel any real sympathy for the man, and
her lack of compassion embarrassed her. She'd
been a nurse before she became an administrator,
and she never wanted to lose her empathy for anyone in pain, be it emotional or physical.

As patient rep, her job involved the resolution of
conflict—she was the bridge between the system
and the individual. She dealt with anger every day,
she even gave seminars on anger management, and
still she couldn't entirely resolve the ambivalent
feelings she had toward O'Connor.

One of his first campaigns when he came to St.
Joe's last February was to try to do away with her
position. She understood that budget cuts by the
government were at the root of his reasoning, but
he'd been unsupportive in the extreme, suggesting
that having an employee whose sole function was
to resolve patient and staff problems was both friv-
olous and unnecessary. Her salary was a waste of

money, he declared openly at one meeting where she was present.

Fortunately, she had powerful support on the hospital board as a result of a dispute she'd resolved just before Christmas that had saved St. Joseph's from what might have become a lengthy and expensive lawsuit.

When he learned of it, O'Connor had grudgingly withdrawn his objections to her position. He no longer actively opposed her, but neither had she felt any positive support from him.

At the time, she'd felt betrayed and deeply angry. She'd tried to let it go, but it was there, just under the surface, whenever she was around him, which was often. She saw him regularly at staff meetings, and they were on several committees together. It had been necessary many times to meet with him and discuss various concerns that had been brought to her attention involving patients and staff. Although he'd always been fair, he'd certainly never gone out of his way to be understanding, and she resented him for it.

Why, then, was she so powerfully, physically aware of the damned man? Sometimes he had a way of looking at her from those unreadable brown eyes, as if there was no one but the two of them in the room. She was all too conscious of the graceful, athletic way he moved, and she'd noticed that his unruly dark hair curled a little above his collar, and his hands were big and muscular.

It was such a waste. In Kate's opinion, Tony O'Connor had been richly blessed with compelling good looks, and he'd gone and sabotaged the package with a personality that could only be described as unsympathetic. Offputting, she amended. Downright objectionable? Yup, at times he could be a proper pain in the butt.

She certainly didn't want O'Connor to suffer any real pain from his injury, she assured herself as she closed the door of her windowless office and sank into the comfortable chair behind her narrow desk. Clicking on her answering machine, she started listening to the dozen messages that had accrued that morning, making careful note of the ones that required immediate responses.

Pain, no. She wouldn't wish that on anyone. But a dose of what it felt like to be caught up as a patient in the machinery of a big hospital wouldn't hurt Dr. Tony O'Connor one tiny bit.

FOR THE FOURTH TIME in ten minutes, Tony glanced at his watch. He'd now been in Emerg for one hour, twelve minutes and forty seconds. He'd had to ask a nurse to call and make his apologies for the ten o'clock meeting he'd missed. His cell phone was in his pocket, but when he'd tried to use it, a nursing aide had snatched it from him.

"Pacemakers, Doctor. The man in the very next cubicle has a pacemaker. You know you aren't allowed to use a cell phone in Emerg."

He did know, of course, but he'd forgotten. His irritation had reached the borderline of outright fury by the time Alf Jensen burst through the door with the results of the X rays.

"It's about time," Tony growled. "Fractured, right?" He'd resigned himself to the fact that he'd be hobbling around on a cast for the foreseeable future. His ankle was swollen to more than twice its normal size, and it was so painful he could barely stand the weight of the ice pack a nurse had slapped on it.

Alf closed the door and perched on the side of the bed.

Tony frowned at him, wondering why the hell Alf had such a grim look on his face. "Well? What's the verdict? If it's fractured, I know I'll have to wait for the swelling to go down before we can cast the bloody thing. Let me have a look at the X ray." He grabbed for it, but Alf quickly moved it out of his reach.

"The ankle looks fine, Tony, no fracture."

"Well, that's good news." It didn't make it any less painful, but at least a sprain would heal faster. "So let's just bind it up with a tensor bandage, and I can hobble around on crutches."

"I'm afraid the X ray picked up something we hadn't expected." Alf got up and slipped the negative into the viewing frame. "See this shadow right here?"

Tony frowned and studied the film. It showed an

ankle and part of a leg. Alf was pointing to a spot on the fibula, just above the ankle joint.

"There's a lesion right here, Tony. I had Crompton take a look at it—that's what took so long. He was up in Surgery and I had to wait until he could break for a minute. He agrees with me that it looks like a possible sarcoma."

Stunned, Tony gaped at the other doctor. "You've got to be joking. Sarcoma? That's not possible."

"I wouldn't joke about a thing like this, Tony, you know that."

It was a struggle for Tony to keep the utter horror he felt from showing on his face. The ramifications sent a bolt of fear straight into his gut. Sarcoma was a fast-acting cancer. He could lose his leg.

No, he corrected as his stomach knotted and bile wormed its way up into his throat. No *could* about it. If this were sarcoma, he *would* lose his leg. He swallowed hard and did his best to control his expression.

"I've ordered a CAT scan. They'll come and take you over there in a minute." Alf looked uncomfortable and didn't meet Tony's gaze. "We could well be wrong. Let's just keep our fingers crossed. And we have to be grateful for the X ray. If it is sarcoma, the sooner we treat it the better—although I don't need to tell you that, Tony. You know as well as I do."

He did, but it wasn't any comfort. After mouthing another half dozen platitudes, Alf finally left, and for the first time all morning, Tony was relieved to be alone in the tiny room.

He could let go of the rigid control he'd maintained in front of Alf. His fists were knotted, and he realized it was because his hands were trembling. In fact, his whole body was shaking. His stomach felt sick. He could feel his heart hammering against his ribs, as if he'd just run a fast mile, and his breathing was jerky and rapid.

Shock. For the first time in years, he felt on the verge of tears. Jumbled thoughts raced through his head, all of them centered on his small daughter. Losing a leg was one thing, but what if the cancer had spread?

What would become of McKensy if he died? She was only nine, and he was the parent raising her. His ex, Jessica, had left them when McKensy was about to turn four. Jessica wanted to be a jazz singer, and when an offer came to travel with a blues band, she'd taken it.

He and his ex-wife were friends now, but it had been a tough four years. Tony knew Jessica loved their daughter, and she came to visit whenever time and distance permitted, but the life she'd chosen to lead wasn't one that could include a child.

After his divorce, and after two bad experiences with housekeepers, Tony had asked his mother, Dorothy, to move in with him and McKensy. The timing was right. Dorothy had just sold the family home and bought a condo, which she promptly rented out. The extra income meant she was better off than she'd ever been, and of course Tony paid her well for caring for McKensy.

He was grateful to his mother, but for very good reasons he absolutely didn't want Dorothy raising his daughter single-handed. His mother was a kind and loving grandmother, but she was also a neurotic and bitter woman, still obsessed with the fact that Tony's father had walked out on her years before.

He had a brother and two sisters, but to which of them would he entrust his daughter? They all loved McKensy, but their lives were busy and full. Two of them had children of their own. His single sister was plowing her way through med school and had another grueling three years to go.

For a moment, he gave in to the despair that overwhelmed him, and felt the strange sensation of tears welling up in his eyes. Horrified, he used his fist to swipe at the moisture that escaped down his cheeks.

With no warning knock, the door opened. "Tony O'Connor?"

He scrabbled for a tissue and turned his head away until his eyes were dry.

A white-smocked young woman ignored his distress and gave him a wide smile. "Hi, I'm Lisa Bently. I'm here to take you down for a CAT scan." She released the brakes on the bed and whizzed him out the door and down the hall, chattering as they sped along.

"Wrecked your ankle, huh? I did that last year, out jogging. I fell off the edge of the sidewalk. Hurts like fury, doesn't it? Here we are. Looks like you'll have a bit of a wait—this place is crazy today." She angled the bed against the wall, one of four others.

"Look, Ms.—" Tony had to squint at her name tag. "Ms. Bently, would you just go in and tell the tech that I need this done stat?" He hated to pull rank, but there was no choice in this case. "Tell them the chief of staff is waiting and needs to be seen immediately."

"Oh, they know, Doctor. But see, it's first come first served. You'll have to wait your turn like everybody else. Here's a couple magazines."

She plopped two outdated copies of *Newsweek* on his lap and was gone before he could say another word.

"Hell of a thing, ain't it?" The elderly man in the bed across the hall propped himself up on his elbow and twisted his head around to talk. "S'posed to be the best medical system in the world, here in Canada, and still you gotta lie around goin' rotten waiting for some test or another. What're you in for?"

"My ankle." Tony tried to be distant without being rude, but the old man was oblivious to subtlety. For the next thirty-five minutes, he regaled

Tony with the entire history of his bowels and gall bladder operation. By the time an attendant finally came and wheeled him in, Tony felt numb. He went through the test without saying a single word, grateful for the silence, anxious for the results. When it was over, he asked to see the negatives, but the female attendant insisted that Jensen had to see them first.

"Look, I'm a doctor," Tony insisted. It was getting harder to summon up his usual authoritative tone. He felt exhausted, and his stomach was upset again. The sense of unreality that had begun with the X ray intensified. Still, he tried. "I'm the chief of staff at this hospital. Surely I have the right to see my own results."

"Sorry, Doctor." The older woman shook her head. "You're Dr. Jensen's patient, and he didn't leave any orders of that sort."

By the time he'd been wheeled back to Emerg, Tony was seething again, focusing on the ridiculousness of the rules rather than thinking about what the results of the scan would reveal. But underneath the justifiable anger, he could feel anxiety eating away at his gut like acid.

Jensen came bustling in after another twenty-minute wait, a brown envelope clamped under his right arm, and Tony's stomach cramped hard. The bile in his throat burned, and he had to swallow repeatedly before he could croak out, "Is it sarcoma?"

"Tony," Jensen began in a hearty tone, avoiding eye contact again, "I don't know how to tell you this. There's been one hell of a mix-up—I owe you an apology. When I looked in the computer for the results of your X ray a while ago, I had no idea another Antony O'Connor had been seen in Emerg this morning. He was complaining of a sore lower leg, and he had an X ray shortly before you did. Turns out it was his X ray we were looking at, not yours. He does indeed have sarcoma." With a triumphant gesture, Jensen whipped out the negatives from the envelope. "Now, *this* is you, and as you can see, there's no fracture, and definitely no sarcoma. We can safely assume all that's wrong is a severe sprain."

The relief that flooded Tony was so intense he felt dizzy. It took several moments before utter fury edged out the thankfulness. How could such a gross mistake happen in *his* hospital? He opened his mouth to ask and the turmoil in his stomach intensified.

Suddenly he knew he was going to vomit. He stretched across Jensen, groping for a kidney basin. Jensen shoved one at him only seconds before he threw up.

With each expulsion, the burning in Tony's chest intensified, and he began to have difficulty catching his breath. His intestines were on fire, and as his stomach convulsed in agony, he moaned and bent double.

"Easy, Tony." Jensen was checking his blood pressure. Two ER nurses materialized and took over the task of monitoring vital signs.

"Acute GI symptoms," Jensen concluded. "You have any history of intestinal problems, Tony?"

Tony gasped and shook his head. "Tylenol," he managed to croak. "Four Tylenol…empty stomach…need water…"

Jensen gave him a small paper cup of water, and Tony swallowed it in one sip. "I just need some food," he groaned, his eyes streaming from the pain in his chest and abdomen. "That Tylenol I took is killing me."

Being told he probably had sarcoma hadn't helped, either, but Tony didn't have the breath to say so.

"Go down to the kitchen and ask for a bowl of clear broth," Jensen barked at an aide, "and be quick about it."

The burning subsided enough so that Tony could straighten. A nurse stayed with him, and when the aide arrived with a large bowl of broth on a tray, she cranked the back of the bed higher so he could sit more comfortably.

Tony had never been as grateful for a simple bowl of beef broth. He spooned it up, and almost immediately the pain in his chest and abdomen began to ease.

"Better?" The nurse smiled at him, and he was able to give her a facsimile of a smile in return.

He finished the entire bowl in less than two minutes. The nurse set the tray on a cart. Sinking back on the bed, he heaved a sigh—and with the speed and intensity of a killer wave rolling in, a sensation of extreme heat rushed over him. It grew more and more intense, and as he felt his throat begin to swell, panic overwhelmed him.

"Allergy," he whispered with the last of his breath.

He heard the nurse shouting and was dimly aware of bodies surrounding him and voices talking in urgent tones. In the few moments before he lost consciousness, he knew he was about to die, after all.

CHAPTER THREE

"DID YOU HEAR THAT O'CONNOR'S now on a respirator in ICU?"

Leslie was taking hungry bites of her tuna sandwich. It was past two in the afternoon, and she and Kate were sitting in the hospital cafeteria.

"The whole story's been flying back and forth on e-mail all day," Kate said with a shake of her head that sent her auburn hair flying. "It's hard to believe there could be such a series of problems, and with the chief of staff, of all people."

"It would be funny if it hadn't almost been tragic," Leslie agreed. "The final straw was that new French chef in the kitchen."

"Rene Lalonde," Kate said. "I heard that he put eggshells in the beef broth. Now, why would he *do* that?"

"Apparently it's a traditional French custom. It clarifies it or something. How was he to know that O'Connor was violently allergic to eggs? We had his allergy marked down on the admitting form, but none of us suspected there'd be eggshells in the broth. I tell you, I've seen some panic situations in the ER, but today took the prize. Practically every doctor in the entire hospital was down there at one point. Nobody could see any obvious reason for such extreme symptoms. It was Jensen who finally asked for a detailed list of what the broth was made of.''

"Tony's going to be okay, isn't he?" Kate felt ashamed of her earlier lack of sympathy for his medical problems. He certainly didn't deserve to be in ICU on a respirator.

Leslie nodded. She finished her sandwich and gulped some of her coffee, swearing when it burned her tongue. "He's stable at the moment, but it was touch-and-go there for a while. They even called next of kin—his family's upstairs right now. Apparently his mom is really up in arms. According to the nurses, she's been making noises about suing the hospital for malpractice.''

They looked at each other and shook their heads.

"Can you imagine the headlines?''

Kate could, only too well. "Sounds like Tony's mom is really scared," she mused. She struggled again with her personal feelings, but she knew what her professional role was. "I'll go up and see what I can do. Maybe just talking to somebody would help her feel better about things.''

"Better you than me," Leslie said, sounding skeptical. "One of the nurses up there told me the woman's a real piece of work.''

"Well, I'd rather have her unload on me than on a lawyer.''

Leslie raised her eyebrows. "Anybody ever tell you that the normal reaction to a bad scene is to run the other way?"

Kate grinned. "Yeah, but I get paid good money for standing still and deflecting bullets. Back when I was nursing, I told myself I could do a lot more for emotional issues than I ever could for physical ones." That conviction had inspired her to go back to school and take one course after the other in psychology and conflict management. "And you're a great one to talk about running away from emergencies, Les. Besides, I'd like to meet Tony's mother. Talking to someone's mother can give a lot of insight into why their kids are the way they are." Kate chewed the last of her bun, reflecting that she could use all the help she could get as far as Tony was concerned. It was humiliating to be able to resolve everyone else's anger but her own.

"Yeah?" Leslie gave her a narrow-eyed look. "So that's what you and Galina talk about each time I go to the bathroom, huh? You're trying to analyze me."

"Don't flatter yourself. Your mom tells me how sexy the guys in Rehab are and asks why you and I don't spend more time down there. Beats me. By the way, how's Galina doing with rehab these days, Les?"

Leslie's mother, Galina Poulin, was in her seventies, stubborn, opinionated, funny and delightful. In January, she'd decided to wash the bathroom walls in the town house she and Leslie shared, and she'd fallen and broken her hip. Galina had stubbornly refused to consider physiotherapy until the night Kate came to dinner.

It had taken a great deal of persuasion to convince Galina to even visit the rehab unit. When at last she agreed, Kate introduced her to the therapists, and one of them, Isaac Harris, had charmed her and talked her into coming twice a week for therapy.

"She loves Isaac—she giggles and blushes when I tease her about him," Leslie laughed. "She's really making headway. I wondered there for a while if she'd ever walk again, but now she's off the crutches, just using a cane. I owe you for that one, Kate."

"Hey, your mom's done it all by herself. I only hope I have half her energy when I'm her age."

Leslie beamed. "Me, too. She's one of my best friends."

"Not many people can say that about a parent." She never could, Kate reflected sadly. "It says a lot about the kind of person you are, Les, that you and Galina get along the way you do."

"Yeah, doesn't it? Divorced single female, emotionally dependent, insecure and tied to my mom's apron strings."

They looked at each other and chorused, *"Not."*

The hospital's PR system came on. "All ER staff

please report back to Emerg, all staff back to Emerg, stat."

Leslie groaned, gulped the last of her coffee and got to her feet. "I'm not sure I even wanna know what that's about."

"Good luck."

"Today we need it," Leslie sighed. "Let me know how you make out with Mother O'Connor."

"I will. See you later." Kate watched her friend hurry off, then finished her coffee and reluctantly made her way up to the Intensive Care Unit.

The nurse at the desk indicated which waiting room the O'Connor family were in and confirmed that Dr. O'Connor was steadily improving. As Kate headed down the hallway, she could hear a woman's loud, angry voice.

"—never heard of such a thing, eggshells in soup. It had to be deliberate. God knows Tony has enemies here—he's in a position of power and that always means stepping on somebody's toes. Did you call the pastor like I said, Wilson? I'd like Reverend Anderson to come. I know they say Tony's improving, but did you *see* his color? White as a sheet."

Kate paused in the doorway. There were five people in the room, two men and three women. The plump, older woman with the tightly permed white hair must be Tony's mother, Kate deduced. She'd been the one talking when Kate came in.

They all turned toward her. "Hello," she said

with a reassuring smile. "I'm Kate Lewis, the patient rep." She directed her attention to the older woman, stepping toward her and extending a hand. "And you are...?"

"I'm Dorothy O'Connor. I'm Dr. O'Connor's mother." She gave Kate an assessing look.

Dorothy's eyes were red rimmed behind her pink-framed glasses, and her face had settled into what Kate thought were permanently dissatisfied lines. "How do you do?" Kate kept her hand extended, but Dorothy ignored it, so she turned to the others with a questioning smile.

Dorothy immediately took control. "This is my oldest son, Wilson O'Connor, and my son-in-law, Peter Shiffman."

The men mumbled greetings, and then Dorothy introduced the two women. "And these are my daughters, Judy Shiffman and Georgia O'Connor."

Judy was obviously older than Georgia, but both sisters were slender and of medium height. Judy had Tony's dark hair, and was wearing a tailored dress, stockings and heels, her makeup meticulous. Georgia's hair was fiery red, drawn up in a careless knot at the back of her head, and she wore jeans and no makeup. They each gave Kate a strained smile and a nod, although neither said anything beyond hello.

"I wonder if there's something I can help you with?" Kate began. "Do you have any questions you need answered regarding Dr. O'Connor's care?

Any concerns you might have that you'd like to talk over? I know this is a very stressful time for you, and I'd like to make it easier in any way I can." She directed her remarks at Dorothy.

"And just how can you make anything easier?" Dorothy's voice was sarcastic. "This hospital won't get away with this fiasco, you know. You just tell me how my son could sprain his ankle this morning and then end up in intensive care with his life slipping away from him." She raised her glasses and dabbed at her eyes with the lacy handkerchief she held clutched in one hand, but anger overpowered tears. Her voice rose. "Why, it's malpractice, plain and simple, any idiot can see that. My son's a doctor, and he's chief of staff here, too. It makes you wonder what happens to the ordinary Joe when he walks in off the street. What would the papers do if they got hold of this news? I can tell you there'd be an uproar, and rightly so."

Tony's brother, Wilson, stepped forward and put an arm around his mother, nodding in agreement and looking at Kate as if it was all her fault.

"Maybe we ought to give the *Vancouver Sun* a call," he said to Kate in an accusing tone. "You people need to know that gross carelessness of this sort simply won't be tolerated." He sounded pompous and self-righteous. "Like Mother says, it's malpractice, and someone should pay."

Kate waited until he was finished speaking, reminding herself that this wasn't about her. She took a deep breath and kept her voice even, her tone friendly and nonjudgmental. "It sounds as if you're all very upset and angry, and you have every right to be. This must be terribly stressful for you."

Dorothy snorted. "Darned right it's stressful. My poor son is lying in there not able to talk—" she pointed dramatically toward the Intensive Care Unit, and her voice wobbled "—and not one person is doing anything about it. As far as I can tell, nobody even cares."

Kate had to bite her tongue hard in order to keep from telling Dorothy that she was totally wrong, that the entire hospital was in an uproar. Specialists had been called in, and every physician, nurse, tech and aide was horrified at the series of events that had led to this emergency.

Everyone, down to the newest member of the cleaning staff, cared a great deal. But Kate knew that blocking Dorothy's anger would only exacerbate it. Listening and sharing information were tried-and-true ways to defuse that anger, difficult as they were.

Now Georgia O'Connor stepped toward Kate, and she sounded more worried than angry. "Could you find out exactly what's going on with Tony? They asked us to leave because a couple of doctors were examining him, and the nurse said they'd speak to us when they were done. They came out, but so far, nothing." She drew in a shaky breath, obviously on the verge of tears. "We just want to know how he's doing.'' Her large brown eyes were filled with concern, her forehead creased in worried lines.

"Absolutely," Kate said. "I'll go now and check with the nurse, then I'll come right back and let you know exactly what she says."

Kate found four doctors grouped around the nursing station, and when she asked, they assured her that the chief was improving rapidly. She suggested that the family needed reassurance, and Dr. Clark agreed. He walked to the waiting room. Kate followed, listening quietly as the doctor, with admirable candor, explained the entire sequence of events to the O'Connor family without making a single excuse.

Dorothy interrupted repeatedly, her tone accusing, her manner confrontational, and Kate had to admire the way Clark listened with patience and forbearance and then each time quietly reiterated the fact that the patient was improving rapidly and it looked as if there'd be no further side effects. Tony would remain in intensive care overnight, but there was every reason to believe he'd be back on his feet within a day or so, and the medical staff were doing everything in their power to help him recover.

"Exactly what does that mean?" Wilson O'Connor demanded. "It sounds as if my brother's at death's door already because of the incompetence of the staff around here."

"What's happened is unfortunate," Clark said. "But we really are doing our best for Tony, I assure you. I consider him a friend as well as a colleague."

Tony's mother gave another snort. "With friends like he's got here at St. Joseph's, I'd like to know who needs enemies."

Dr. Clark's face flushed at this obvious insult and he gave a pointed glance at his watch, nodded to everyone and walked out of the room, murmuring excuses about being late for an appointment.

"Can't stand to hear the truth," Dorothy said in a self-satisfied voice.

"Actually, you were pretty rude to him, Mom." Georgia's chin rose, and she returned her mother's belligerent gaze. "He was only trying to be helpful."

"Well, we all know whose side you're on, don't we?" Dorothy's skin flushed magenta, and her eyes narrowed as she glared at her daughter. "Just because you're hoping to be a doctor yourself doesn't mean you ought to defend something like this."

Georgia swallowed and it was obvious she was holding back tears. "I'm on Tony's side. All I care about is that he gets better. I don't think laying blame on anybody is helpful."

Kate silently applauded.

"Well, I'm sure you'd handle everything so much better than I do," Dorothy said in a sarcastic voice. "Although two divorces aren't exactly what I'd call an example of good judgment."

Georgia's face flushed and Kate felt a rush of sympathy for her.

"I don't think this is any time to be jumping down Mom's throat, Georgia," Wilson admonished, again taking his mother's side. "She's under a lot of stress here."

"We all are," Georgia said in a trembling voice. "Why does everything always have to turn into a huge fight? We're in this together. We're all worried about Tony."

There was silence for a few seconds.

"Georgia's right," Judy agreed. "We should pull together instead of arguing at a time like this. And it sounds as if the worst is over, which is a good thing because Peter and I are going to have to leave now, Mom." Judy pointed at her watch. "Otherwise we'll get caught in rush hour traffic and be late picking up the kids from school."

"School! Oh, my goodness." Dorothy clapped a hand over her mouth. "I forgot all about McKensy. How could I do such a stupid thing? She'll be waiting for me when her class gets out. She won't know why I'm not there."

This time, Kate noted, Dorothy's hysterics rang true.

"When that call came, I got so upset I didn't think to make arrangements for her," Dorothy wailed.

"We'll go and get her," Judy soothed. "We have to pick up Ryan and Tricia anyhow, and we can collect McKensy on the way. Her teacher knows me. We'll take her home with us for the night, Mom.''

"She'll need her teddy and her quilt and some clothes,'' Dorothy said, rummaging in her purse. "Here's the house key—just drop it next door with Mrs. Draycott.''

After Judy and Peter left, Wilson explained that he had to go back to his office, but he promised he'd come and drive Dorothy home later on.

"I can drive you, Mom,'' Georgia offered. "I've got my car.''

"Oh, I'd rather go with Wilson,'' Dorothy said. "There're things I need to talk over with him.''

Georgia shrugged. "Whatever you like, Mom.''

When the nurse told Dorothy she could go in and see Tony for ten minutes, Kate was left alone with Georgia.

"Sorry about all that,'' Georgia said in an embarrassed tone. "I guess it's pretty obvious Mom and I rub each other the wrong way.''

"It's a tense time for all of you.''

"Yeah, it really is,'' Georgia sighed. "I should try and be more patient with her, I guess.''

Kate felt that Dorothy was the one who should do the trying, but she didn't say so. "It seems as if you all have busy lives and lots to think about,'' she remarked. "Do you have kids, Georgia?''

"Nope. I was smart enough to know that wasn't a good idea for me.''

"McKensy is Tony's daughter?" Kate knew very little about Tony's personal life. She vaguely remembered hearing through the hospital grapevine that he had a child and he was divorced, but she'd assumed the child lived with his ex-wife.

"Yeah. McKensy's nine, she's a great kid. Mom lives with Tony and takes care of McKensy for him." Georgia's eyes reflected the affection she felt for her niece. "Tony's the best father any little girl could have." Kate thought she detected a wistful note in the other woman's voice.

"Sounds as if you and Dr. O'Connor are really close." It was Kate's turn to sound a little wistful. Her only sister lived in San Diego. Marie was eight years older than Kate, and the age difference had meant that they'd never really gotten to know each other. Kate sent gifts to her niece and nephew for birthdays and Christmas, and now that they had a computer she e-mailed them regularly, but she missed being close to family.

Georgia nodded. "I always say Tony's my guardian angel. When my second marriage fell apart, he was there for me, and when I wanted to go back to graduate school and study medicine, he offered to support me." She swiped at her eyes. "Mom thought it was totally nuts, me going back to school. But Tony convinced me I could do anything I set my mind to. I'd never have made it through the first year if it weren't for him."

Kate was beginning to see Tony O'Connor in an entirely new light.

"What branch of medicine are you planning to practice?"

"Obstetrics." Georgia's face became animated. "I think bringing babies into the world has to be the most exciting way anyone could spend their working hours."

"I agree." Kate smiled, but deep inside was the usual twinge of sadness and regret that nipped at her whenever babies were mentioned. Because of an ovarian cyst and a resulting hysterectomy when she was nineteen, she could never have babies of her own. Ironically enough, she'd been the kind of little girl who'd had dozens of dolls and played with them long past the time she should have lost interest in them. She'd always dreamed of growing up and having lots of kids, and the operation had sent her into a depression that lasted on and off for several years, until she met Scott and his daughter, Eliza.

Dorothy came bustling back into the room. "Well, they say he's improving, but I can't see it. Go in and see what you think, Georgia."

Georgia hurried off and Kate tried again to get to know Dorothy O'Connor. "Georgia was telling me about your granddaughter, McKensy."

Kate hoped it was a topic that would steer Dorothy in a more positive direction, even if only for a few moments. The woman was difficult, no doubt about it.

"McKensy's my darling girl." The angry set of Dorothy's mouth softened into a smile, the first Kate had seen. The older woman looked pretty when she smiled, and the frown lines between her eyes eased.

"She's thoughtful, and so smart. Straight A student, just like Tony was." In the next moment the smile faded and the frown lines reappeared. "It's just a blessing she took after him and not that fly-by-night mother she has."

Kate heaved a mental sigh. It seemed that nothing was entirely positive in Dorothy's view. She didn't want to pry further into Tony's private affairs, but she found herself paying close attention when his mother continued with a disapproving sniff. "Fancied herself a singer, Jessica did. Everybody knows what kind of life those singers lead, what with dope and liquor and men. No morals whatsoever." Her mouth pursed into a prim line. "At least she had enough sense to leave McKensy for Tony to raise, only sensible thing she ever did. I told him before he ever married her what the outcome would be, but he didn't listen."

"How nice that you have a chance to get to know your granddaughter," Kate persevered. "My grandparents lived too far away for me to visit more than once every couple of years, so I never really got to know them at all."

Dorothy's chin lifted, and her voice was filled with pride. "My own children were lucky. They had the best grandfather in the world. My father was a wonderful man. He supported me and the children after my husband deserted us.'' Her voice became bitter again. ''He walked out before Georgia was even in school.''

It was hard not to think that Dorothy would drive anyone off.

''That must have been very difficult for you, raising a family on your own.'' Kate was trying to get a better sense of Dorothy's life.

''Oh, it was hard.'' Dorothy shook her head. ''Four kids, and no husband to help raise them. It was a struggle.''

''You must have been very self-reliant. What sort of job did you have?''

''I taught piano,'' Dorothy announced with great pride. ''I come from a very musical family. My father was a professor of music at the University of British Columbia.''

''How wonderful. I love music, but I can't play any instruments.''

''All my children play—my father and I taught them. Piano, violin. Georgia had promise as a professional pianist, but she didn't pursue it.'' Dorothy's mouth turned down in a disapproving line. ''She only plays the guitar these days—a total waste of God-given talent, if you ask me. And of course Tony was very talented as well. He took up the saxophone.''

In her mind Kate immediately saw his tall figure,

knees bent, eyes closed, passionately playing Dix-
ieland jazz. By now she felt a bit like a voyeur, but
she couldn't help asking, "Does he still play?"

"Oh, yes. He used to be part of a jazz group that
played in piano bars all over the city, but now that
he has McKensy, he no longer has the freedom to
go out at night. Once you have children, your life
changes."

"Yes, it does." Kate was thinking of her stepdaughter, Eliza. She hoped her ex-husband had remembered about the birthday party the little girl
was attending this afternoon.

Kate glanced at her watch. Her workday was almost over. "I'm going to be going home soon. Is
there anything more I can do for you, Mrs.
O'Connor?"

Dorothy gave Kate a look that said she didn't
think Kate had done anything to begin with. "No,
I really don't see what anyone *can* do. There's no
way that what's done can be undone, is there?"

"Unfortunately, no." Smiling at Dorothy was
becoming more and more of a struggle, but Kate
did her best. "I'll leave you, then, and I hope Dr.
O'Connor continues to improve."

"So do I." It was plain from the tone of her
voice and her deep sigh that Dorothy expected
nothing of the kind.

As she hurried down the hall to the elevator, Kate
wondered what made some people so negative.
She'd met plenty of them in the course of her job;

they were the ones who found the most to complain about, so they were the ones she dealt with on a regular basis.

She loved her job, she reminded herself as she finished the day's work, then retrieved her purse from her drawer and headed out to the parking lot. Defusing hostility was challenging, and Kate knew she did it well. But that didn't mean she wasn't glad to leave her work behind her and head home at the end of the day.

She was relieved that the late afternoon meeting she'd had scheduled was canceled. It was the weekly one the chief of staff held with department heads, and Kate had been asked to attend because of a staffing complaint. Tony O'Connor was obviously in no shape to conduct a meeting.

After all that had happened, Kate felt she knew him better than she had that morning. She was sorry now that she'd been unsympathetic toward him. He had a lot of family issues to deal with, and she knew how that felt.

So he played the saxophone, huh?

Kate sent him good thoughts and headed home.

CHAPTER FOUR

TWENTY MINUTES LATER, she pulled up in front of her modest frame house, annoyed that her ex-husband, Scott, had once again parked his battered car in the paved driveway. The ancient vehicle sat there, flaking bits of rust, its hood up and various pieces of its innards spread across the lawn, which Kate had mown and trimmed just two days before.

But it wasn't the battered car that made Kate frown and hurry up the walk. Eliza was sitting on the front steps, her bare knobby knees clasped between her arms, tears trickling down her cheeks.

Her golden blond hair, clipped fashionably close to her skull by Kate's hairdresser, stood up in stiff peaks, carefully sculpted in place with the mousse Kate had given her, and she was wearing her bright pink party dress. Kate knew the birthday party she was supposed to attend must have started at least half an hour before.

"Eliza, what's wrong, honey?" Kate raced up the steps and sank down beside her stepdaughter. "I thought you were supposed to be at Melanie's party."

Eliza nodded, her wide blue eyes overflowing. "I

was, but Daddy forgot to get me a gift. He said he would when I got home from school, but then he couldn't drive me because the car's broken again." She rubbed at her face with the palm of her hand. "I made her a card, but I can't go without a gift. Everybody got her something special—they all told me what they got her in school today." Her voice wobbled. "I wanted to give her some of that sparkly lotion from the Body Shop, but it's too late now."

Frustration at her ex made Kate's heart pound. She had to struggle to keep her tone neutral. "And where's Daddy gone?"

"He went to see if he could borrow Mike's van. But he's been gone a long time."

Kate could guess why. Chances were good Mike's van was out of gas or had some problem with the carburetor or the battery or the alternator. Scott's friends could have been his clones. None of them could organize anything except getting together for a beer at the pub. Last-minute emergencies with vehicles were the norm rather than the exception. And like Scott, none of them held down a steady job.

"Would an unopened package of kid's bubble bath and dusting powder do for a gift, you think?"

"Yeah." Eliza's little face brightened. "But where will we get it?"

"I just happen to have some in my dresser drawer." Eliza's own birthday was coming up soon, and Kate had bought the items on the weekend.

She rushed in the house and found them, then grabbed some purple tissue, tape and a pink ribbon as well. Eliza could wrap on the way to the party.

They hurried to the car and Kate slid behind the wheel. She didn't bother leaving Scott a note—he'd know she'd bailed him out yet again. Eliza concentrated on wrapping as Kate drove swiftly to the address the little girl recited from the printed invitation. Fortunately, it wasn't too far away. Eliza would be late, but not hopelessly so.

Kate went to the door with Eliza, and a cheerful young woman answered.

"Hey, you must be Eliza," she said with a wide grin. "Melanie's going to be so happy that you're here—she's been missing you." She rubbed her hand on her jeans and then stuck it out to Kate. "Icing sugar, sorry. Hi, I'm Belinda Rogers. You must be Eliza's mom."

"I'm Kate. Sorry she's late."

"No problem, the girls are still in the pool. You did bring your swimming suit, Eliza?"

Kate's heart sank, but Eliza nodded. "It's under my dress."

"Off you go, then."

Eliza gave Kate a fast, fierce hug and then ran off to join her friends.

"She doesn't have a towel." Kate felt like a negligent parent. Eliza had forgotten to tell her it was a swimming party.

"No problem, there's a whole stack of them by the pool."

"What time should I come and collect her?"

"Seven-thirty's good."

Kate thanked Belinda and then drove home, trying to get past the irritation that simmered in her. She'd made a point of reminding Scott about the party, and the fact that she wouldn't be able to drive Eliza because of the meeting. He'd promised he'd do it.

Why, just once in his life, couldn't he carry through on the promises he made so glibly and then never kept?

You know he's unreliable, so why do you go on expecting him to change? They'd been divorced four years now, after five troubled years of marriage during which Kate gradually and painfully gave up her illusions, admitting at last that Scott Bauer didn't want to be anything other than what he was, an unemployed bum.

Kate was the one with dreams, the one who'd chosen to believe his oft-repeated promises about getting a job, buying a house, trading in the battered car for a decent one.

She realized now that she had only herself to blame. Scott had been a means to an end for her. She'd liked the amiable young man, but she'd fallen head over heels in love with Eliza, six months old when she met Scott. The baby needed a mother so desperately it almost broke Kate's heart to look at her, dressed in mismatched and discolored clothing, sucking on a pacifier, her huge blue eyes staring hungrily into the face of every stranger. To this day, Kate couldn't read the Dr. Seuss book, *Are You My Mother?* without crying.

Eliza's teenage mother had died of a drug overdose when Eliza was two months old. Scott had sworn he hadn't known his wife was using, but Kate thought now that he probably had, and in his usual fashion, simply chose to ignore it.

Thankfully, there was no indication that Eliza's natural mother had used drugs during her pregnancy. Eliza was bright, usually cheerful, the most normal of little girls.

Because of the baby, Kate overlooked things she should have noticed, such as the fact that Scott, who had a degree in chemical engineering, was out of a job when she met him. He'd never had a steady job, and Kate knew now he probably never would.

But during the years of their marriage, she'd continued working as a nurse, volunteering for night duty several times a month so she could afford classes at university. She'd gone on believing that when the right job came along, he'd take it. She'd been patient and understanding when one opportunity after the next came to nothing. She'd agreed that Eliza needed a parent around, and she'd been willing to work so that Scott could be their daugh-

ter's caregiver. But it hadn't taken long to realize
that although he took reasonable care of Eliza during the day, he did absolutely nothing else.

Arriving home exhausted after a twelve-hour
shift on the geriatric ward, Kate would find the
breakfast dishes still on the table, clothing scattered
wherever he'd seen fit to drop it, no groceries in
the house. He never once made dinner, cleaned the
house, did the laundry or mowed the lawn. All
household tasks were left for her to do. She paid
all the bills and she also did all the housework,
indoors and out. The moment she was home, he
handed over Eliza, as well.

When Eliza started kindergarten, Kate had had
enough. She gave Scott an ultimatum. Find work in
three months, or the marriage was over.

By this time Scott was grossly overweight and
made no effort at all to look for a job. Kate at last
faced the facts. She was married to a man who had
no ambition and who had never really loved her—
at least not in the way she wanted to be loved.
Somewhere during the five years of their marriage,
she'd lost all respect for him, as well as any affection. He refused to move out of the apartment they
shared, so Kate packed her belongings and left, but
the pain of leaving Eliza had nearly killed her. She
saw a lawyer, explaining that she and Eliza adored
each other. She was the only mother the little girl
knew, and Kate wanted custody.

The lawyer explained that she had a fair chance,

but it might mean a long and costly court battle. Scott was the girl's biological father, and despite his laziness, he did take reasonable care of her. Kate couldn't deny that Scott loved his daughter. The apartment they'd shared, which she'd painted and decorated, wasn't in any way an unsuitable home for a child.

After three months of painful visits with Eliza and tearful partings, Kate came up with a plan. Her own parents, dead for some years, had left her a small legacy, so Kate took the money and bought a house on Vancouver's east side, one with a bright and spacious basement apartment. Banking on his laziness, his cheapness, and his penchant for always taking the easiest route, she'd offered the suite to Scott at a reduced rent. He and Eliza had moved in and had lived in Kate's house ever since.

The arrangement was far from ideal. Scott took flagrant advantage of the situation, using Kate as a built-in baby-sitter, relying on her to buy the majority of Eliza's clothes, even borrowing Kate's car to drive his daughter to the dance classes Kate paid for. She tried not to get angry with him, but it was a challenge.

When Kate drove up in front of her house, Scott's ample rear end protruded from under the hood of his car.

No blame, she reminded herself. *The problem is the problem. Errors are just opportunities to learn and forgive.* But the mantra wasn't working. She remembered Eliza's tearful little face and wrath took the place of reason.

Slamming the car door unnecessarily hard, Kate stalked over to Scott. "I've just taken Eliza to her birthday party," she snapped. "She was crying her heart out when I got home, and she was late by the time we got there. I thought you said you'd take her to buy a gift and make sure she made it to the party?"

Slowly, like a turtle emerging from a shell, Scott's jowly grease-smeared face appeared from the car's innards. He had the nerve to smile at her. "Oh, hi, Kate, how's it going? That's good you took Eliza, because I couldn't get Mike's van. He'd promised to deliver furniture with it."

His nonchalance infuriated her.

"Eliza was excited about that party. You let her down."

"I knew you'd get her there. No harm done."

Don't blame. Don't accuse. Kate knew her own rules, but somehow Scott pushed her into situations where she couldn't apply them. "How can you do that to your own daughter?" Her voice rose. "You just assume I'll come along and pick up after you. Well, Scott, I've had enough of it."

It felt good to explode. But they'd been down this path before, and Kate knew more or less what was coming.

"Chill out, Kate. If you feel that way about it,

I'll take Eliza and go. My cousin called about a job in Nova Scotia. He promised me a place to live.''

Did he even have a cousin in Nova Scotia? Kate had never been certain, but the very possibility of his taking Eliza away made her stomach tighten. She'd never see Eliza again, and she couldn't bear that.

As always, she backed down. Trembling, she stabbed a finger at the greasy auto parts now littering the lawn. ''I want you to get this mess off the grass and find another place to work on this wreck of a car. The neighbors are complaining—the whole front yard is an eyesore this way.''

''Hey, hey, temper, temper. Aren't you the one always preaching patience?'' His grin was snide, and for an instant Kate longed to bring her hand up and smack him hard. With every ounce of self-control she possessed, she walked around him and up her front steps. Closing the door behind her, she collapsed in an armchair as the full effect of the quarrel washed over her.

She'd engaged, breaking rule number one. She'd accused, and she'd blamed, and she hadn't listened. How could Scott push every single button the way he did? And not once, but every single time something like this came up.

At least she could take a cool bath and eat some dinner before she went to pick up Eliza. She tried to concentrate on those pleasures and ignore Scott's goading. She hadn't asked him to pick up his daughter, because she knew he'd simply borrow her car to do it.

Times like these, she felt trapped and hopeless. Also defeated and a failure, she admitted as she kicked off her shoes. Whatever made her think she could defuse anger? She couldn't even manage it in herself. She thought of Dorothy, of the deep-seated anger that had surfaced when she mentioned her husband deserting her.

If she went on this way with Scott, would she eventually end up like Tony's mother, a bitter, sour, resentful woman?

The very idea made her long for something sweet. Kate headed for the kitchen. She needed chocolate chip cookies, and she needed them right away.

CHAPTER FIVE

THE FOLLOWING AFTERNOON, Kate set the home-made cookies she'd brought Tony on the bedside table, hoping she didn't appear as awkward as she felt. "Hi, Tony. It's good to see you looking so much better."

"Cookies?" His voice was gravelly and still weak.

"Yup. I baked them myself, I guarantee there're no eggs in them. I found a recipe in an allergy cookbook."

"Thanks, Kate." She was rewarded with a smile, but she still felt uncomfortable. Maybe she should have brought him flowers or a magazine instead of the cookies. They seemed too—too intimate.

Cookies are cookies. There's nothing sensual about them.

She was relieved that he was alone, but she was also disturbed by it. He was lying on top of the sheets, wearing a pale blue short-sleeved T-shirt and a pair of loose-fitting black track shorts. He had great muscles in his arms—and his legs, too. She swallowed. She'd never really seen his body this uncovered.

His silky hair was rumpled, but he'd had a shave. Although he was still pale, he looked more like himself again. She noticed that he was too long for the standard hospital bed. His uninjured foot stuck out of the bars at the end of the bed. It was long and narrow. Elegant. Sexy.

Sexy? Get a grip here, Lewis. How could a foot be sexy? She jerked her attention away from his foot and cleared her throat.

"They told me at the desk they'd sprung you from ICU this morning. This room is nice, great view." She walked over to the window and pretended to gaze down on the small interior courtyard, giving herself time to collect her ridiculous thoughts.

"If you've got to be a patient, I guess this is as good as any." He sounded grumpy, and Kate's guard went up. If the tightness of his jaw and the narrow-eyed look he gave her were any indication, he was in a bad mood.

She decided to get down to business. "The nurse said you wanted to speak to me?" Kate turned from the window and sat down in the chair beside the bed. She tried to put aside the slight nervousness she felt. There was also the stupid sexual tension that zipped through her, caused by her ridiculous awareness that he was in bed. She could smell the shampoo he'd used on his hair. Or maybe it was aftershave?

For heaven's sake, Lewis, concentrate on his concerns and get your mind out of the gutter.

After all, he was a patient first, chief of staff second, attractive male third—way, way down the list. It was her job to do everything she could to set his mind at ease. And just because he was lying in bed, there was no reason to think lascivious thoughts.

"You're the only person I could think of who might pay attention and treat me like an adult," he began in a disgruntled voice. "I'm finding out first-hand just how few rights patients have in this place. It's appalling." He tried to sit up straighter and swore when the movement hurt his ankle.

It was petty to feel triumphant at the fact he needed her, but she couldn't help it. Ashamed of her reaction, Kate made a move to assist him, but he waved her away with an impatient gesture. She flopped back down in the chair and tugged her skirt closer to her knees. Why had she worn this snug knit thing, anyhow? She should have put on something loose and long around him.

"I asked to see my chart this morning," he continued, totally oblivious to the way her mind was deviating from the issue, "and I was refused." He sounded irate. "In the ER, I demanded a look at the CAT scan and was told that wasn't possible. Well, that's just not good enough." His eyes darkened and he said between gritted teeth, "I want a full accounting of what happened, Kate. I want to know exactly who screwed up and why. Some of it I already know. The mix-up with the X rays—now that was a fiasco.'' He shook his head in disgust. ''The whole thing's a damned fiasco, come to that. What's gone on in my case is exactly the sort of thing I've done my best to prevent at this hospital. It's inexcusable, from start to finish.'' He smacked a fist down on the bedcover and roared, ''There'll be a full inquiry the moment I'm out of this bed, I can assure you of that.''

Kate had anticipated this, but the full effect of his wrath was still disconcerting. She'd come prepared, however. She breathed deeply, drew a small notebook out of her jacket pocket, recrossed her legs and referred to it as she outlined, in a quiet voice, the exact series of events that had led to his respiratory arrest.

''You slipped on a candy wrapper in the lobby and went to the ER several hours later, where there was a mix-up with the X rays.''

''Inexcusable. Absolute inefficiency.''

She let him emote, and then she went on with the accounting.

''You had a severe gastrointestinal response to the acetaminophen you'd taken for pain.''

''Are you trying to insinuate that what happened was my own *fault?*''

It would have been easy to cower. He was intimidating, the way he was glowering at her. She retaliated with dignity. ''Absolutely not. In fact, what

I'm trying to establish is that we should forget fault altogether.''

"Easy for you to say. You're not the one lying in this bed." He gave her a pitying look, as though she was some dimwitted do-gooder beyond sensible reasoning.

But at least he listened without interrupting after that.

Each time she glanced at his face, however, she could see that he was growing more outraged by the moment. His skin was flushed, his dark eyes glared, the frown between his brows deepened.

She swallowed and went on with the recital. She referred to everyone involved by name so he'd be reminded that they were individuals.

"The cook, Rene Lalonde, was in my office this morning. He's terribly upset. He feels personally responsible for what happened with the broth, and he's also really worried about his job. He's recently moved his family out here from Quebec, and now he's afraid he'll be out of work. He has three small kids and his wife is pregnant with their fourth.''

Tony snorted. "He must know I can't just fire him, he's a member of the union. Anyhow, I have no intentions of firing him. But it was negligent of him to add those damned eggshells to what was supposed to be a clear broth. He definitely deserves a reprimand, and I intend to be the one to give it to him.''

Kate knew she shouldn't defend the man, but she

couldn't help it. "He was doing the best he knew how. Mistakes are simply opportunities to learn."

"Literally over my dead body. I came that close, Kate," he said, eyes narrowed, finger and thumb millimeters apart.

She was tempted to say that close only counted in horseshoes but managed to restrain herself.

"Fortunately, you've made an amazingly fast recovery," she said instead. Was he really like his mother, always expecting the worst?

Kate thought of his sister, Georgia, and reminded herself of the things she had revealed, how good and kind Tony was to his family, what a great father he was to his daughter. Maybe Kate could appeal to that generous part of him.

"People make mistakes," she began. "No one did anything deliberate."

"What about that mix-up with the X rays? That was inexcusable. That was negligence. I actually thought for a few hours that I had sarcoma. Thank God the other patient didn't get my results. I blame the ER staff for such incompetence."

"I can imagine how terrible the whole thing was for you, but blaming only makes *you* the problem. The thing we should concentrate on is the solution, don't you agree?"

He didn't respond, and he didn't seem mollified by her sympathy or her appeals to reason. She reverted to facts. "The ER was unusually busy that morning. There were dozens of Shriners with gastroenteritis, as well as the usual run-of-the-mill patients. And the other man did have the exact same name as you.''

He grunted.

It was wicked of her, but she did it, anyway. ''Each and every individual who was involved with your case has asked me if they can visit you to apologize,'' she said in a sweet voice. ''Shall I tell them to come in today?''

He jerked upright, then swore, rubbing his sore leg. ''God Almighty, not on your life. Tell them no.'' He was horrified, and she hated herself for enjoying it. ''I can't face all those people trooping through here, making excuses.''

''But they feel responsible. And it would make them feel better.''

''Well, it wouldn't do a damned thing for me. And it's not up to me to make them feel better about nearly killing me, is it?''

He was a tough case. ''Absolutely not,'' she agreed. ''But keep in mind that it was a system failure. Mistakes were made, but there was no malice whatsoever involved. Everyone is deeply concerned and upset over what occurred.''

''Which makes it all the more frightening,'' he said with vehemence. ''Concerned and upset aren't what we're aiming for at St. Joseph's, warm and fuzzy as the words might make you feel, Kate.''

His sarcasm finally got to her. She had to struggle to stay calm. She reminded herself that an angry person was asking for love, but it wasn't easy to believe that of the large man glaring up at her from the hospital bed.

"What is it you *really* want, Tony?"

Did she imagine it, or did his eyes flicker to her breasts?

He recovered fast and she couldn't be absolutely sure.

"What I want for St. Joseph's," he finally ground out between his teeth, "is professionalism, competence, the best medical care humanly possible. And what I want from the staff is assurance that they aren't going to *screw up this way again.*" His voice rose, echoing in the small room.

"Exactly how do you see that assurance? In writing?"

He frowned. She'd confused him. She felt wickedly pleased.

"What do you mean, 'in writing'?"

"Well, you just told me you want assurance from the staff. In what form do you want it?"

"Are you putting me on? I'm not being literal here, for God's sake. This isn't kindergarten."

"I understand that." Ah, the power of sweet reason. "I'm simply trying to pinpoint what would make you feel better about all this. Would you like to meet with the staff and tell them how you feel?"

For a moment he considered that. Kate was relieved to see that his anger had diminished.

"Yeah, I sure do," he finally said in a gruff

voice. "Not right away, but in a few days. When I feel better, when I've got my strength back, then I'll meet with them all and lay it on the line."

Her heart sank. He was going to blast them, in spite of her efforts.

"Great." It was anything but. "I'd be happy to arrange that meeting for you, if you want me to."

"Yeah. Get hold of my secretary. She'll help you set it up."

There didn't seem to be anything left to say. Kate stood up and started toward the door just as it swung open and a young girl skipped into the room. She had a mop of stick-straight strawberry-blond hair escaping from a ponytail, an engaging freckled face, and a smile that was like a magnet. Kate couldn't help but respond to it.

"McKensy begged me to bring her to see you, Tony." Georgia followed Tony's daughter into the room and waved her fingers at Kate. "We're both on our lunch hour, so she can only stay fifteen minutes. The traffic's a nightmare and I promised her teacher she wouldn't be late getting back. I'm going to grab us each a sandwich from the cafeteria. Be back in a few minutes." With that, she hurried out the door.

"Papa, Papa," McKensy squealed, racing for the bed. She threw herself up and into Tony's welcoming embrace, covering his face with smacking kisses. "Oh, Papa, I'm so sorry you hurt your foot. I missed you *so* much. I was scared when I heard you had to stay here. Auntie Judy took me home with her. She drove me to school this morning. Uncle Peter took us all to Pizza Heaven for supper last night and I won a free root beer. Are you better now? When can you come home?''

''Hey, duchess, how you doing? Slow down a little, okay? We'll take one question at a time.''

Kate was fascinated to see that Tony's features had undergone a remarkable transformation. The frown had disappeared, and a wide grin lit his face. He had dimples in his cheeks that Kate had never been aware of, and the usual guarded expression in his eyes was replaced by warmth and such obvious affection it made her catch her breath when he turned to her, still smiling.

God, he was downright hazardous to her health when he looked like this.

''Kate, I'd like you to meet my daughter, McKensy. McKensy, this is Ms. Lewis.''

The shape of McKensy's mouth was the same as his. She had his exact smile, but hers had no restraint. It was spontaneous, trusting and generous. It made her animated little face radiantly beautiful, even though, feature by feature, she wasn't quite.

''How do you do, Ms. Lewis? Do you work with my papa?''

Kate smiled in return. ''It's a pleasure to meet you, McKensy. And yes, I do work with him. Please, call me Kate.''

''May I, Papa?''

What an endearing child, Kate thought, returning McKensy's megawatt smile. And such beautiful manners.

"Yes, of course you may. Kate's just said it's okay."

"Goody." She clapped her hands. "I love it when grown-ups let me call them by their first name. It makes them more *intimate*."

Tony rolled his eyes and Kate laughed. "I think you're right," she agreed. "It certainly makes it easier to get to know one another."

"That's what I think." McKensy nodded enthusiastic assent.

"Which school do you go to, McKensy?" Kate was enchanted by the little girl.

"St. Regis Academy. It's *so-o-oo* fun."

"I'll bet it is." It was known as one of the best private schools in the city. Kate had tried to convince Scott that Eliza should go there, but he'd balked at the cost, even though Kate had offered to pay half.

"Do you have any kids, Kate?" McKensy was perched on the side of Tony's bed, her gray eyes taking in every detail of the room.

"A stepdaughter, Eliza. She'll be nine next month."

"I was nine in April, we're nearly the same age. Which school does Eliza go to?"

"Collingwood."

"I think that's the school right across the street from where I go to dance classes, isn't it, Papa?"

Tony nodded.

"DanceCo?" Kate asked. "Eliza goes there, too. What are you studying, McKensy?"

"Ballet and tap."

"So is she," Kate exclaimed. "She just moved up into Madame Bloor's class for the last couple of weeks."

"I take that class," McKensy squealed, her eyes huge. "There're two Elizas in my class. Does yours have brown braids or blond, sticky-up points?"

"Sticky-up points," Kate said.

"Oh, super." McKensy threw herself back on the bed, not noticing Tony's grimace when she bumped his sore leg. "I'm *so* glad. She's the one I like. The other Eliza's sort of snobby."

"McKensy," Tony admonished in a gentle tone.

"I'm not being rude, I'm just telling the truth." She sat up and gave her father a wide-eyed innocent look. "And I wouldn't have said it if she was the other one," she assured him in a whisper.

Kate met Tony's eyes and this time they both laughed.

"Why haven't I seen you at DanceCo?" he asked.

"Eliza's been going on Wednesdays. She's just started the Thursday class, and her father often drives her."

"I go Thursday, right, Papa?"

Tony nodded, and Kate got up. "I'll be off now and let you two have some time on your own." She moved toward the door, but before she reached it, Georgia was back, carrying a bag of food.

"Sorry, McKensy, but we've gotta go now," she said. "I'll bring you back tonight so you can have a nice long visit with your dad."

Again, Kate was struck by the child's manners, and her good nature as well. She didn't argue or complain, but simply kissed Tony and hugged him hard before she slid off the bed and walked over to where Georgia was waiting.

"Bye, Kate." The smile flashed. "It was nice meeting you." She gave Kate a quick once-over. "I really like your hair."

"Why, thank you, McKensy. I like yours, too. It's a fantastic color. It was fun meeting you."

With one last dramatic wave of her hand and a loud kiss blown in Tony's direction, Eliza left with her aunt.

"What a super kid you have," Kate remarked.

"Thanks." Tony couldn't disguise his pride. He was slumped back on the pillows, totally relaxed.

"I wish Eliza had such good manners," Kate sighed. "She's a bit inclined to have sulks and tantrums when something doesn't suit her. McKensy seems so good natured."

"Oh, not always," Tony said. "She was on her best behavior today. She can sulk and tantrum with the best of them when the mood strikes her. She *is* female, after all. And she has that touch of fiery red in her hair. A bit like yours.'' He winked.

Kate almost gaped. Could he actually be teasing her?

There was a twinkle in his eye as he grinned at her. ''So, you gonna cite me now for sexual discrimination, Ms. Lewis?''

''The female thing was probably just a slip of the tongue,'' Kate purred. ''After all, we have to make mistakes in order to learn. And do call me Kate. It's so much more *intimate*.''

He laughed aloud, and Kate did, too. The invisible barrier that had always been between them seemed to evaporate.

''You got time to talk for a few minutes? Apart from the infernal paperwork my secretary brings, there's nothing to *do* in this damned place.''

The request, a little plaintive, amazed her.

''Sure, I always have time to talk,'' she responded. ''Talking is a major part of my job, you know that.''

''So pull up that chair again and sit back down,'' he invited. When she had, he said, ''What does your husband do, Kate?''

''Oh, I'm not married. I was, but we divorced. Four years ago now.''

''Aah. You, too.'' He thought for a moment and frowned. ''You did say Eliza was your stepdaughter? I thought perhaps she lived with you.''

She could see him trying to figure out the relationship.

"My ex-husband, Scott, rents an apartment in my house."

He thought that over and then raised an eyebrow. "That's a unique arrangement."

"I know it is. And it's not always easy." She wondered how much to tell him. The gossip mill at St. Joe's was formidable, and she hadn't really confided in anyone except Leslie. She found herself wanting to talk to Tony, though. Somehow she knew she could trust him to keep her confidences private.

"When Scott and I first separated, I realized I wouldn't be able to see Eliza every day, or be part of her life the way I had been, and it broke my heart," she began.

He nodded and waited.

"I could see that it was affecting her, as well. She started having nightmares and trouble getting to sleep."

"Your ex never remarried?"

"Nope." Kate shook her head. It was something she'd wondered about after the split. Although Scott had dated from time to time, nothing permanent had developed. She surmised that the women were simply smarter than she'd been, and could see that he wasn't prime relationship material.

"The thing is," she explained, "having Scott and Eliza living in the same house keeps her in my life. We married when she was a tiny baby. I'm the only mother she's ever known."

He thought about that. "You don't think you'll have other children?"

She shook her head and heard herself say in a level tone, "I can't have kids."

"I'm sorry." His deep voice was gentle. "For a woman who so obviously enjoys children, that's too bad."

Again, he surprised her. She'd thought he might say, as so many others had done, *Oh well, you can always adopt.*

And of course it was true, she could. She *had*, in a sense, with Eliza. But Tony seemed to understand that not being able to grow a child in her own body had nothing to do with adopting. The two were separate, just as she supposed the love parents felt for their children differed from one child to the next. Not more, not less. Just different.

"Your ex is a fortunate fellow to have you mothering Eliza," Tony continued. "I'm a single father, and I know how tough it is to raise a daughter by yourself. I'm lucky because I have a large family around, and now my mother's living with us. But before that happened I went through a series of housekeepers."

"Your mother adores McKensy." Whatever else Dorothy was, she'd come across as a doting grandmother.

"I'm grateful to her for being there when I can't

be.'' Tony raised an eyebrow and a small smile came and went. "You met my mother, Georgia said.''

Kate nodded.

"Then you understand why it isn't always easy to explain to McKensy that Mom's attitudes aren't the ones I want her to copy. You must have noticed my mother can be difficult to be around.''

His openness surprised and touched her. It was hard to know how far to go with this, though. "Dorothy seems to be quite angry,'' Kate ventured tactfully. "I wonder if she'd agree to some counseling? It can't be easy for her to feel that way all the time.''

"Counseling's crossed my mind several times, but she'd never go. Besides, what good would more talking do?'' He blew out an exasperated breath. "Mom already wears everyone out with talking.''

"It's a difficult step to take.'' Something in her was relieved to know that Tony could view his mother in an impartial, albeit loving, manner. His brother Wilson didn't seem to see her clearly at all. "It can't be comfortable for her, feeling such strong negative emotions all the time.''

"What worries me is that McKensy will pick up some of her negativity.''

"I doubt it. I think kids come with their own personalities pretty well intact,'' Kate remarked. "I used to worry that Eliza would take after her father in some of the ways I found difficult, but that hasn't happened. She's very much her own person. And from the little I've seen of your daughter, I'd say she has a delightful personality all her own."

"It's comforting to hear you say that," he said with a sigh. "It's impossible to be impartial about your own kid, isn't it?"

She nodded agreement. "Raising kids is a challenge, but it's also the best game in town as far as I'm concerned. Which is lucky, seeing how much time and energy it takes."

"It's a full-time job, all right," he agreed. "Sometimes I envy the couples I see on Sundays at the park or the science center. It has to be easier, having a partner you can talk stuff over with, someone who cares the same way you do about your kid." He added quickly, "Not that my ex doesn't care about McKensy, she does. We're good friends. It's just that she's never been around to do the actual parenting."

"Well, Scott's there every day," Kate said with a shrug, remembering the previous night and the birthday party. "But it doesn't seem to help much."

Tony waited, but she didn't go into detail. She didn't want to sound like a typical ex-wife listing the shortcomings of the person she'd once chosen to marry. "It makes for a certain amount of conflict," she admitted.

God, that was the understatement of the century. The truth was, Scott managed to drive her to the brink of homicide. She wondered what Tony would think if she admitted to having fantasies about hitting her ex in the head with a tire iron.

She happened to glance at her watch and leaped to her feet. "My gosh, look at the time. I'm late for a meeting." An hour had sped past in what she could have sworn was ten minutes.

"Don't run to get to it," he counseled. "You could slip on a candy wrapper in the lobby," he said with a wry grin. "I was on my way to a meeting that morning and I was late, which is how I ended up flat on my back in here."

"I'll keep that advice in mind." She gave him a wide smile and a wave. "I enjoyed our conversation, and I really enjoyed meeting McKensy."

"Thanks. Come again when you get a minute, okay? I never realized how mind deadening it is to be a patient in this place."

"You'll be going home soon, won't you?"

He shrugged and held out his hands, palms up. "How would I know? These doctors never tell you a damned thing."

She was laughing as she raced for the elevator.

CHAPTER SIX

MAYBE IT WAS LYING IN BED this much that made
him so damned horny. Or maybe it was the perfume
Kate wore, a light, flowery scent that reminded him
of summer picnics with his first real girlfriend.
Whatever it was, he'd been uncomfortably conscious of her the whole time she was in the room.
And that ridiculously short skirt hadn't helped any.
Not that women with legs like that should wear
anything *but* short skirts.

He wasn't complaining, though, and it was
hardly the first time he'd felt aroused when Kate
Lewis was around. Usually he'd been grateful that
their differences of opinion irked him enough to
take his mind off her sex appeal.

Still, there was something irresistible about the
contrast between her wide, open smile and that way
she had of tilting her head down and looking up at
him as if she was just a little shy. Her body didn't
hurt, either. It curved in and out in all the right
places, and he'd had to make a special effort to
appear totally businesslike and professional around
her.

But today McKensy had made him forget about

professional behavior. The rascal had charmed Kate, and he was positive that his daughter would be giving him a rundown on how *super* Kate was, and how *pretty,* and didn't she have *green eyes,* and wouldn't it be nice if he took her out to *dinner?*

McKensy had been on a campaign for some time now to get him married. When she was little, she'd talked about her mommy coming back to live with them, but in the past couple of years she'd shifted focus. Now she simply wanted him to find her another mommy.

It wasn't that she didn't love Jessica. And she adored Dorothy. But an absentee mother wasn't enough, and already McKensy was balking at Dorothy's conservative ideas about fashion and hairstyles. He'd heard her asking Georgia about periods and how old she'd been when she started, for God's sake.

Marrying him off wasn't a bad scheme in theory, Tony thought. But the reality was that the few women he'd dated since his divorce weren't interested in taking on a man with a young daughter. They had career goals, busy lives with no room for a needy little girl.

Besides, he'd tried marriage once, and it had been such an emotional roller coaster, such a series of crises and disappointments and confrontations he didn't think he'd ever get himself mired that way again. It wasn't worth it, even to make McKensy happy. Even for regular sex, he added with a wry grin, although that particular aspect was appealing.

Tony shifted in bed, wincing when his ankle hurt. Of all times to be laid up, this had to be the worst. He had a busy medical practice, he was still new at his job here at St. Joe's, still trying to implement the changes he thought necessary to move the medical center into the technological age.

He didn't have the full support of the hospital board; there were a couple of mastodons who considered him too young, too radical, too confident. And at the same time there was this unholy mess going on in his personal life.

Fumbling in the bedside drawer, he found his wallet. In it was the airmail letter that had upset the whole family. It had arrived several weeks ago, but he'd avoided telling his mother about it until yesterday, the morning of his accident.

It was because of this letter and the ensuing row with Dorothy that he'd been late for work. He'd raced in, hurrying to a meeting with the sound of his mother's angry voice still ringing in his ears.

Now he unfolded the fragile airmail pages and scanned the words, even though he knew exactly what they said.

His father's handwriting had always been large, bold—easy to read. In this letter, it was cramped and crooked. In places it faltered, as if the person writing had wavered.

Dear Tony,

I hope all is well with you, as it is with us, and that McKensy is over the chicken pox. I remember when you were a nipper and had them, how itchy you were. I've enclosed a funny card for her. Betsy picked it out. She's better with cards than I am.

How's the new job panning out? Chief of staff sounds like a load of responsibility, and I know you'll do a fine job for St. Joseph's. They're lucky to have you. I'm mighty proud of you, lad. I tell all the old codgers down at the pub about you and your success.

Now, there's some news I need to give you. Betsy and I are planning a trip to Canada. As you well know, I've never come back since I left your mother, but now it's time. If it's okay with everyone, I want to meet all you kids. It's hard to think of you as grown-ups with young ones of your own. Even though you sent photos, I still remember each of you the way you were when last I saw you. Probably works both ways, so be prepared for a shock. I'm a lot older than I was when you were little. (Joke.)

We'll be coming in six weeks' time and staying at a hotel one of Betsy's friends recommended, the Barclay on Robson Street. Seems it's a nice cozy place without costing the earth. I don't want to cause upset for any

of you, Tony, but it's past time I came home
for a visit. Aren't any of us getting any
younger.

If I thought it would help, I'd drop your
mother a line, but I know from past experience
it'll only upset her. I'm relying on you to know
what's best where she's concerned. Sorry to
put the weight on you, lad, but I don't know
what else to do.

Looking forward to seeing you soon,

Your affectionate father,
Ford O'Connor

Tony remembered in vivid detail the last time
he'd seen his father. He was eleven. It had been a
hot summer afternoon, and he'd been thrilled when
Ford had taken him down to the Fraser River fishing. He'd felt he was one up on Wilson, getting to
go off with Ford alone, even though he knew Wilson didn't like fishing, anyway. His brother preferred going to concerts with Dorothy to doing
things with Ford.

They'd baited the hooks and hung over a piling
with their rods in the water, and that's when Ford
had told Tony he was going away.

"Your mother and I have our differences," Ford
had begun after much throat clearing and fiddling
with the line. "She's a fine woman, but I've always
been a disappointment to her, son, and try as I may,
I can't make it right. I am what I am, and I can't

be what she wants. And I can't live with the failure any longer—it's taking the heart out of me."

Tony had known that his mother and father didn't get along. He'd lain awake many nights, squirming in sympathy as he listened to Dorothy's shrill voice detailing every one of his father's faults, from his smoking all the way up to the fact that, in her opinion, he didn't earn enough money to support his family the way she thought they ought to be supported, and why didn't he have the gumption to try and better himself. Didn't he know he was a poor example for his sons, and wasn't it lucky the children had her father to show them what a man should be?

It was so many years ago, but Tony shuddered even now, remembering the empty feeling in his gut, the physical hurt in his chest when his father blurted, "I'm going away, son, to Australia. My friend Tommy has a sheep farm there and he's loaned me the fare and offered me work." Ford's weather-beaten face twisted with emotion and he swallowed hard. He laid a hand on Tony's shoulder and squeezed, the closest he ever came to an embrace. "I wish I could take you with me, boy, but I can't. Your mother would fight me to the death on that one. Besides, you're a clever boy. It's best for you to stay here and get your education."

Hot tears had burned behind Tony's eyelids. To keep from crying, he'd concentrated hard on a tugboat churning up the channel with its load of logs.

He'd hated his mother at that moment with a fierceness that consumed him.

Ford had cleared his throat once again and coughed hard. "Damn fags. Your mother's right— they're a filthy habit. Don't you ever start, promise me that."

Tony had promised. He'd kept that promise. And he'd never gone fishing again.

"Now, I'll write you, I'll send it care of your auntie Lully, so you'll always know whereabouts I am. You give her a call in a week or ten days and she'll have a letter for you. Look out for your sisters, son. And in a few years, when you're finished your schooling, you can come and be with me if you want to."

The next morning when Tony woke up, Ford was gone. Georgia and Judy bawled their eyes out, and Wilson, bossy and self-important, phoned their grandfather, who rushed over and comforted Dorothy by assuring her she was better off alone.

The letter Ford had promised arrived fourteen days later, and subsequent letters followed regularly, one for each of the children. Dorothy had a fit of hysterics when she found out, and forbade them to have any contact with their father or their auntie Lully, Ford's sister.

Tony defied her, and so did Georgia. They both kept up a steady correspondence with Ford, and once they were teenagers, they'd visited their aunt

Lully as often as they could sneak away. She'd died two years ago.

When Tony was older, Ford told him about the money he'd sent regularly to Dorothy for their support, money Dorothy never admitted receiving. As the years passed, Ford also cautiously told Tony about Betsy, the much younger woman he lived with. Ford never said, but Tony knew his mother had heard about Betsy and stonewalled a divorce, which kept Ford from marrying the woman he so obviously adored.

Dorothy was still legally Ford's wife, and she'd never stopped hating him for what she labeled his desertion of his wife and family. Her bitterness and anger had centered around a ring of her father's. She'd given it to Ford at their wedding and felt he should have returned it to her when he left. The subject came up with tiring regularity, and when it did, Dorothy castigated Ford to her adult children, just the way she'd done all during their growing-up years.

The situation between his father and mother had divided his family. Wilson grew up siding strongly with Dorothy, and Judy refused to take sides, agreeing with her mother when she couldn't avoid it.

Tony and Georgia sympathized with their father, and several times they'd openly said so to Dorothy. The ensuing scenes were horrific.

When Dorothy came to live with him, Tony had told her he respected her feelings, but he wouldn't allow any negative comments about Ford in front of McKensy. Ford was her grandfather, and that was that. He wouldn't have his daughter torn between warring camps.

Dorothy had promised, but of course she hadn't been able to keep her word. Her feelings about Ford were like an abscess that never healed, and even before she learned of his plan to visit, she and Tony had had several confrontations about his relationship with his father. Tony couldn't help but worry what effect Dorothy's deep-seated anger was having on his daughter.

Shortly after the letter arrived, he'd told Judy and Wilson about the impending visit. Ford had, of course, written to Georgia.

Tony said that what his siblings decided to do was their own affair, but he was hosting a dinner at a downtown restaurant in honor of his father and Betsy, and they and their kids were invited.

All hell broke loose when Tony told Dorothy about the visit and the dinner. He explained that he wanted McKensy to get to know her grandfather. Dorothy had thrown a fit of hysterics the morning of his accident, and hadn't mentioned Ford or the visit again, but Tony knew she would the moment he was home.

"Here're your meds, Doctor. Dinner will be along in a short while. Is there anything I can get you?" The nurse handed him the paper cup and the water, waiting like a warden to be sure he swallowed the array of pills.

He recognized Tylenol 3 and Rithonol, but the other one eluded him. He gave up trying to identify it and gulped the pills down. In answer to her question, he felt like asking for a voucher for a peaceful life, but he knew this particular nurse was lacking a sense of humor, so he kept quiet.

When she left, he opened the box of cookies Kate had brought, smiling at the hand-drawn certificate she'd enclosed. Certified egg free, she'd printed with a gold pen. He munched several down, thankful that he had something to kill his appetite before dinner arrived. The food here was not inspiring, in spite of Rene Lalonde and his innovations.

If the opportunity presented itself, Tony wondered if he'd ask Kate's opinion about the problems in his family. She'd been open with him about her unusual living situation, her love for Eliza and her problems with her ex. What sort of an absolute fool would force a woman like Kate to divorce him?

A total idiot, he concluded, reaching for another cookie.

She could be difficult, though. In his dealings with her he'd recognized an intractable stubborn streak. As he lay there, he thought about the conversation they'd had concerning his accident, and then he fantasized for a while about certain salacious aspects of being married to Kate, but even in his imagination, the idea of bringing her into the hornet's nest of his family deterred him, so he revised the imaginary relationship into a hot affair. Really hot.

Cool it, O'Connor. Maybe the aide who delivered his dinner wouldn't notice his erection. He reminded himself that long ago he'd decided to put his own personal needs on hold until McKensy grew up. Life was complicated enough without adding a lover into the mix.

But what the hell, there was no law he knew of against fantasizing.

CHAPTER SEVEN

A LITTLE OVER A WEEK LATER, Leslie shut the door to Kate's office and sank into the comfortable chair kept for visitors.

"O'Connor's back at work today, and everybody's waiting for the other shoe to drop. The word is out that heads will roll at the meeting he's called this afternoon. Everybody who was involved with his case will be present and trembling in their trainers."

Kate nodded, pouring hot water over the tea bags she'd dropped in the mugs. She handed one cup to Leslie and blew on her own to cool it. "I wanted to go over any concerns you have about what happened in the ER that morning. Just so we're on the same page."

"You figure he'll ream the whole lot of us out?"

"I don't really know what's going to happen," Kate said, shrugging. "He asked for a meeting with the staff involved in his case and I arranged it for him."

"But you'll be there?"

"Absolutely. He was still pretty angry about everything the last time we spoke, so I don't have a clue how he plans to handle it.''

Leslie groaned. ''We could all be out of a job by four o'clock. Except the docs, of course. They don't work for St. Joe's, anyhow. Lucky them.''

At Leslie's morose expression, Kate laughed. ''It won't come to firing, that's what unions are for. I think he just wants to hear exactly what happened from the people involved.''

''Too bad somebody doesn't stand up and say, 'We're all part of a conspiracy, O'Connor, but something went dreadfully wrong and you survived.'''

''C'mon, Les, he's not that bad.''

Leslie shot a look at Kate. ''Hey, that's a new line. Where's this benevolent attitude coming from? Isn't this the same O'Connor who tried to get your position canceled not too long ago?''

Kate flushed and nodded. ''The very same. But I've gotten to know him a bit better since his accident.''

''Aha.'' Her friend gave her an appraising look. ''And you'd like to get to know him better still, am I right?''

''C'mon, Les, he's not that good.''

They giggled at their own nonsense.

''Seriously, though, he's liable to put comments on our files that won't be exactly flattering,'' Leslie said glumly.

''You don't know that for sure. Think positive.''

Sitting in the boardroom later that afternoon and noting the tense expressions on the faces of the staff who'd been involved in Tony's care, Kate was having trouble following her own advice. She felt apprehensive about this meeting, and she reminded herself that she didn't have to fix anyone's feelings. Feelings just are, she reiterated silently.

The staff assembled a little early, but Tony had yet to appear. Kate knew his reputation for being on time.

No one was talking much, but when the door opened and he came in, voices stilled and the silence grew heavy and foreboding.

The crutches he was using because of his ankle didn't slow him down as he swung around the table and took a seat across from Kate. He was wearing gray dress pants and a lightweight sports jacket over a pale blue shirt, and as always, the clothes were expertly tailored and fitted him beautifully.

Kate decided she much preferred him in the shorts and T-shirt he'd been wearing the last time she saw him.

"Thanks for taking time out of your busy day to come," he began. "The purpose of this meeting is simply to ascertain what went wrong during my recent admission, and figure out how best to keep such things from happening to some other poor victim." He smiled, and when it was clear he was joking, there was an audible sigh of relief.

"I have to tell you, I felt pretty steamed over this

whole affair, and I was all prepared to arrange for a firing squad, but I've cooled off, thanks to some good advice.'' His eyes met Kate's for a long moment, and he actually smiled at her.

Warmth spread from her toes to the top of her head, and a sense of satisfaction came over her. Sometimes her job was difficult, but it was at moments like these, when a catastrophe had been averted, that she knew exactly why she did what she did.

One by one, the staff members explained exactly what had occurred when Tony was being treated by them. Without making excuses, they related the way mistakes had happened, and what they felt could be done to avert similar mistakes in the future. And each and every one included a heartfelt apology.

Kate was touched by them all. She'd talked to each of them separately and tried to help clarify for them how they felt and what they wanted to say to Tony. She'd given them the direction, and now they were going the distance.

Instead of confrontation, there was a growing sense of camaraderie as the meeting progressed. When it was over, each person who'd attended lined up to shake Tony's hand and express their pleasure at his recovery.

''In spite of our best efforts,'' Alf Jensen joked, and Kate was relieved when Tony laughed.

The meeting over, Kate got up and was almost

out the door when Tony walked past her on his crutches and closed it, then turned to face her. The room was empty except for the two of them.

"Kate, do you have a moment?"

"Sure." She tensed, aware of standing close to him, and moved back a step or two.

"I just wanted to say this was a good idea, after all. And you were right—blaming wasn't the way to go." He held her gaze and added, "I was wrong when I devalued the job you do here, Kate. I want to apologize for that, and thank you for getting everyone together."

"Apology accepted." She could tell that it was hard for him to admit that she'd been right. She felt a rush of admiration for him. It took a strong man to admit he'd been mistaken. More than that, his recognition of her efforts sent her heart soaring. She gave him a grateful smile. "Thank you so much, Tony."

"My pleasure." His grin flashed, and Kate's heart skipped a beat as their eyes met and held for several long moments before he glanced at his watch and shook his head. "I've gotta run. I've got patients lined up at the office waiting for me. See you soon, Kate."

She waited until he was gone and then sank back down into a chair and blew out the breath she'd been holding.

What exactly was going on with her and Tony O'Connor? Was the attraction she felt toward him reciprocal, or was she imagining things? And what had he meant by "see you soon"? Was he referring to work, or was he hinting at maybe meeting her away from the hospital?

What would she do if he asked her out? Besides the inherent dangers of dating someone she had to work closely with, there were the complications of her personal life. Having Scott living in her home and Eliza needing a great deal of her time had ended her association with the only two men she'd dated since her divorce.

Tony knew up front about Scott and Eliza, but he wouldn't fully understand how they affected her life until—

Lordy, Lewis, give it a rest. She shook her head and got to her feet. *Talk about a rich imagination.* All he'd done was smile at her, and she'd manufactured a whole romantic drama. Pathetic, she berated herself. Was she really that desperate...that lonely?

There wasn't time to give an honest answer, because she, too, had people waiting to talk to her, and she had to hurry or she'd keep them waiting. She needed to finish work on time today, because it was Thursday and Eliza's dance class started at five-thirty.

Since the birthday party fiasco, Kate had stopped relying on Scott to take Eliza anywhere. It cut down on conflict, but it meant that Kate had to fine-tune her schedule. Fortunately it was almost the end of

June, and dance lessons and school activities would be over for the summer. Kate was looking forward to the break.

Putting all thoughts of Tony out of her mind, she raced off down the corridor.

IN SPITE OF HER BEST EFFORTS, Kate was late getting home. Eliza was waiting impatiently, and after a hectic drive through rush hour traffic, they pulled up in front of DanceCo five minutes late.

"See you in an hour, Kate." Eliza tumbled out of the car and raced for the entrance. Kate was planning a grocery list in her head. There was a supermarket nearby, and she could do her weekly shopping while waiting for Eliza.

A tap on the car window startled her.

Tony, balanced on his crutches, smiled at her through the glass. She rolled down the window.

"Care for a coffee while we wait? There's a place just down on Tenth, but you'll have to drive. I can't with this ankle. We took the bus over here."

"Sure." Her heart gave a bump. She'd forgotten about McKensy and Eliza being in the same dance class. The shopping list went into a mental garbage can. "Get in."

The place he indicated was small, with an awning and four round tables out on the sidewalk. He ordered coffee and pastries, and when they were settled, he sighed and lifted his right foot up on a spare chair.

"I can't believe how much this bum ankle slows me down."

"Injuries tend to do that." She leaned back and sipped her coffee, enjoying the late afternoon sunshine, the people strolling past, the unexpected pleasure of being with Tony away from St. Joe's. "Maybe it's nature's way of telling us we're going too fast in the first place," she mused.

"You could well be right." He gave her a long, considering look and then shook his head.

"What? I've got spinach in my teeth?"

"Nope. I was just thinking that you see things in a different light than I do. It's refreshing."

"Thanks. I think." Maybe he just figured she was weird.

"I'd like your advice on something, Kate."

She gave him a wide smile. "It's free, but maybe that's what it's worth."

"I'll take my chances." He was quiet for a time, and she waited.

"My father is coming from Australia for a visit in August," he said at last. "I haven't seen him since I was eleven. He's bringing the woman he's lived with for the last twenty years or so, and his visit's turned my family into two hostile camps. Georgia and I are eager to see him and meet Betsy, but Wilson and Judy feel it would be disloyal to my mother." He sighed. "Dorothy's pretty worked up over this whole thing, and it's affecting everybody, particularly McKensy."

Kate listened as he explained more about his parents' marriage and described the resentment Dorothy had harbored since the day Ford left. She was both surprised and touched that Tony felt comfortable confiding in her like this.

"My mother's totally unreasonable about anything related to my dad. I've tried to explain that whatever the guy did, he's still my father, still McKensy's grandfather. But she doesn't see it that way at all."

"Sounds as if she's really insecure," Kate observed.

"Insecure?" His tone was incredulous. "That's about the last word I'd use to describe my mother. She has strong opinions about everything, and she's vocal about them. She does her best to get everyone on her side." He shook his head. "I sure wouldn't label her insecure."

"It was just a suggestion," Kate said in a mild tone. "Insecurity sometimes looks like overconfidence. Fear can take a lot of different forms."

"So what do I do about it?"

"What do you want to do?"

"See my father, naturally. I don't want to hurt Dorothy, but I won't give in on this, either." He blew out a frustrated breath. "I'm sick of arguing with her about it."

"It usually helps to just quietly state where you're coming from, without getting involved in arguments. Assertive people repeat the same thing calmly until the other person realizes that they mean it."

He thought that over. "You mean just keep saying I'm going to meet Ford, and I'm taking McKensy?"

Kate nodded. "The theory is that when you stick to your truth, without accusing or engaging, the other person has no choice but to accept it."

"You don't know my mother very well," he said, looking skeptical. "She doesn't listen. She'll go on and on until I lose my temper, and then I say things that hurt her, and I feel like an asshole." He raised an eyebrow. "Do you practice what you preach, Kate?"

She grimaced and shook her head. "Don't I wish I could. Theory's always a lot easier than practice. I still can't use my own methods on Eliza's father. My temper gets the best of me, and as soon as I get angry, I lose control of the situation."

"How did you get so interested in all this stuff about anger management, anyway?"

She'd asked herself the same question many times. "It was something I knew I had to learn how to handle." She sipped her coffee, took a bite out of a cream bun, and ignored the clutch in her belly that memory always brought. "My dad used to rage at my sister and my mom and me. I grew up feeling apologetic. I used to think that if I'd behaved differently he wouldn't have gotten mad in the first place.'' She'd grown up with a perpetual knot in her stomach.

The expression in Tony's eyes grew hard. ''Was he violent? Did he hit you?''

''Oh, no.'' Kate shook her head. ''Just verbally. But words can do almost as much harm as physical blows.''

''Yeah, you're right about that.'' Tony was obviously thinking of Dorothy again. ''So have you worked things out with your father?''

''Nope.'' Kate shook her head. ''He died before I'd figured out what I needed to say to him. I've always been sorry I couldn't resolve things with him, though, because he taught me a lot, even if it was all negative.''

''How about your mom? What's she like?''

''She's dead, too.'' Remembering made her sad. ''Mom was gentle, totally intimidated by my dad. She used to do her best to be invisible. She always stuck up for us girls, though. Unfortunately she died of a heart attack within a year of my father.''

''So there's just you and your sister now?''

Kate nodded. ''Marie's older than I am, married to a lawyer. They live in San Diego.''

''Any kids?''

''Two. I only see them once a year or so. I don't really know them as well as I'd like to. Marie's a very reserved person, super smart, but emotionally removed. She wanted to be a lawyer, but she got pregnant with Sara before she graduated.''

Tony nodded. "Shot herself in the foot, you think?"

"I can't help wondering about that."

"I watched Georgia do that, get married because she wasn't self-confident enough to go back to med school. I guess we've all done that from time to time, taken one road when we should have gone down the other." He gave his own foot a rueful look and muttered, "And then some of us wreck ourselves on a mere candy wrapper."

Should she say what she was thinking? What did she have to lose? "I'm grateful to that piece of foil, Tony."

"Oh yeah? Why's that?"

She was heading out on a limb here, but she did believe in being honest, didn't she? "I wouldn't be sitting here eating cream buns with you if you hadn't slipped. I like it."

He tipped his head back and laughed. She laughed, too, relieved that he hadn't read more into her remark than she'd intended.

"I guess I owe the damned thing a debt of gratitude myself, looking at it that way." Their eyes met, and the expression in his belied the lightness of his words. Kate felt again that indefinable tug that happened each time they really looked at each other.

"More coffee?"

About to agree, Kate glanced at her watch and

did a double take. "Omigod, the kids' class is over. We're ten minutes late picking them up."

"They'll wait." He didn't seem concerned. "We're gonna have to stop meeting like this."

"Think so?" She felt absurdly disappointed.

"Absolutely not." He grinned. "I don't know when I've enjoyed an hour more. Same time, same place, next class?"

"I'll be here." She probably should have given it some thought, but her acceptance was immediate and instinctive.

When Kate drove up in front of the dance studio, Eliza and McKensy were sitting on Eliza's red sweater on the grassy lawn.

Tony stuck his head out the window and called, "Hey, ladies, sorry we're late."

"Hi, Kate, hi, Daddy." McKensy came skipping over to greet him. She kissed him and helped him rescue his crutches from the back seat.

Eliza followed much more slowly. Kate got out of the car and came around to introduce Eliza to Tony.

"Hello, Eliza," he said, smiling and putting out a hand to her. "It's nice to meet you at last. Your mom's been telling me all sorts of nice things about you. I see you and McKensy know each other."

"How do you do," Eliza mumbled, staring at her feet and ignoring his outstretched hand. She shot Kate an accusing look and then climbed in the front seat of the car and shut the door with a bang.

Kate gaped at her. Eliza wasn't usually rude. Maybe something had happened in class to upset her.

Remembering what Tony had said about the bus, Kate asked, "Would you two like a ride home?"

"Thanks, but Georgia's coming to pick us up," Tony said. Then he added with a grin, "She's always late—she'll be here in a minute or twenty."

Kate got in the car, noticing that Eliza didn't respond to McKensy's cheerful wave. The little girl sat staring straight ahead, slouched down so her head barely showed above the window.

"What's wrong, Eliza?" Kate asked as they drove home. "Did you have problems at dance class?"

There was a recital coming up, the finale of the term. Maybe Eliza hadn't been chosen for a part she wanted.

But Eliza shook her head and remained mute.

"You were rude to Mr. O'Connor, Eliza. When you act that way it embarrasses me."

"I didn't know you were friends with McKensy's daddy." The words sounded more like an accusation than a comment.

"He's a doctor at St. Joe's, of course I'm friends with him. Does that bother you?" Kate was still confused as to what this was about.

Eliza shook her head, but her mutinous expression belied the denial.

Kate pulled into the drive of her house.

"I want Daddy to take me to class next time," Eliza blurted out as she scrambled from the car. She didn't wait for Kate the way she usually did. Instead she ran around to the back of the house, to the entrance to the apartment.

"Change your clothes and come and have some soup—I made that carrot stuff you like," Kate called after her. So she *was* a little jealous, Kate realized with a pang of sympathy.

Seeing McKensy with Tony had probably done it, Kate realized. Scott hardly ever took Eliza to her lessons. Her heart ached for her stepdaughter. Eliza had such difficult situations to come to terms with, and she was only a little girl. Scott had disappointed her so many times, and would again. And there was nothing Kate could do to prevent it.

She sighed and went inside. Walking into her house never failed to give her pleasure, even when she was feeling sad. She'd painted and decorated her home exactly as she wanted, using various shades of yellow for the living area, from a cheerful sunny color in the kitchen to muted amber in the living room. She loved plants and flowers, and greenery spilled down from an ornate old ladder she'd rested against the kitchen wall. The bamboo table and chairs she'd bought secondhand and then painted white looked inviting in the eating alcove.

It had taken her a long time to decide what she wanted her home to look like. Married to Scott, she'd been too busy earning their living to pay attention to her surroundings. When she'd bought this house, she'd spent money first on making the basement suite comfortable and bright, particularly Eliza's bedroom, so the little girl could invite friends home for sleepovers.

But in the last two years, Kate had begun to work on her own surroundings, and she'd found she enjoyed the process. She haunted secondhand stores and made use of inexpensive items to turn her house into a home. She'd planted a vegetable garden out back, and flowers along the borders, taking heed of the advice in women's magazines not to wait for a man in her life before making a home for herself.

Somewhere in the past few years she'd pretty much given up on the idea of ever marrying again. The fact that she couldn't have children and the situation with Scott and Eliza didn't enhance her appeal as a desirable partner.

But tonight, as she heated the soup she'd made that morning and waited for Eliza, she admitted how lonely her life was at times.

Eliza was wonderful, but Kate longed to have an adult to talk with, to exchange ideas, to confide memories. Being with Tony, even for one brief hour, had emphasized that longing. She missed having a sex life. She knew she'd be passionate with the right man. What happened to passion if it didn't get used? Did it just dry up and disappear?

Before she could get too maudlin, she reminded

herself that she had Eliza, she had her work, she had her friendship with Leslie. She had a great deal to be thankful for.

Cultivate an attitude of gratitude here, Lewis. You've got another date with him on Thursday, while the kids have dance class.

It wasn't a real date, though, she reminded herself.

It was just a way to pass an hour while the girls were in class. She mustn't make too much of it.

She liked it, though. She really liked it.

"I LIKE ELIZA, PAPA. She's got a sense of humor."

Tony was sitting on McKensy's bed. She was bathed and ready for sleep, wearing an old rugby shirt of his as a nightgown.

"A sense of humor's essential, all right." Tony had to struggle not to smile. McKensy had been assessing various friends and members of the family for weeks now, gauging their possession of, or lack of, a sense of humor, after seeing a television special on how humor affected illness.

"Does Kate have a sense of humor?"

"Yeah, she does." The memory of Kate teasing him with that engaging twinkle in her eye pleased him. Sitting with her and hearing her talk about her family had been interesting. Her view of people's actions and her acceptance of their differences was both touching and endearing.

"Do you like Kate, Papa?"

"Yeah, duchess, I do. I like her a lot." Kate's wide smile and endearing dimples came to mind. There was a softness about her voice and her manner that he found seductive.

Of course, he wasn't about to explain the seductive aspect to McKensy.

"So are you maybe gonna *date* her?"

Here there were dragons. Tony knew all too well the desperate need his daughter felt for the kind of family that included a mother and a father, and more children than just one.

He didn't want to raise McKensy's hopes at all.

"I don't think so, sweetie. We're good friends, but dating's not on the agenda."

She tipped her head to one side and gave him an exasperated look. "You're gonna stay single your whole *life* unless you date *some*body, Papa."

Her logic was sound. "I'll get around to it one of these days."

"That's what you always say."

Time to change the subject. "So is your class getting all prepared for the big dance recital coming up?"

Her gray eyes widened, and her face lit up. "Guess what? I nearly forgot. You'll never guess."

"You got the part of the princess?" He had no idea whether or not there even was a princess in this one, but judging by the two recitals he'd sat through already, it was inevitable. McKensy had wanted desperately to be the princess in the last production.

"Phooey." She blew a raspberry and shook her head. "Who wants to be a dumb princess? I get to be the *troll*. There's only one and it's such fun, and I got it."

The troll? For an instant, his protective hackles rose and he wanted to blast the idiot who'd cast his enchanting daughter as a troll.

"I'll show you how I'm gonna do it." She started to climb out of bed, and he restrained her.

"Better wait until tomorrow, honey. It's pretty late, and you need music to do it properly."

She lay down again and she was silent for a moment. "You're right, Papa. No music tonight. In case Grammy's headache still hurts."

The lightheartedness Tony had been feeling crashed like a suddenly becalmed kite at the mention of his mother. His brother Wilson had paid them a visit that evening, and although McKensy was in her bedroom when the argument started, Tony suspected she'd overheard a good part of it.

"Tony, I want you to reconsider this ridiculous business of having a dinner for Ford and that woman," Wilson had pontificated in his loud voice.

Dorothy had made coffee, and she was pouring mugs for the men and herself. Her lips tightened and her face took on a martyred expression as she took her place beside them at the kitchen table.

"You and Margaret can come or not, just as you

choose," Tony replied, keeping his voice as even as he could. Kate's words echoed in his head. *Assertive people repeat the same thing calmly until the other person realizes they mean it.*

"I don't know how you can be so pigheaded about this," Wilson continued in his pompous voice. "You're insulting Mother by having anything to do with him."

Wilson obviously hadn't read the same books Kate had.

"The dinner isn't open for discussion, and neither are my actions," Tony said, holding up a warning palm.

His older brother was oblivious. "Just out of respect for Mother, you ought to cancel," Wilson insisted.

Tony was hanging on to his temper by a thread. "That's not gonna happen, Wilson," he reiterated in an even tone. "And like I've said already, the dinner isn't open for discussion."

"You're deliberately causing trouble in the family over this," Wilson accused. "And you're causing Mom a lot of pain."

That was Dorothy's cue, and she didn't miss a beat. "Goodness knows I've done my best all these years for all of you," she whined. "And I don't see how you can go behind my back like this and even think of speaking to that horrible man. He deserted us, he walked out when Georgia was little more than a baby. He has no right to come back now and cause trouble like this.''

Tony couldn't stay calm any longer. ''He sent money to help support us all,'' he stated, knowing that his voice was rising. ''You always leave that little detail out, Mom. He could have just disappeared, but he didn't. He wrote letters and tried to keep in touch.'' The usual frustration and anger were building in him. He'd been through this countless times with his mother, and it typically ended with her in near hysterics and him wanting to put his fist through the nearest wall.

He could have repeated word for word her next salvo.

''What kind of father leaves his family and goes off to Australia without a backward glance? And takes a precious ring that doesn't belong to him? My father gave me that ring, and now that floozy your father's shacked up with is probably wearing it.''

As happened whenever this subject arose, Dorothy's voice vibrated with angry passion. ''And now you plan to greet him with open arms, as if he never did anything wrong. How can you do this to your own mother, Tony? After all I've done for you?''

He had to bite his tongue until it nearly bled to keep from telling her that the doing was a two-way street. She'd raised them, and she'd worked hard to do it, he didn't discount that. But for years now he and his brother and sisters had done whatever they could for their mother, financially and emotionally. They'd paid for a trip to Hawaii for her birthday, they'd surprised her with special dinners on Mother's Day, they'd made certain she had enough money in her pension plan to more than provide for her needs.

Tony paid her a generous salary for caring for McKensy, and he looked after all the household expenses. But he was coming to realize that Dorothy was like a black hole, which no amount of affection or gifts or money or reassurance could fill.

Remembering the escalating voices and the loud and angry quarrel that ensued, Tony felt ashamed. He knew by her troubled expression that McKensy had heard at least some of it. Afterward, Dorothy had donned a martyred expression and murmured about a vicious headache, and Tony, as usual, had felt like a jerk.

"I'm sure Grammy's head is better by now," Tony assured his daughter. "If it's not, I'll give her something for it and send her to bed early."

"Okay." McKensy's frown didn't go away, however. "My grandfather Ford who's coming to see us? He was *your* daddy, right?"

"Right."

"Was he nice to you when you were little, like you are to me?"

"Yes. He was a nice man, and a good father. He *is* a nice man."

"Then why did he steal from my grammy?" McKensy's gray eyes were puzzled. "She says he took something from her that didn't belong to him. That's not right, is it? That's stealing, right?"

Tony felt defeated. How did he explain to his child his family's conflicting views of the same event. "Grammy gave my father a ring when they were married," he said. "It was a ring that had been passed down in her family from her great-grandfather. When we give something, we don't expect it back. But Grammy thinks that because my father went to Australia, he should have given the ring back. Because it had been a family heirloom."

"What's an air loom?"

"It's something old that has been in a family for a long time and is valued by them because it represents their past."

"Do I have any air looms?"

"You have that photo album Grammy gave you, the one with all the old babies in it."

For her ninth birthday in April, Dorothy had given McKensy an ancient album that contained photos of their ancestors as babies and children, rolling hoops and dressed in outlandish costumes. Tony remembered looking at it when he was a child himself. It enthralled his daughter the way it had him, and she'd declared it her favorite gift.

That was the thing about his mother, Tony thought. She could sometimes do the most original and meaningful things, and at the same time be so narrow-minded and impossible he couldn't bear to be around her.

"And of course you have me," he sighed dramatically, getting up and balancing on his wretched crutches. "Some days I feel old enough to be an heirloom."

"Oh, Papa," she giggled, arranging her stuffed toys all around her in preparation for sleep. "Sometimes you're so funny. I'm glad you have a sense of humor."

Except it doesn't show often enough. Tony suspected that at St. Joe's, there were many who considered him grim. Lately he hadn't found much to laugh about, certainly not with his family. He'd made Kate laugh today, though. The thought pleased him.

"Could Eliza come over and see Fats's babies?" McKensy's pet hamster had produced a litter the day before. "I told her all about them. She said she was gonna ask if maybe she could have one. And I want to show her my room."

Dorothy had given McKensy a wall-size poster of a sun-filled forest glen, and made sunny yellow curtains. The window seat was filled with dolls and stuffed animals. The white dresser contained trays of hair accessories and nail varnish. It was all as alien to Tony as the surface of the moon, and a reminder of how much he relied on his mother to fill in the blanks for him.

"Sure, Eliza can come if she wants to. If Kate

says it's okay.'' *And why couldn't he ask Kate over to see his room?* The ridiculous lewdness of that brought a crooked grin to his lips, and when he went downstairs he was able to greet his mother with a kiss and a cheerful remark.

CHAPTER EIGHT

"LESLIE, GOOD MORNING, c'mon in. Have a cup of tea, the kettle's on." Kate looked up from her computer with a smile that faded as she got a closer look at her friend's face. "What's wrong, Les? You look pretty down."

Leslie closed the door of Kate's office and sank into a chair. "I had to bring Mom into Emerg last night."

"Is she okay? What was wrong?"

"When I got home yesterday, she was dizzy and staggering around. I was scared she'd fall and break her hip again. She'd been nauseous, and her right eye was moving involuntarily—nystagmus," Leslie explained, giving the symptom its proper medical label. "As you know, nystagmus can relate to an inner ear disorder, or it might also be a neurological symptom."

"Was she admitted?" Kate set a cup of peppermint tea in front of Leslie.

"Nope." Leslie shook her head. "Hersh was on, that new guy that nobody likes."

Kate nodded. She'd already heard more than a few complaints about the new resident in Emerg.

Nathanial Hersh was young and supremely confident, which was a good thing in an ER physician who was called on to make snap decisions. But from the reports Kate had received, Hersh was also impatient and brash, unwilling to listen to anyone else's input. He wasn't a team player.

"He examined Mom, and he diagnosed labyrinthitis."

"Ear inflammation?"

Leslie nodded. "She's had a case of the flu, and she's still a bit stuffy. He gave her some antibiotics and sent us home, even though I asked him if he'd admit her and run a few more tests. At her age, the same symptoms could easily indicate something a lot more serious. But he was definite about the diagnosis. He as much as told me to butt out and let him do his job. I got mad and said some things maybe I shouldn't have, but I felt he was way too casual and offhand about the diagnosis."

"So you're mad at him and you're worried about Galina."

Leslie gave an emphatic nod. "You better believe it. She seemed a little better this morning, but it's hard to tell. I got one of my neighbors to stay with her today."

Seeing how agitated Leslie was, Kate felt anxious herself about Galina. She was fond of the older woman. "Can you maybe get your family doctor to make a house call?"

Leslie shook her head. "Wouldn't you know he's

on holiday, and Mom won't agree to see a stranger. You know how stubborn she can be.''

Kate nodded, pondering what she could do to help. ''Do you want me to drop by after work?''

''Thanks, Kate,'' Leslie said after a moment's hesitation, ''but I really don't think it would make a difference.''

''What would make you feel better about this?'' It was a question Kate asked constantly.

''I don't know,'' Leslie admitted after some thought. ''I just have this bad feeling that I can't seem to shake.''

''If I can help in any way, just ask.''

A sharp knock at the door surprised them both.

Kate got up and opened it.

''Hi, Tony.'' She masked the surprise she felt. He'd never come to her office before. They always met in his, or at meetings. ''C'mon in. You know Leslie Yates.''

''I sure do. Hi, Leslie.'' He nodded and smiled, but he looked uncomfortable. ''I should have called instead of just dropping by, Kate. You're busy, I'll come back another time.''

''I've gotta be going right this minute,'' Leslie said, getting to her feet. ''It's probably bedlam down in the ER.'' She gave them a distracted wave and hurried out the door.

''Sit down, Tony.'' Kate indicated the seat Leslie had just vacated. ''I see you got rid of the crutches.'' He was using a cane instead.

"Yeah, the more I exercise this, the faster it'll get better. Sorry to barge in on you," Tony said, sinking down in the chair. "I'm here with a message from my daughter. She wanted me to ask if Eliza could maybe come home with her after dance class on Thursday. I think it has something to do with the hamster's babies. And I have to warn you, McKensy's looking for foster homes for them."

Kate laughed. "Sure, she can come. I'll check with her father, but I don't see why not. As far as the hamster goes, I half promised Eliza one for her birthday, anyway. It's coming up in July."

He nodded and smiled. "McKensy will be thrilled. And I'll drive Eliza home right after dinner."

Silence fell. He was a big man, Kate noted. Her office, already cramped, seemed to shrink still further with him in it.

"I like that print." He motioned at the wall. "It's one of my favorites."

"Mine, too." It was Monet's water lilies, and it soothed Kate to look at it.

"We still on for coffee on Thursday?"

"Absolutely."

"Good. See you then."

When he left, Kate realized she had a ridiculous grin plastered across her face. He could have called her instead of dropping by. The fact that he'd made an effort to see her pleased her, and for the rest of

the day she found herself smiling more often than
usual.

She raced down to the ER just before Leslie was
due to go off shift to find out how Galina was.

"She's about the same," Les sighed.

"If there's anything at all I can do, call me."

Leslie promised, but the phone didn't ring all
evening.

KATE MADE A POINT of being early for Eliza's class
on Thursday. She dropped Eliza at the entrance and
drove to Tenth. Tony was waiting, sitting at the
same table they'd had the previous week. Kate
parked right in front of the coffee shop, and he
smiled at her and waved. A spark came to life and
glowed inside of her.

When she sat down, the waitress came by and
Tony ordered. He remembered exactly how she
liked her coffee, and he ordered the pastries she'd
enjoyed. The glow intensified.

"You look pretty in blue," he commented, admiring the summer dress she'd put on after work.

"Thank you." She flushed with pleasure. It was
the first time he'd commented on what she wore.
She liked what he was wearing, too, although she
didn't say so. He had khaki walking shorts on, and
his legs were long and strong, nicely dusted with
dark hair, the way she remembered them from the
hospital. A shiver of awareness went through her.

What would it be like to have those long legs entwined with hers?

He was giving her a quizzical look, and she felt the color rising in her cheeks. *Idiot. Don't keep on blushing. He doesn't know what you're thinking.*

But there was a spark of humor in his eyes, and a hot intensity to his gaze that made her wonder if maybe he suspected. To break the awkwardness of the moment she blurted, "How's the ankle?"

"Much improved, thanks. I've started working out again. I can't jog just yet, but walking doesn't seem to hurt it, as long as I don't go fast or far."

"Do you like to jog?" Her glance went automatically to his legs. That was probably what made them so powerful.

"Yeah, I stay pretty active. I've done a couple marathons, but the training's intense and it takes up too much time. I still play the odd game of rugby, and I bike when I can. But since I came on board at St. Joe's I haven't had much time for anything but work. How about you, Kate? What types of exercise do you enjoy?"

This was tricky. She didn't dare admit that weeding her vegetables and her flower beds was her usual workout. Although she *did* go swimming with Eliza fairly regularly.

"Gardening. Swimming. Walking," she embellished. It wasn't much of a lie. She walked quite a lot at work. "I'm like you, it's hard to find the time."

"Want to start a routine, real slow, with me?"

Real slow. With him. Her heart lurched. "Sure. Doing what?"

"Walking. Let's figure out a time that might work for us both. You a morning person?"

She definitely wasn't, but no way would she admit it just now and endanger her prospects. "I could be." Would it kill her to get up half an hour earlier?

"Great. What about a walk tomorrow at, say, five-thirty?"

"Five-thirty?" Her voice was faint. "In the morning?" She knew she sounded like an idiot, but *was* there a five-thirty in the morning? And was this a date? "Yeah. I guess so. Sure."

"Okay, it's a date."

There, he'd said it. It just wasn't the kind she'd had in mind. Was she going to regret this? She glanced again at his legs and got a tingly feeling in her stomach. "Where?"

"How about Queen Elizabeth Park? It's equidistant from both of our houses, and it's got good paths."

It also had hills, if she remembered correctly. "Great." She did her best to sound enthusiastic and gave him a bright, phony smile. "I'll be there."

Maybe she'd just stay up so she wouldn't have the challenge of climbing out of her warm bed at that ungodly hour.

He took a swallow of coffee and she did, too.

Then he smiled at her. He had the greatest smile.

"Eliza was fine with the idea of coming home with McKensy after class?"

"Yeah, she's looking forward to it." Actually, Eliza hadn't been as enthusiastic about it as Kate thought she would, but the hamsters had clinched the deal.

He was studying his coffee cup. "I tried my best to put your advice into practice the other night."

"What advice was that?" Kate was still thinking about Eliza.

"Your wise words about how assertive people handle themselves at critical moments."

"Oh, that. And did it work?"

"It might have if I'd stuck with it," he admitted in a rueful tone. "Trouble was, I lost my temper."

She grinned at him. "Welcome to the club. Don't be too hard on yourself. Remember, we always get another shot at it."

He pulled a face. "Oh, yeah, I've no doubts about that at all."

She wondered what specific incident had triggered him, but she didn't ask, and he changed the subject. "McKensy's thrilled because she got the part of the troll in the recital. What part did Eliza get?"

"She's a rabbit."

"Was she disappointed?"

"Yeah, she really was." Kate shook her head. "She wanted to be the wicked stepmother."

He looked puzzled. "Isn't there a princess in this one?"

Kate frowned. "There must be, there always is. At least in the ones I've watched. Eliza didn't say."

"Why do you suppose our girls don't have any hankering to be the princess?" He sounded honestly confused, and Kate had to laugh. She was also touched at his reference to *our girls*.

"I'd say it's an indication that we're raising them right. I mean, what future is there for a princess? All a princess can aspire to be is queen."

He shrugged. "So what's ahead for a troll? Or a stepmother, for that matter?"

"Character parts on sitcoms?"

They both laughed. Kate noted that she laughed a lot when she was with Tony. She could only hope she'd still be laughing at five-thirty the following morning.

CHAPTER NINE

HOSPITAL EMPLOYEE DIES of Hypothermia.

Kate imagined the headlines as she slogged up the path behind Tony. She hadn't anticipated rain, even though this was Vancouver. It had been hot and sunny for several weeks, and she'd expected more of the summery weather. But when her alarm blared at four-forty-five and she managed to unglue her eyes, the clouds outside her window were thick and it was already sprinkling.

She'd waited for him to call and cancel. Instead, he called and confirmed. And now, twenty-three long minutes into the walk, the sprinkle had turned into a full-scale downpour. Her jacket was dripping. Her bare legs were freezing. Her new trainers were sopping.

"This is invigorating." Tony was marching along the pathway, using his cane, but still moving at a pace that made her pant, although at 6:00 a.m. the only pace she was truly capable of was a stationary one.

Horizontal and stationary.

"Feels good, breathing in all this fresh air." He drew in a deep lungful and expelled it.

She was trying not to breathe. All that chilly air made her shiver. "It's waking me up, I'll say that for it." She swung her arms back and forth to get her circulation going. The effort exhausted her.

He trudged upward and onward. "The kids had a great time last night. They named all the hamsters after the dwarfs in Snow White."

"Eliza told me. She also said that your mom spoiled them silly. She let them make sugar cookies and decorate them, and she made them burgers and fries for dinner, but she let them eat their dessert first."

"Mom's big on ice cream as an appetizer. She has shares in Baskin-Robbins."

"She's a pretty cool grandma by the sounds of it. In fact, Eliza said she was *way cool*. She's green with envy that McKensy has hamsters *and* a grandma." It had been fascinating for Kate to learn of this entirely different side of Dorothy.

"Your ex doesn't have family?" He held a bush back so she could pass. Drops of water trickled down his unshaven face.

"Nope. He grew up in foster homes." The path was rising at an astonishing rate, and Kate tried her best not to sound winded. "He married young, and then his first wife died when Eliza was only three months old. Scott had no experience at all with babies, and no one to turn to for help."

"So you came along and rescued them both."

"Yeah." She tried to ignore the water dripping

down her neck. "Nurses are great rescuers. It's one of the things in our makeup that causes us the most difficulty. It's so hard to resist the impulse to rush in and fix everything."

"So do you think you've got it licked now? That fixing addiction?"

She laughed. "I'm in recovery." But was she? She thought of Scott and decided she had a ways to go. "I do one day at a time and I still have my slips."

"And where does your job fit in with recovery? Seems to me you spend all your working hours fixing things between people."

"Nope." She shook her head. "I don't fix anything. All I do is give people guidelines on how to fix whatever it is by themselves. There's a big difference."

Thank goodness they'd finally reached the top of the hill. Kate's heart was pounding. Clouds of mist obscured the city, so there was no view. She thought longingly of a hot shower, coffee, breakfast. In a tentative voice she said, "Tony, think we should head back?"

"God, I thought you'd never ask." He gave a huge sigh of relief. "I didn't want to be a wimp, but I'm soaked and I've had enough of this walking in the rain."

Kate threw back her head and gave a victory shout that startled Tony and echoed to them from the mists.

They made their way down the hill faster than they'd come up. Except for their two vehicles, the car park was deserted.

"Same time tomorrow morning?" He gave her a challenging look.

"Tomorrow's Saturday." Weekdays were one thing, but getting up before dawn on the weekend horrified her. "I have to cut the lawn if this rain clears, so maybe we'd better stick to weekdays."

"Sounds good to me."

They stopped beside her car. As she fumbled in her pocket for the keys, she felt his hand on her shoulder. She turned and looked up at him, and her breath caught in her throat. He was going to kiss her.

Getting up had been worth it, after all.

She tipped her head back, sighed and closed her eyes.

SHE'D HAD HIS FULL ATTENTION from the moment she'd climbed out of her car looking dazed and sleepy, hair tied in a messy knot at her neck, face shiny and free of makeup. It was a turn-on, because he'd never before seen Kate anything but perfectly groomed.

The green waterproof jacket she wore came below her shorts, which for some weird reason he found sexy as hell. As she'd walked ahead of him on the trail, he couldn't keep his eyes off her long, slim legs. He couldn't keep from fantasizing that she had nothing on under the damned coat.

Now he slid a hand under her wet hair and drew her toward him.

She came willingly.

Tipping his head, he brought his mouth down on hers.

Her skin was wet and warm, her lips full and soft. She tasted of the coffee he'd brought her, and of the toothpaste she'd used, and of something subtle and sweet and intimate that was strictly Kate.

As he tasted her more fully, she made a small appreciative noise in her throat, and the sound excited him. Deepening the kiss, he dropped his cane and used his free hand to draw her closer, and her arms slid around him. Then she pulled back a little, unzipping his jacket and her own and sliding her arms inside.

It was intimate and thrilling. He could feel the water from her coat wetting his sweatshirt. He could feel her hands, warm and tentative and arousing, touching his back.

He closed his eyes and moved his lips from her mouth to her cheek, nuzzling her jawline, breathing in the fragrant, sweet smell of her neck when she tipped her head back.

"Kate. Katie. Katherine." He breathed the variations of her name, liking the sound of it, the feel of it on his lips. He felt the shudder that ran through her when he claimed her lips again, more aggressively this time.

A sharp clap of thunder startled him.

"Hell's bells." He opened his eyes and squinted up at the sky just as rain began pounding down on them. "It's a bloody deluge."

After helping her unlock her car, he hurried around to the passenger side and clambered in beside her. She started the engine and turned on the heater as rain pounded against the roof. For a while they sat side by side in silence, watching the torrent pour down the windshield.

"I like kissing you," he finally said in a companionable tone.

"I like being kissed by you." Her voice was as matter of fact as his had been.

He tried not to let his apprehension show. "So where do we go from here?"

"I'd say to work." She pointed at the clock on the dash and grinned at him. "Wouldn't you?"

"Right." She *was* right. There was no need to analyze what had happened. He reached over and touched her wet, sleek hair, smoothing it back behind her ears. He liked her ears, delicate and pinned close to her head. "I'll see you at the Admin meeting at ten, then."

"I'll be there." She smiled at him. "Dried off and properly dressed."

"More's the pity." He got out and made a dash

for his car, and by the time he got it started and the wipers going, she was driving away.

He sat with the motor running, thinking about Kate.

It's a big mistake, he reminded himself, getting involved with a co-worker. You know all the reasons, you've always claimed it wasn't something you'd ever do. And besides, she's not someone you can just have an affair with, O'Connor. She's got a kid, just like you do. She's responsible and respectable. McKensy likes her way too much.

For heaven's sake, man, it was only a kiss, not a roll in the flower beds. It was erotic, though. He thought of the way her breasts had pressed against him, nipples hard from the chill—maybe from more than the chill—and he shuddered. If the sun had been shining, he might have gone nuts enough to drag her into the flower beds, after all.

He smiled at his own insanity. *Me Tarzan, you Jane.* Sex for the sake of sex. Wasn't that supposed to be every man's fantasy?

One thing about it, fantasy sure as hell took his mind off other things. He hadn't thought about his mother or his father or Wilson or the impending visit for all of two hours now.

Get moving, O'Connor. You're gonna be late for work.

KATE'S PHONE RANG that afternoon.

"For some reason," Tony began, "I forgot to

ask you this morning if you'd sit with me at the kids' recital on Monday night? Mom usually comes, but she's got a bowling tournament.''

Kate hesitated. Scott had always come with her to the recitals, and Eliza loved having them both there. But if it came to a choice between sitting with Scott or sitting with Tony—no choice.

''I'd like that,'' she said.

''Shall McKensy and I pick you two up, or do you want to meet us at the studio?''

''We'll meet you there.''

''Good. I'll get tickets and watch for you. I'll try to get us seats front row center. How often will we have the chance to see our very own troll and rabbit cavorting around a stage?''

''Not again in this lifetime, I fervently hope,'' she said.

''The girls can't eat much before they perform, so I thought we'd all go out for dinner afterward— if you agree. There's an Italian place that's good for families. It'll be quiet on Monday night.''

Now, *this* was sounding a bit more like the kind of date she fancied. ''I'll check with Eliza, but it sounds perfect. Thank you.''

Families, he'd said. She visualized him and McKensy, her and Eliza, waving from the windows of a green cottage with a white picket fence and a huge tree in the front yard. But then just where did Scott fit into that cozy picture?

CHAPTER TEN

"DADDY'S COMING WITH US, right, Kate?"

It was Monday afternoon, and Kate was doing a final fitting on the rabbit costume Eliza would wear in the recital.

She'd hurried home, but it was already 5:20, and the show started at six-thirty. The costumes the school provided weren't new, and the fur had a tendency to molt.

Kate sneezed for the third time. "Hold still, I need to take this in a little right here." So she was avoiding an answer, so what?

"Daddy's coming, isn't he?" Eliza was nothing if not persistent.

"Did you ask him?"

"Of course I did, a long time ago. He said he was gonna talk to you about it."

Scott had. He'd said he hadn't had time to get a ticket and asked her to pick one up for him. He'd meet her at the studio but he'd be a little late. It was his usual system to avoid spending his own money.

Kate had told him he'd have to get his own

ticket, that she had a date. Scott had looked surprised, and then he'd laughed.

"You got a date for a kid's dancing thing? What is he, a little light in the loafers?"

Give herself credit, Kate thought, she'd managed to walk away without saying anything.

"Daddy *is* coming, isn't he, Kate?"

She was feeling uncomfortable. She resented being Scott's messenger. "I don't know, sweetie." Why should she feel responsible for the bloody man? But it wasn't Scott she felt responsible for, she reminded herself. It was this beautiful little girl.

Eliza looked enchanting with her spiky hair freshly done, her cheeks pink with excitement, her long, gangly legs sticking out the bottom of the ridiculous costume. Now, if Kate could only get this darned tail to stay in the right place—

"But he always comes with you, you always watch me together." Kate sighed. Eliza wasn't going to let it go.

"Not this time." *The truth shall make you free.* "This time I'm not going with your daddy. Mr. O'Connor asked me to sit with him. I told you that, remember?"

Eliza jerked away and Kate stabbed a needle into her middle finger.

"Ouch, Eliza, you've got to hold still." She sucked her stabbed finger. "We have to leave soon and this tail is drooping."

"That's not fair." Eliza's face was scarlet, her

blue eyes mutinous. "You should sit with my daddy, not with Mr. O'Connor."

Kate struggled to remain calm. "Eliza, you know your daddy and I aren't married anymore. When people aren't married, they have other friends."

"But you and Daddy are friends. You always sit with Daddy at my dance things."

"I always have, yes. But tonight I'm not going to. That doesn't mean your daddy can't come on his own." Kate was feeling worse and worse about this whole thing.

"But he won't." Tears poured down Eliza's face. "You know he won't come by himself. He likes to come with you. And I want him to be there."

"Then you need to tell him that."

"*You* tell him. You're the grown-up, not me." Eliza tore off the costume, splitting several seams that Kate had painstakingly stitched.

"If my daddy doesn't come, it's all your fault," she hollered as she tore off in search of her father.

Kate sewed the costume together and had a quick shower, feeling tense and edgy. She put on a pair of amber silk trousers and a matching top, gave her hair a quick brush, and went looking for Eliza.

"All ready, sweetie?" The girl was sitting in Kate's kitchen, her costume stuffed in a carrier bag. Crossing her fingers mentally, Kate said, "Is your daddy going to come watch you perform?"

"He said maybe." Eliza shot Kate an angry look,

and she didn't say another word during the drive to the studio.

Tony was waiting just inside the entrance. He looked at Kate and silently whistled, and for an instant she felt a rush of pleasure. But Eliza ignored his cheerful greeting, and once again Kate felt embarrassed by her stepdaughter's behavior.

Eliza didn't respond when Kate gave her a good-luck hug and assured her she was going to be the best rabbit that had ever danced a tap solo.

One of the dressers came and took Eliza backstage, and for the first time she could remember, Kate was relieved to see her go.

"I've snagged us the best seats in the house," Tony said. "Is Eliza having a little attack of stage fright? I thought McKensy might, but she said she's enjoying herself too much to be scared. She disappeared the minute we got here." He escorted Kate through the maze of chairs, seating her as he'd promised, front row, center. "Can I get you a drink? They have soda or coffee, and bottled water."

"I need something cold and wet. Water, please."

Tony left her, and Kate turned and anxiously searched the crowd for Scott. Surely he wouldn't let Eliza down. But there was no sign of him.

The noise level increased as more and more parents and friends arrived, and by the time the lights dimmed and the recital began, the small room was filled to capacity. Kate looked around several more times for Scott. She knew it was unlikely in the extreme that he'd appear now, but for Eliza's sake she kept hoping.

"Here we go." Tony reached over and took Kate's hand in his as first McKensy, wearing a green costume covered with scales, and then Eliza, with her bunny ears, fur bodysuit and crooked tail came on stage.

Kate caught a glimpse of Tony's face. It was filled with humor and intense pride as he watched his daughter capering across the stage. McKensy had spotted Tony, and although she wasn't allowed to wave at him, Kate could tell she was dancing her heart out for her father.

Eliza also saw Kate. Their eyes met, then Kate watched the girl scan the crowd, searching for Scott. When she didn't see him, she went on with her dance, but there was no energy in it.

Like all the dance recitals Kate had attended, this one went on far too long, but this time she wasn't bored at all. She was far too conscious of Tony holding her hand, of the way he'd threaded his fingers through her own, cradling her hand on his thigh, stroking his thumb across her skin and making her shiver. But she knew, too, that Eliza's sharp gaze had spotted them holding hands. There was no reason in the world to feel guilty, but she did.

When at last the final number was over and the curtain calls came to an end, they got to their feet and waited for the girls to finish changing and find them. McKensy was first out of the dressing room. She flew to her father and threw her arms around his waist.

"Hey, duchess, you were the best dancing troll I've ever seen." He stuck his hand in his pocket and pulled out a small box tied with gold ribbon. "My compliments, mademoiselle."

"Ooh, Papa, thank you." Eyes shining, McKensy tore open the box, revealing a delicate silver chain with a pewter troll dangling from it. "I love it, I love it," she crowed.

Kate cursed herself for not doing something similar for Eliza, who walked slowly out of the dressing room just as McKensy asked Kate to fasten the troll around her neck for her.

"Eliza, over here." Kate thought for a moment the girl hadn't seen them, because she stopped some distance away and stood in the middle of the crowd.

"Eliza?"

At last, she came slowly toward them.

"Eliza, you were wonderful," Kate enthused. She drew the girl into her arms and hugged her close, kissing her cheek. Eliza's body was stiff, her expression stony.

Tony added his congratulations, and then pulled out another small box with the same gold ribbon from his suit pocket and handed it to Eliza.

"For the best of the bunnies," he complimented.

"Open it, Eliza, I'll bet it's like mine," Mc-

Kensy urged. "Only you'll have a bunny instead of a troll, right, Papa?"

"I don't want it." Eliza thrust the gift at Kate without even glancing at Tony or McKensy. "I want to go home now."

"But we're going out to dinner." Kate had to hold on to her temper. Eliza's deliberate rudeness was becoming intolerable

"I'm not hungry. I want to go home, Kate."

"Would you excuse us for a moment, please?" Kate took Eliza's arm in a firm grip and marched her into the crowded washroom, searching for a corner that afforded a bit of privacy.

There was none. Every cubicle was full, and people were waiting in line. Kate bent down to Eliza's level, and in a quiet voice she said, "Okay, young lady, just what's going on with you?"

Eliza's mouth opened wide and she let out a shriek that had everyone in the room staring. When Kate tried to put her arms around her, Eliza lashed out at her with her fists and her feet, screaming, "Go away. I don't want you, I want my daddy."

A blow to her cheekbone made Kate's eyes water. Then Eliza's foot connected with her shin, and Kate gasped in pain. She grabbed Eliza's fists in her own and held on. "Eliza, stop that this minute. Hitting is not allowed."

"She needs a good smack, in my opinion," an older woman declared, shaking her white head in disapproval. "In my day, children weren't allowed to act like that."

Two small girls watched from a few feet away, eyes wide. One of the mothers smiled at Kate, her expression sympathetic.

Kate took a deep breath, trying to focus on Eliza rather than her audience and her own exasperation. Eliza was still shrieking at the top of her lungs, and then the shrieks turned into words. "I hate you. Go away. I want my daddy."

A cubicle was vacant, and Kate tugged Eliza inside and shut the door. Eliza slumped down on the floor, arms over her head, her shouts turning into sobs.

Kate waited for what felt like an eternity. She stroked Eliza's head and tried not to think about Tony and McKensy waiting outside. She tried to rationalize the frustration and outright anger she felt. She wanted to go out to dinner with Tony. She wanted Eliza to behave well, the way McKensy did. She wanted a chance tonight at a life that approached normal.

When Eliza had calmed somewhat, Kate said, "Okay, kid, we can't stay in this toilet all night. Tony and McKensy are waiting outside. It's not fair to just let them wait."

"I don't care about them. I want to go home," Eliza sobbed. "I want my daddy."

"Okay." Kate thought for a moment. "I'll drop you at home before the rest of us go for dinner."

Eliza's head shot up and she glared at Kate with swollen, teary eyes. "I want you to stay home, too."

Kate's patience was slipping. "Sorry, Eliza. I promised I'd go out to dinner with Tony and McKensy, and that's what I'm doing. I'll drop you at home first, though, if you're really sure that's what you want."

"That's not fair." Eliza began to wail again. "I don't want you to go with them."

"Eliza, I'm losing my patience with you. Get up and we'll wash your face with some cool water, and then we're out of here."

But Eliza stayed huddled in a ball on the floor.

At her wit's end, Kate got to her feet and lifted the heavy girl into her arms. It was like carrying a bag of limp, soggy laundry. Good thing she was strong, Kate thought, struggling her way out of the cubicle. Deciding to skip the face washing, she staggered into the reception area, which was now deserted except for Tony and McKensy, waiting on a bench near the door.

Tony got up and came toward her, extending his arms in an offer to take Eliza. The girl's face was buried in Kate's neck, but she must have seen through the corner of her eye what was happening, because she wound her arms so tight around Kate's neck it became difficult to breathe.

"Eliza, loosen up, you're choking me to death." Kate's patience was nearing an end. She managed to get a breath and gasped, "I'm sorry, but she's decided she wants to go home, so could I meet you at the restaurant?"

"We can follow you home, and then you can ride with us," Tony offered.

Kate thought it over. "You're already late with your reservation. I'll meet you there." She was furious with Eliza for causing such problems.

"Fine." He wrote down the address and then put a hand on Eliza's head. "Bye, Eliza. I'm sorry you're not feeling well."

Stony silence.

He slipped the little package he'd brought for Eliza into Kate's handbag and held first one door and then the other so she could dump her burden into the passenger seat of her car. Eliza curled into a ball and wrapped her arms around her head.

"See you in about half an hour," Kate promised in a bright tone that belied the way she was feeling. It took every bit of her self-control to keep silent on the drive home. When she pulled up in front of her house, she felt the urge to scream. For the first time in weeks, Scott's beaten up old car wasn't in the driveway.

Foreboding filled Kate even as she snapped, "Okay, Eliza, here we are. Let's go find your daddy."

But that was impossible, because Scott wasn't home.

THERE WAS NO WAY KATE could leave Eliza by herself, and four frantic calls confirmed there were no baby-sitters available at the last moment.

Feeling mad enough to smash something, Kate called the restaurant and told Tony she couldn't make it. She could hear the same disappointment in his voice that she felt.

Eliza was sitting on the living room couch, tears dry now, shoulders slumped. For the first time ever, Kate found it difficult to summon up sympathy for the little girl.

To calm herself, she put the kettle on and found a chamomile tea bag. Taking a deep breath she prayed for patience. Once the tea was steeped, she returned to the living room and sat down beside her stepdaughter.

"We need to talk about this, Eliza."

But Eliza, her expression closed tight, got to her feet. "I'm going to have a bath and put my jammies on." She started to walk away and then turned and gave Kate a woebegone look. "Please, please can I sleep in your bed tonight, Kate?"

Her voice quavered and she looked so pathetic Kate's heart melted. What was there to say except yes? There'd been enough drama for one night, she decided. They could discuss this whole thing another time.

She poured her best bubble bath into the tub and washed Eliza's back. While the little girl got her pajamas on, Kate warmed a glass of milk for her and made them each a grilled cheese sandwich. Neither of them mentioned the scene at the dance studio.

When Eliza was asleep at last in Kate's bed, her blankie against her cheek and her tattered old teddy tucked under one arm, Kate stood looking down at her. The blond spiky hair was still damp from the bath, and Eliza's skin looked translucent in the soft light. Her long lashes were dark shadows on her rosy cheeks. The last vestige of Kate's anger melted and overwhelming love filled her heart. She bent and pressed a kiss against Eliza's temple. She loved this child with all her heart. She often thought she'd give up her own life for the girl.

And then a traitorous little voice in her head whispered, *Aah, but isn't that exactly what you're doing?*

Shocked, Kate tiptoed out of the bedroom and sank into one of her comfortable living room chairs. She'd built a trap for herself by having Scott and Eliza live here, in her house. How would she ever get free?

She was attracted to Tony. Hell, that was the understatement of the year. She wanted to get naked with him, she wanted to know what he looked like, last thing at night and first thing in the morning.

And how was she going to accomplish that with Eliza in her bed and Scott in her apartment? A wave of depression threatened to engulf her. It was hopeless. It would be years before Eliza was grown, and until then she was stuck with Scott.

C'mon, Lewis. You're good at solving problems. You do it all day at work. So why, no matter how hard she tried, couldn't she see a clear solution to her own situation? She sat pondering over it, and jumped when the phone rang. It was Tony, it had to be.

"Kate?" Leslie's voice was thick and high, almost unrecognizable.

"What's the matter, Les?" Kate was instantly alert. She'd talked to Leslie twice on the weekend, and again this morning.

"It's Mom." Leslie's voice broke. "She's—she's gone, Kate."

For an instant, Kate didn't understand.

"She—she died an hour ago." Leslie broke down in great, gulping sobs. It took several moments before she regained enough control to tell Kate what had happened. "When I got home from work, her voice was slurred. She couldn't walk, her right side was paralyzed. She—she was there alone. I thought she was getting better…today was the first time I didn't have my neighbor stay with her. I rushed her into Emerg and they did everything they could, but she—she's gone, Kate."

While she was frantically trying to figure out who she could get to stay with Eliza, Kate heard Scott's car pull into the driveway.

"Les, where are you?"

"I'm at St. Joe's. The staff lounge in Emerg. I can't seem to think straight or figure out where to go or what to do."

"Stay right where you are. I'll be there in fifteen minutes."

Kate hung up and raced downstairs.

Scott was just coming in the basement door.

"Eliza's asleep in my bed, I have to go out." She glared at him. "She was devastated that you didn't come to her recital."

"I meant to. But then one of the guys dropped by, and it got too late." He looked sheepish and hangdog.

"How can you live with yourself, letting her down like that? Eliza was really upset."

"Well, you were there, weren't you? With your boyfriend," he added with a sly grin. "I figured three's a crowd. And I didn't really promise Eliza I'd come, anyway, I just said maybe."

He was an idiot. He didn't deserve a daughter like Eliza. Kate stared at him, her temper barely in check. She had to leave, she reminded herself. She had to be with Leslie. There was no point in getting into anything with Scott.

"I don't know what time I'll be back," she snapped. "Make sure you set the alarm and get her up and ready for school in the morning."

"I always do, don't I?"

"I seem to recall a lot of times when you've slept in, and I've driven her to school," Kate reminded him. He was infuriating. Without another word, she turned on her heel and went back upstairs, grabbed her handbag and raced out to her car.

LESLIE LOOKED ON THE VERGE of collapse. Kate put her arms around her friend and held her. Les was trembling, and her breathing was fast and shallow. She was obviously in shock.

Several nurses came in and began heating soup in the microwave and talking among themselves.

"Let's go up to my office," Kate suggested. "I'll make some tea, and we can talk." She took Leslie's arm, and the other woman followed her like an automaton, down the hall, into the elevator, upstairs.

Kate unlocked her office door and switched on the floor lamp.

"Sit down, Les. I'll plug the kettle in."

"I want to kill him," Leslie burst out. "I want to kill him with my bare hands."

Puzzled, Kate turned to her. "Kill who, Les?"

"Dr. Hersh," she spat out. "Remember, I told you that when I brought Mom in to Emerg, Hersh diagnosed labyrinthitis? She didn't have that at all. She had an aneurysm, I'd bet everything on it. There'll be an—" her voice broke "—an autopsy, and it'll show that I'm right, I just know it. Hersh didn't even bother doing tests on her. I asked him to, and he brushed me off. I told you, remember?"

Kate did remember. She sat down and took Leslie's cold hand in hers, and her concern for her friend grew. "You think if Hersh had done the tests, it might have made a difference?"

Leslie's head bobbed up and down in violent assent. "Of course it would have. She should have been admitted. They'd have found out what was really wrong. But he wouldn't. He brushed her off as just some—some old Russian woman who wasn't worth taking time over—" Her voice broke again, and it was some time before she could go on. "He didn't like me. I argued with him. And now because of *him,* my mom—" Her face crumpled. "Because of him my mom's *dead.*"

To Kate, the reasoning wasn't rational. But Kate wasn't feeling rational herself. Galina's sudden death was a shock.

Leslie laid her head on Kate's desk, her fists clenched. "I can't stand it, I can't. Mom was my best friend, what am I gonna do without her? She was always there for me. When I lost the baby she stayed with me day and night. When that jerk I was married to walked out, she brought me fl-flowers. She had a hot meal waiting when I got home, no matter what time it was."

Kate didn't know what to say that would be comforting, so she simply listened as Leslie went on and on.

"Mom scrubbed offices at night to earn enough money so I could get my nursing degree. She was so proud when I graduated." Leslie lifted her wrist, her face ravaged with grief. She tapped her nurse's watch. "She bought me this and gave it to me that day. God only knows what—what she did without to get it for me." Leslie dissolved again into floods of tears, the words coming out in choking gasps.

"She—she h-had one g-good dress and she wore it for years, just so I could have clo-clothes."

Now Kate's own tears flowed freely. She'd loved Galina, and she'd miss the sweet old lady. And her heart ached for her friend. As she listened, she rubbed Leslie's back. There didn't seem to be much else she could do to help.

"I'll—I'll g-get him for this, so help me God, I will."

It took Kate a moment to realize Leslie was once again talking about Dr. Hersh. The degree of anger in her voice was frightening.

"Sounds like you're really mad at him," she whispered.

Raising her head, Leslie gave Kate a cold, hard stare. "Don't you *dare* use your anger techniques on me. Don't you *dare* try to get me to calm down about this. It won't work, Kate." Her eyes filled again and she choked back another sob. "I *hate* him. And I'm gonna get him for this." Her voice quavered. "For my mom's sake." Sobs overcame her once more. "I'll—I'll do whatever it takes…I'll go to a lawyer."

Leslie's whole body was shaking. Kate put her arms around her and held her until Leslie regained some control. She blew her nose and sat back in her chair. "You need to go home, Kate, it's really late. And I need to go home, too."

Kate shook her head. "Les, you can't be alone tonight. Come home with me. Let me take care of you. Or let me come home with you—Scott's with Eliza."

But Leslie shook her head. "Thanks, but I really need to be by myself for a while. And there're people I need to call—old friends of Mom's who'll want to know, my dad's sisters. And there're arrangements to make for the—" She swallowed and struggled for control. "For Mom's f-funeral. She told me how she wanted it to be."

Although she was reluctant to leave her alone, Kate understood what Leslie was saying.

"Okay. But if it gets too much to handle, if you feel like you want someone to talk to, any hour, phone me. Promise?"

Leslie nodded, and Kate walked with her to the parking level. She gave Leslie a final, fierce hug, then made her way to her own car.

Driving home, Kate realized she was trembling. Sobs overwhelmed her when she thought of Galina. The old woman had been kind to her. She'd crocheted a throw for Kate's sofa and given her recipes for borscht and perogies.

When she got home, Kate's call display registered several calls from Tony. He hadn't left a message, however, and by now it was nearly midnight, far too late to phone him. Kate's spirits sank even lower.

He must have wondered why she wasn't answering, she realized. She'd told him she had to stay with Eliza because no one was home. He couldn't possibly think that she'd been dishonest with him. Could he?

The whole evening had been jinxed, Kate thought with a sigh. She could only hope that tomorrow would be better.

For her, probably it would, Kate thought. But for Leslie it would be a long and difficult time before she had anything approaching a good day again. Kate's heart ached for her friend.

In spite of the lateness of the hour, she couldn't get to sleep when she finally slid into bed beside Eliza. She was anticipating a call from Leslie, she told herself.

But the truth was, ridiculous as it might be, she kept hoping Tony might phone again.

CHAPTER ELEVEN

TONY PICKED UP THE PHONE and then glanced at the clock. It was almost midnight, far too late to call Kate again. He felt uneasy and dissatisfied with the way the evening had gone. He'd been looking forward to having dinner with Kate and the two girls, and although he and McKensy had pretended it was fine eating by themselves, she, too, was disappointed.

She was also good and mad at Eliza. "She acted like a baby."

"She wanted her daddy to be there, and he didn't come."

"So?" Her expressive face was disdainful. "Lots of times I waited for my mom, and she didn't come. But I didn't have a screaming fit over it."

She had when she was younger, Tony recalled. He didn't remind her, though. It hurt them both too much to recall those times.

"She felt let down, McKensy. People have different ways of showing their disappointment."

"I used to like her, but now I don't." McKensy's chin took on a stubborn set, and although he did his best to reason with her, it didn't have much effect. Eliza had spoiled their special evening, and McKensy wasn't ready to forgive her for it.

And Tony, too, couldn't help but feel annoyed at the child, ridiculous as that was. The simple fact was he'd wanted Kate with him, he'd wanted their daughters to get along. He'd been shocked at the intensity of his reaction when she called the restaurant and said she couldn't come, and he was still feeling let down when he and McKensy got home.

Dorothy was watching television. Once McKensy went to bed, she'd switched off the sound and turned to him.

Tony waited, his stomach knotted. He knew by the expression on her face what was coming.

"I talked to Judy tonight. She said that she and Peter are fighting about this dinner you're having for *that man*."

He'd wanted to get up and walk out of the room, but he stayed where he was and managed to say, "Oh, yeah? Why is that?"

"Peter thinks the children should meet their grandfather, but Judy says she's thought it over and she doesn't see why he's coming back now after all these years just to cause trouble."

Tony wondered if that was indeed what Judy had said, or if his mother had twisted the message to suit herself. It wouldn't be the first time.

"I'd say that's something Judy and Peter need to work out on their own." He'd clicked the television sound on again and pretended to be fascinated by a news broadcast, but the loud sighs and meaningful glances from his mother finally got to him.

"I'm going to bed, Mom. Good night."

"Tony, I know you don't want to listen to this, but—"

"You're absolutely right, Ma. I don't want to listen." He'd walked out of the room, ignoring her shocked exclamation and her voice calling his name.

Up in his room, he'd called Kate, but she didn't pick up. Was she there, just not wanting to talk to him? He'd called again, half an hour later, and there was still no reply. He began to wonder if perhaps there'd been something more seriously wrong with Eliza than a temper tantrum.

Or maybe there was more going on with Kate than she'd admitted to him. The thought upset him. He couldn't imagine what that might be, and whatever the answer, there didn't seem to be anything he could do about it tonight.

But after he'd showered and crawled into bed, he couldn't sleep. Where the hell was she?

He'd finally dug into his briefcase and brought out journals and brochures he hadn't had a chance to read. If anything would put him to sleep, he thought with a grimace, these suckers would.

He was flipping through a pamphlet listing upcoming conferences when he spotted a two-day session, Friday and Saturday, that weekend in Edmonton. The topic was Medical Error and the Need to

Inform. Considering his recent experience at St. Joe's, the subject matter was relevant. One of the speakers was a guy who'd gotten his MD and then gone on to become a lawyer.

McKensy was going to a weekend sleepover with her cousins, and if Tony stayed home he'd be alone with Dorothy. Without McKensy's presence, his mother would be certain to harangue him about the upcoming visit from Ford. That alone was incentive enough to register for the seminar.

Tony decided he'd do it first thing in the morning.

He closed his eyes and another idea sprang to mind.

Why not talk Kate into coming to the conference, too? No kids, no ex-husbands, no Dorothy, no St. Joe's. His imagination got the better of him, and he began to visualize adjoining hotel rooms, whirlpool baths, Kate in his arms. In his bed.

He'd better start with the conference and let fate do its thing. How early in the morning could he phone her and suggest it?

"TONY?" KATE CLEARED HER croaky throat and tried to wake up. "Hi, Tony. What time is it?" She sat up and yawned, shoving her hair out of her eyes and squinting at the bedside clock.

"Seven-twenty." He sounded contrite, and a bit stiff. "I figured you'd be up by now. Sorry for waking you."

"I must have slept in." She was such a liar. She never struggled out of bed before seven-thirty, but she felt like a slug saying so. She had her morning routine down to a fine art. "Thanks for the wake-up call," she said, attempting to sound alert.

Eliza was like Kate, not a morning person. She was still sleeping soundly beside her, the quilt pulled right over her head.

"You called last night and I wasn't here." Kate told him about Leslie's mother's death, adding that Scott had gotten home in time to baby-sit while she went to St. Joe's.

"That's rough. Did you know Leslie's mom?"

"Galina, yes." Kate had to fight back tears. "She was a dear lady, I liked her a lot. She and Leslie were really close. Les is taking it hard."

"Losing a parent has to be tough. And speaking of parenting, is Eliza okay this morning?"

Kate glanced at the lump under the covers. "She's fine. She's sleeping right here beside me. I feel bad about dinner, Tony, I really wanted to be there."

His voice was relaxed now. "Me, too. But I take rain checks."

"That's good news." She smiled and snuggled down, drawing the duvet up to her shoulders. This was delicious, talking to him first thing in the morning. She could get used to this real fast.

"I'd take you out for dinner this coming weekend," he was saying, "but I've decided on the spur of the moment that I'm going to a conference in Edmonton. Medical Error and the Need to Inform. Sounds like something that would be valuable for the next time I'm a patient.''

''I saw the brochure.'' She'd noted the conference because it was a subject that applied directly to her job.

''Why not register? I know it's short notice, but I'll bet they still have room for more participants. These things are never that well attended.''

Her first thought was of Leslie. Her friend needed her. But her imagination stirred at what it would be like to be in Edmonton with him. They could have dinner together with no time lines attached. They could talk without either of them having to rush away. There'd be a place to kiss where it wasn't pouring rain.

Regret filled her. There was Les, and there was also Eliza. Friday was their special evening together—girls' night for shopping, an early movie and pizza. Before she could say anything to Tony, the bedroom door opened.

''Time to get up, honeybun,'' Scott's loud voice boomed out.

''Daddy, Daddy. Morning, Daddy.'' Eliza must have been awake all the time, because she popped out of the blankets now, arms held wide for Scott's hug. He lumbered over to the bed.

''I missed you last night, Daddy.''

''I missed you, too, baby.'' Scott plopped his

wide bottom down on Kate's bed. Eliza extended one arm to include Kate in the hug. "Morning, Kate." She made loud smacking noises as she kissed first one parent, then the other.

"I'm on the phone, Scott. Eliza, go with your daddy."

"But I'm not awake yet." She stretched and snuggled under the blankets.

Kate was horrified, knowing that Tony was hearing all this. There was strained silence on the other end of the telephone, and then he said, "Sounds like you're busy at the moment, Kate, I'll talk to you later." The line went dead.

Kate scowled at her ex, wanting to throw the phone at him.

"Exactly what do you think you're doing, barging into my bedroom like this? You know the rules, my living space is off limits. And get off the bed."

He gave a shrug, his face a mask of innocence. "You were the one who told me to get Eliza up for school this morning. You said to be sure and come and wake her because you weren't going to be home, remember?"

She did remember. Why, this one time, had he done what she'd asked? "I suppose you didn't think to look in the driveway and see if my car was here before you came barging into my room?"

"As a matter of fact, I didn't."

But she knew by the studied innocence on his

face that he had. He was just trying, as usual, to test her patience.

"Eliza, go with your daddy this minute and get ready for school."

The two of them left, and Kate slumped against the pillows, feeling furious and defeated. A glance at the clock indicated that she'd better get moving, and she dragged herself out of bed, her earlier exuberance gone.

When she finally staggered into the kitchen, Eliza came dancing in.

"Guess what, Kate?" Her eyes were glowing, and she couldn't stand still. She bounced from one foot to the other. "My daddy's taking me camping. Thursday's the end of school, so we're going Friday morning. We'll be gone till Sunday. Daddy's going to show me how to catch a fish."

So much for girls' night out. Kate summoned up a smile and told Eliza she was happy for her, and then she dialed Leslie's number.

Her friend answered on the first ring. The funeral would be on Thursday, she announced in a lifeless voice. It would be a small, quiet ceremony followed by cremation, which Galina had requested.

"I'll arrange food for after the funeral," Kate offered, "and I'll come over this afternoon. We can talk or go out for a walk or something." She'd take a few hours off. Leslie shouldn't go through this alone.

Leslie's voice took on a hard edge. "That's not

necessary, Kate. I'm not having anyone over after the service. And I'm busy this afternoon.''

People dealt with grief in different ways, Kate reminded herself. ''Then how about coming to dinner Saturday, Les? Eliza's going camping, we'd have a chance to talk.''

''I won't be here on the weekend,'' Leslie said. ''I'm going away for a few days. My aunt is coming and I'm taking her to Victoria.''

''Maybe that's a good idea.'' And maybe not, Kate thought, trying desperately to figure out a way to reach her friend. ''If anything happens and you change your mind, though, I'm free. We'll go wherever you want, my treat.''

''Thanks.'' Leslie sounded distant and distracted. ''I've got to hang up now. I'm waiting to hear from a lawyer. I'm going to make a formal complaint to the college about Hersh, and if this lawyer agrees, I'm also going to sue him in civil court.''

Kate's heart sank. She'd hoped that by this morning some of Leslie's anger might have given way to grief, but it was obvious that hadn't happened. What could she say to her friend? What could she do to help?

''How about talking to Hersh first, Les? I'm sure he'll feel terrible when he hears about your mom. Would it make you feel better if I arranged a meeting—''

''No. I told you last night, don't even try that route with me, Kate.'' Leslie's reaction was definite, her voice suddenly cool, as if Kate had betrayed her. "I never want to lay eyes on that man again, unless it's in court. Look, I've got to go now. I've got a million things to do." And for the second time that morning, the phone line went dead in Kate's ear before she could respond.

CHAPTER TWELVE

TONY TOLD HIMSELF HE wouldn't seek Kate out at work that morning. It wasn't any of his business why her ex-husband would be in her bedroom so early.

It didn't matter a damn to him, he seethed. There'd been an intimacy to the overheard scene that shocked him, emphasizing just how much of a stranger he was in Kate's life, and how familiar this Scott guy was, barging into her bedroom first thing in the morning.

Which of course logically brought out the urge to race over there and punch Kate's ex in the gut. *Absolutely rational response, O'Connor, you raving lunatic.*

He registered for the seminar, and then at 9:00 a.m., he sat through a meeting where the main issue seemed to be the question of why plastic instruments were being autoclaved when they were supposed to be disposable. The answer, of course, involved finances. He made what he hoped were intelligent noises as he tried to figure out why he'd be jealous over a woman he hadn't properly dated yet.

Not that he hadn't tried, Goddamn it. He'd wanted to take her to dinner. With the kids included. He should have known that dating with kids around was impossible.

Or at least, it was with Kate's kid around, he revised. McKensy was another story. She'd happily set up a wedding date for him and Kate if she thought there was any possibility of getting the stepmother she longed for.

At ten, Tony took part in a panel discussion whose primary function was to approve new physicians. He read résumés and asked questions and wondered if Kate had called. He checked his messages during the coffee break and was furious to find she hadn't even tried.

At eleven, he participated in a discussion among staff members on the pros and cons of introducing a policy that would make alternative medical practices available to patients at St. Joe's. He asked questions about acupuncture and decided he'd find out if she were free for lunch. They had a lot of things to sort out.

To his enormous relief, she answered when he dialed her office.

"Kate? It's Tony." Now, wasn't that self-confidence for you? Surely by now she ought to recognize him by his voice. It was a wonder he hadn't added O'Connor. "Kate, could you meet me for lunch?"

'Oh, Tony, I'm so sorry. I have a luncheon meeting with Libby Baker.''

Libby Baker was the social worker in Rehab. And he could tell from the formal tone of Kate's voice that she had someone in her office at that moment.

"Not a problem," he said in such an upbeat tone he almost made himself nauseous. "I just wanted to go over the, uh—" he racked his brain for something viable "—your ideas regarding the new consent forms in admitting." It was fairly lame, but it was the best he could come up with on short notice.

"Absolutely. Maybe we could discuss them on the plane," she said.

The plane? For an instant it didn't register. Then he understood. The *plane*. The plane to Edmonton. She was going to the conference. His spirits went from dismal to elated with no intermediary steps.

"I'm booked on the 9:00 a.m. flight with Western Air on Friday morning," she said, just as if he'd had sense enough to ask.

Slack, O'Connor. You're definitely out of practice at this.

"Me, too." He'd booked with Air Canada, but that was about to change. The moment he got off the phone, he'd switch airlines and make certain they had seats beside each other. "Fine, then. That's great. I'll be sure to bring the admission forms along."

Not in this lifetime. His wicked imagination went

straight to other, more salacious things they could do on the plane. Was there still something called the high-flyers club, where you spread a blanket across your knees and— He suddenly remembered that the flight to Edmonton with Western Air was only forty-five minutes in a small plane that probably didn't even have blankets. Last time he took it, which was several years ago, it barely had bathrooms.

"Tony, can I call you back? I'm with someone at the moment. I'll be free in half an hour or so."

"Sure, call whenever you can. I'll be here." He'd been about to head off to the cafeteria, but lunch suddenly didn't seem at all important.

He busied himself with changing his reservations and cajoling Western Air into seating him and Kate side by side. Then he scanned reports until the phone rang. He pounced on it.

"Tony, it's me." Her voice was low and intimate. "Sorry about before. I had someone with me and couldn't talk. Look, I want to apologize for this morning."

"No apologies necessary." The Edmonton trip had taken the heat out of his anger, although he still wanted to murder her ex, just on general principles.

"Well, let me explain exactly what happened, then." She did, and by the time she was through he felt much better, although he still didn't appreciate her ex-husband having the run of her bedroom. But what right did he have to object?

"Talk about a comedy of errors," she sighed in his ear. "You see why I'm looking forward to Edmonton. It feels like a holiday for me."

"I'm looking forward to it, as well. And Kate, I'm going to have to cancel our morning walk for the rest of the week. I have early meetings and a dental appointment."

"Oh, too bad." Was that a trace of relief in her voice? "I wouldn't be able to make it on Thursday, anyway. Leslie's mom's funeral is in the morning."

"Do you have the name of the funeral parlor? I'll send flowers. I wish I could attend, but what with taking Friday off, I'm swamped."

She gave him the number and he made a note of it.

"Until Friday, then."

He loved the husky timbre of her voice on the phone. "By the way," he asked, "do you need a ride to the airport?"

"That would be nice. If we're going on the same flight?"

"We are. I'll pick you up at six-fifteen."

There was a pause. "Six-fifteen? Doesn't the flight leave at nine?"

"I always like to leave time for emergencies."

He heard her swallow. "Of course. I'll be ready. Six-fifteen."

He hung up the phone, locked his hands behind his head and spent five precious minutes anticipating Edmonton.

LESLIE WAS A MODEL of perfect control during Galina's funeral. She sat with an elderly woman Kate assumed was her aunt. Kate wept during the church service, but Leslie was dry eyed. At the burial site, she made a point of personally thanking each person for coming, but politely refused Kate's offer to take everyone out to lunch and promised she'd call later in the day.

Feeling uneasy about Leslie and sad about Galina, Kate went back to work, but the moment she was finished that afternoon, she drove to Leslie's apartment. She'd worried all day that Leslie would be sitting by herself, crying, but Leslie was composed when she answered the door. She said that she and her aunt were leaving for Victoria and they had to go to the airport right away, so she couldn't invite Kate in.

Kate suggested she drive them to the airport. "You must be exhausted, Les, and I'm worried sick about you."

Leslie refused to let Kate drive them. She wanted her car waiting when they got back, she explained.

It was hard for Kate not to feel rebuffed, but she reminded herself that Leslie was under a great deal of strain.

When she got home, she had a ton of things to do herself, laundry and ironing and her own packing, as well as help Eliza get ready for her camping trip. Still, Kate made a point of calling Leslie twice more that evening, using her friend's cell number.

There was no answer either time. She was probably out with her relatives, Kate surmised. She left a message asking her friend to call the moment she got in.

But by the time Kate headed for bed, the phone still hadn't rung.

"MORNING, KATE." Tony lifted her suitcase as if it didn't weigh a ton and put it in the trunk of his sleek black car. He was wearing close-fitting jeans and a short-sleeved checked shirt, and he looked totally wide-awake.

Kate could smell the fresh, outdoorsy scent of his aftershave, which was a good thing, she thought blearily. It might help wake her up. The shower she'd taken hadn't done much in that regard.

She'd helped Eliza pack the night before, and it was late before she got around to her own packing. And then she couldn't decide what to take, which was why her suitcase was so heavy. Around midnight, she'd become desperate and simply decided to take almost everything she owned in the way of decent clothes. Once that decision was made, it was just a matter of packing her largest suitcase. But then she'd had a bath and gone through the entire female beauty ritual of plucking her eyebrows, shaving her legs and giving herself a manicure and pedicure.

As a result, she hadn't gotten to bed until two-thirty this morning. Then she couldn't get to sleep, and now she couldn't wake up. But man, was she well groomed.

"Here we go." Tony opened the car door for her and she slid inside.

She figured anybody that could drive at six in the morning would probably want to hold a conversation, and she hoped it would be something that didn't require much gray matter. Her brain didn't feel any more awake than the rest of her.

"Looks like rain," he commented.

She made an agreeable noise in her throat.

"I hope it's hot in Edmonton, I like the heat."

She got away with the same noncommittal noise, and leaned back against the padded headrest. "This is a really nice car, Tony," she said in a sleepy voice.

"Glad you like it." He sounded amused.

It *was* nice. The seat was soft. The headrest was comfortable. She could just relax during the forty-minute drive to the airport. She closed her eyes just for an instant, and then someone was touching her face with his fingertips. With an effort, she dragged herself into consciousness. The car was stopped in an echoing underground parking space.

"Kate? Kate, wake up. We're at the airport."

She was slumped sideways against his shoulder, drooling a little. "Omigod. I guess I fell asleep."

He was grinning at her. "I guess you did. I've

never seen anyone go to sleep that fast. I was talking to you and you were dead to the world.''

"Gosh. Did I snore?" Her dry throat told her she had. She cleared it and added, "Much?"

"No, no." He was trying not to laugh. "Not very much, anyhow. You awake enough to walk into the terminal, or should I request a wheelchair?"

"Yeah. No, no wheelchair. Of course I can walk." She cleared her throat again and ran her fingers through her hair. It was probably all mashed down on one side, and her eyes felt gummy.

"I'll get a cart for the bags."

He'd found one and had it loaded by the time she dragged herself out of the car. "I'm starting to wake up now." She tried to sound chipper.

"That's a positive sign." He was laughing at her again, but it didn't bother her. Instead, she felt cared for.

He wheeled the cart into the terminal, found the proper counter and got the luggage checked and their boarding passes without her having to say or do a thing except yawn. The best part about arriving so early was no lineups.

He tucked her hand under his elbow and led her through Security and to the waiting area at the proper gate. He found her a seat—they were nearly the first ones there—and then went off and bought coffee, fixing it just the way she liked it, lots of cream and a touch of sugar.

"This is heaven—pure ambrosia. Thank you."

As she sipped the coffee, she could feel herself begin to come out of the sleepy fog that enveloped her. When she had finished, she visited the washroom and splashed her face with cold water, redoing the minimal makeup that was now smeared and smudged. She brushed her hair, grateful that the shoulder-length mop didn't require much attention.

Tony smiled at her when she came out, and all of a sudden she was awake and aware. God, he was a good-looking man. He had the longest legs and the nicest hands and the warmest smile. And they'd be together all day today and tomorrow. She walked over and sat back down beside him, conscious that he was watching her every step of the way. He winked at her and handed her a fresh coffee, which was exactly what she wanted at that moment.

"So," she said in a bright voice, "what do you think about those new admission forms?"

He grinned at her. "You want the truth? I don't give a tinker's damn about the admission forms."

She grinned back. "What a coincidence. Because neither do I."

"So what does that leave us to talk about on the plane?"

She sipped the coffee, and the jolt of caffeine brought her awake once and for all. "Well, for starters you could tell me how you got in the habit of getting up in the middle of the night. And what kind of complex makes you arrive at the airport hours early?"

"I'm an early riser. It's a carryover from when I was interning and hardly got any sleep at all. As for getting here early, remember when you were a kid and you were so excited about something you couldn't sleep?"

"Yeah. Christmas, my birthday. Sometimes when the moon's full and shining in my window, I still get wired."

"That's how I was about this trip. Wired."

"It's your birthday? You were looking at the moon?"

"I was thinking about Edmonton."

"You're that excited about hearing a lecturer talk about medical ethics?" She thought she knew what he was leading up to, but she couldn't resist teasing him a little.

"Nope. I'm excited about having a couple days to ourselves, Kate. Away from kids and family and work." He looked into her eyes, and he wasn't laughing at all. "I'm excited about spending time with you, getting to know you better. We haven't really had a chance for that."

Warmth spread from her toes to her ears. She couldn't stop smiling, and she felt giddy and breathless. All she could stammer was "I feel the same way."

CHAPTER THIRTEEN

THE HOTEL MACDONALD was old, beautifully refurbished and situated smack in downtown Edmonton. When the bellman left, Kate bounced on the bed. The mattress was better than the one she had at home. Her room was small but elegant, and a glance in the luxurious bathroom confirmed that she'd be wonderfully comfortable here.

Outside the window, the sun shone like a beacon. Getting up early and flying across the mountains had its advantages; it was still midmorning, and the whole day was ahead. Excitement surged through her.

Tony had suggested they meet at the registration desk in fifteen minutes, take care of details and then have brunch together.

So what did sophisticated women wear to brunch in an elegant hotel? Kate undressed and dug through her overflowing suitcase until she came up with a simple knit dress, almost sleeveless, that ended a few inches above her knees. Its color was the same green as her eyes, and she pulled it on, along with a pair of summer sandals. This was fun, not having to think about anything more serious than what to wear.

She opened the door to the corridor just as Tony opened his. He was in a room directly across the hall, and she'd remarked on the coincidence when they got their room cards. The slight flush on his cheekbones gave him away.

"Did you request rooms on the same floor?"

"Yeah." He looked sheepish. "I thought it would be more convenient. Do you mind?"

She didn't mind one bit. But the shiver of desire inside of her made her wish he'd be clearer about what he meant by more convenient. *More convenient for what?* She warned herself not to get her hopes up.

"From my window it looks as if there's the most amazing jogging path right along the river," he said as they headed for the elevators. "I'm not sure how to get down there but there must be a way. I'll ask the concierge about it. I thought if you didn't mind, we could get up early and explore it tomorrow morning."

"Great." She hoped her smile didn't look as phony as it felt.

They registered and then found the dining room. Brunch was being served. The sight of the laden buffet tables reminded Kate that all she'd had to eat so far was a package of nuts on the plane. She was ravenous. As she filled her plate, Tony said, "Did you manage to get into the lectures you wanted?"

"All of them. And you?"

"I only registered for two," he confessed. "I thought it would be nice to take some time to explore the city."

Why hadn't he told her that before she signed up for so many sessions? Well, she could always play hooky for the first time in her life.

As they moved along the buffet table side by side, Kate noticed another couple just ahead of them. They were putting strawberries on each other's plates and smiling into each other's eyes with an intensity that signaled recent sexual activity, or sexual activity soon to come.

Kate was suddenly envious. Were they on their honeymoon? She added strawberries and maple syrup to the pancakes she'd chosen and surreptitiously watched the other couple, feeling a tiny bit sorry for herself.

She'd never had a honeymoon. She and Scott had been married in a registry office. Her best friend, her bridesmaid, had held Eliza during the brief ceremony, and they'd all gone back to Kate's apartment afterward, where she served the fancy lunch she'd prepared the night before. Later that day she and Scott ordered pizza for dinner, and Eliza cried most of the night. She'd been teething.

When she and Tony sat down with their food, Kate blurted, "Did you go on a honeymoon when you got married?"

His eyebrows lifted in surprise, but he said,

"Yeah. We went to Hawaii for ten days. We stayed at an old army encampment on the rainy end of Oahu because we didn't have much money."

"What was your wife like?" She'd often wondered, but never had the courage to ask. "Do you have a picture of her?"

"Nope. I tossed them all out when she left. I was pretty fed up with her there for a while. We're on good terms now, though. When you've got a kid, it makes sense to get along."

"Describe her for me." It was suddenly important that she have a mental picture of this woman he'd loved.

"Petite. Slim. Lots of black curly hair. Very intense."

Kate was surprised. For some reason she'd thought McKensy must look like her mother, but the woman he described couldn't have been more unlike Tony's daughter.

"Pretty?"

"Yeah." It was obvious he wasn't going to elaborate. And she wasn't ready to politely back off, either. For some reason this had become a mission.

"What was her name?"

He was giving her a strange look now. "Jessica. Jessica Diehl."

"Sounds classy. How did you meet?" Kate knew she was pushing the envelope here, but she couldn't seem to stop.

"She was singing in a jazz joint in downtown

Vancouver. A bunch of us docs used to go there. I sat in sometimes with the band.''

"When you were in ICU, your mother told me you play the saxophone.''

"Used to. I don't play much anymore, I don't get time to practice.''

"And that's where you met Jessica?'' She really ought to leave it alone, but it was an obsession.

He nodded. "One of the guys in the band introduced us.''

"Love at first song?'' Kate couldn't carry a tune to save her soul.

He shook his head. "More like lust.'' He gave Kate a deliberate look. "I took her home that night and stayed over. We had a pretty intense time of it, and within a couple weeks she was pregnant. She told me she was using birth control, so I didn't bother. Anyhow, we got married. She stuck until McKensy was four, but she wanted to sing professionally, and she got an offer from a jazz band that had a gig in Toronto. We both pretended at first it was temporary, but after a year she filed for divorce.'' He ate some of his French toast and then added, "If she hadn't, I would have.''

Kate noticed there wasn't any anger in his voice. He just sounded resigned.

"Does she see McKensy often?''

Tony shook his head. "If she's in town, she'll call and take McKensy out. The last time was four months ago. Jessica's totally wrapped up in her career.''

"That must be hard on McKensy." Words were coming out her mouth without any planning at all.

"It was at first. McKensy was still so little and we both thought Jessica meant it when she said she'd be back. Now McKensy doesn't expect much anymore. She loves her mom, but she accepts that singing comes first with her.''

Kate thought of Eliza, who knew she was first in Kate's heart.

She'd asked so many questions, she might as well ask one more—the million dollar one. "Think you'll ever get married again?''

He took a long time to answer. "My daughter wants that more than anything. She asked for a stepmom for Christmas last year, believe it or not, but it's not exactly something you can order from a catalog, is it?'' His grin was wry, his eyes guarded. "The truth is, I don't know, Kate. As you've seen, my family seems to thrive on turmoil. Mom isn't easy to get along with. She hated Jessica, and if I'd allowed it, she would have caused trouble between us.''

"Every family has its problems.'' She thought of herself and Scott and Eliza. They weren't even a family anymore, but they certainly had their share of upsets.

His nod was noncommittal. "I'm going for more hash browns. You want anything?''

"No, thank you." She watched him walk over to the buffet. She had a feeling there was more to his reluctance about marriage than just his family. Maybe he still had strong feelings for Jessica that he was being careful to hide. Or maybe he'd been hurt so badly he wouldn't try again.

The sweetness of the maple syrup turned a little sour.

When he came back, they finished their food and then made plans to meet for dinner, since each of them had a seminar to attend that afternoon.

They rode upstairs in the elevator and walked side by side down the corridor, but he didn't take her hand. He didn't touch her at all.

When they reached their rooms, Kate said in a cheery voice, "See you at six," and closed her door firmly behind her.

Darn. No matter how pretty the room was, it was awfully empty with only her in it.

TONY KNOCKED ON KATE'S DOOR at five minutes before six, and her dimples showed when he whistled in appreciation.

She was wearing high heels—very high—with something short and black that clung to her body suggestively. Her lovely, silky legs went on and on. Her coppery hair was swept up in a loose knot at the crown of her head, and little tendrils floated around her ears and the nape of her neck. The hotel room smelled female, of flowery dusting powder and soft silky fabrics and perfume. The whole effect made Tony dizzy.

"I'm trying to figure out which earrings to wear with this dress." She turned her back and rummaged through a satin jewelry case while he devoured the delightful view with every one of his senses.

"You look—" He searched for a word, but none seemed extreme enough. "I'm trying to find a word that goes beyond *ravishing,* Kate," he finally managed to say.

She was hooking a silver hoop into her ear, head tilted to one side, and she turned toward him with a foxy smile.

"*Ravishing* will do fine. And thank you. You look pretty hot yourself. That's some fancy suit."

He'd packed it especially to impress her, and he was pleased that she liked it. He didn't dare glance at the queen-size bed, but it was like a magnet for his imagination. He tried to keep his mind firmly in the moment as she finished with the earrings and grabbed a soft black wrap from the back of an armchair.

"Ready. Finally."

He held the door and she wafted past him in an intoxicating cloud of something sultry and dangerous. With heels on she came to his shoulder, and he took her hand as they stepped on the empty elevator.

"Handsome couple," he murmured, nodding at the mirrored wall.

"Wonder where they're going?" she whispered back.

"Out on the town. Look at how they're dressed."

"Think her skirt's too short?" Kate smoothed the dress over her hips.

"With legs like that, a skirt could never be too short," he declared, restraining her hand as she tugged at her hem. "She's incredibly beautiful, he's going to be the envy of every guy in the place. Probably have to fight dozens of men off before the night's over," he added in a gruff tone.

She giggled. "I hardly think so."

But he was conscious of the covert male glances she attracted as the maitre d' led them to the table Tony had reserved in the dining room.

The meal was probably delicious, the wine superb, but Tony didn't remember eating. He was concentrating too hard on the lovely woman across from him.

Kate wanted to discuss the lecture she'd attended, called To Err Is Human. "I couldn't help but think about what happened to you, Tony, when you hurt your ankle. The speaker emphasized that the media focuses on medical error and blame. I remember your mom and brother threatening to call the newspapers when you were in ICU. It would have really harmed St. Joe's image if they'd done that."

Distracted from admiring the sparkle in her green eyes and the intriguing curve of her lips, Tony clicked his tongue in disgust. "I didn't know they'd even thought about doing that. Damn, Mom and Wilson can make a tremor into a full-scale earthquake."

"Everybody reacts strongly when they feel there's been a mistake. Leslie feels that way about her mother's death." Her face somber, Kate outlined what had happened, how Nathanial Hersh had sent Leslie's mother home instead of admitting her for further tests. "Leslie won't meet with Dr. Hersh to discuss it. She's really angry."

"I helped hire Hersh. He graduated top of his class, he's an excellent physician." Tony couldn't help feeling defensive. He knew Nathanial and respected the younger man's ability. Admittedly, he was a little rough around the edges, but experience would smooth him. "Maybe Leslie just needs some time."

Kate nodded, but he could see she wasn't convinced.

"Let's not spend the evening discussing work," he pleaded. "Let's talk about really important things, like what you like to read, what music you enjoy, what you want for dessert." He signaled the waiter and the elaborate dessert tray was wheeled up.

After much deliberation, Kate couldn't choose

between petits fours and hazelnut cheesecake. Tony ordered both.

Coffee was served, and a glance at his watch showed that it was still early. He'd given the evening a lot of thought while he was dressing.

"I checked the local papers to see what was on. There's a good jazz group playing not far from here. Would you like to go?"

Her green eyes widened. "I've never heard live jazz."

"Then it's absolutely time you did."

THE CLUB WAS SMALL, noisy, and smoky in spite of the No Smoking sign over the bar. Kate held tight to Tony's hand, feeling excited and a little shy.

The band was taking a break when they arrived. Tony found a table at the back of the room, and since there was no waiter, he went off to the bar to get the glass of white wine she'd asked for. Kate watched as a dark-haired woman materialized beside him, putting a familiar hand on his arm and smiling up into his face.

A stab of pure jealousy shot through her as Tony bent his head and kissed the woman on the cheek. He listened to what she said, then threw back his head and laughed.

So he happened to know someone here, Kate chided herself. Why should that bring on such a strong reaction in her? Because she'd assumed they'd be alone and anonymous. Because she didn't want to share him. Because the lousy woman was pretty, and the way she leaned into Tony and put her hand on his chest hinted at intimacy instead of casual friendship.

Kate did a down-and-dirty survey. The woman wore an ankle-length red dress, bias cut, that fitted close around a tiny waist, emphasized generous breasts and narrow hips and then flared out provocatively at the hem. Over it was a tiny cropped purple silk jacket. The dramatic colors suited her mass of coal-black curls and perfect heart-shaped face.

Damn it all to hell, she was more than pretty. She was beautiful.

And now she was swaying across the room on her stiletto heels, her hand on Tony's arm, making straight toward the table where Kate waited, lips forced into a wide, welcoming smile. What had ever made her think listening to jazz was a good idea?

"Kate Lewis," Tony was saying. "This is Sandy Solem, an old friend. She used to sing at the jazz club in Vancouver when I was sitting in with the band."

Kate put out her hand and Sandy took it. Her palm was warm, and she squeezed Kate's hand in a friendly gesture. "Happy to meet you, Kate." Her voice was low and throaty. "Antony tells me you work at St. Joe's. What do you do?"

Antony? Kate explained her job briefly.

The other woman listened, then said with a warm

smile, "So you keep peace between all the warring factions, have I got that right?"

"That's the idea," Kate said, feeling more comfortable. Sandy was obviously making an effort. "I don't always manage it, but I try."

"There's times the band could use your services," Sandy said, wrinkling her nose. "As we speak there's a bloody feud going on between the drummer and the new guy on the horn. And speaking of the band, looks like I'd better get back."

The musicians were lifting their instruments.

Sandy leaned over, and Kate heard her say close to Tony's ear, "If you're still around when the next set's done, I'd love to have a drink with you."

She was gone before Tony could answer. He reached across and took Kate's hand, linking his fingers with hers and giving a reassuring squeeze.

"I had no idea Sandy was touring with these guys."

The music began, and when Sandy began to sing, Kate was mesmerized in spite of herself. The woman's voice was a riveting combination of little-girl innocence and womanly seduction, a teasing and insinuating lilt that brought an involuntary smile to the faces of her listeners. She had range and power, and she commanded attention, even in this noisy atmosphere.

Kate glanced at Tony, thinking that he and every other man in the room must be captivated by the tiny bombshell with the huge voice. But Tony wasn't looking at Sandy. He was looking at her.

"Dance?" He got to his feet at her nod and guided her to the small, crowded dance floor. As she moved with him to the music, at first tentatively and then with growing confidence and pleasure, Kate wondered for a moment if there was something incestuous in dancing with him to a torchy song sung by a woman she strongly suspected had been his lover at some point.

But soon the pleasure of being in his arms blotted out any concerns. Their bodies were in perfect synch, and together they floated from one rhythm straight into the next. By the time the band took their next break, Kate was totally relaxed, and when Sandy came over and sat down, Kate told her how much she'd enjoyed her singing.

"Thank you." There was something both humble and shy in the acknowledgement. "It's what I was born to do, I guess."

"Do you want a drink, Sandy?" Tony asked.

"Soda water, please."

Leaving the two women alone, Tony made his way to the bar.

Sandy lit a cigarette. Her lovely face was thoughtful as she tapped ash into a napkin with perfectly manicured fingers. "You've got good taste. So is it serious between you two?"

Kate felt her face grow hot. Sandy was nothing if not direct, but she had no right to ask such a personal question. Kate opened her mouth to say that she and Tony were just friends, but instead heard herself confess, "I don't know. Too soon to tell."

"Antony's a great guy, but I guess you've figured that out." Sandy drew on her cigarette and blew the smoke out slowly. "We went out a couple times, but then he met Jessica." She laughed. "She snatched him out of my clutches."

"You know her?" Kate felt her earlier curiosity about Tony's ex resurface.

"Sure, we're friends. Jazz is a small world, everybody knows everybody. I was at their wedding. They were hot together, those two. But it couldn't last, they were going in different directions. He was way too settled for her—their kid was really all they had in common. I saw McKensy once when she was staying with Jessica. She's a crackerjack, isn't she?" There was something brittle in Sandy's voice.

"She really is." Kate wondered where this was going.

"You got kids, Kate?"

"A stepdaughter, same age as McKensy. What about you, Sandy?"

"Nope." The other woman shook her head and changed the subject. "From what I hear, Antony and Jessica stayed friends after they split. I wish I could say that about even one of my exes." Sandy grinned. "How about you, Kate? You got any you stayed buddies with?"

"Not really." She certainly didn't consider Scott a buddy. What was taking Tony so long? What would this woman say next?

When it came, it touched Kate's heart.

"I hope it works out for you two. Antony was there for me once when I needed him. I'd like to see him get lucky, and you look like the kind of steady lady that could manage that."

Tony was now heading back to the table with a tray of drinks. He handed Kate a fresh glass of wine and placed soda water in front of Sandy. She raised it in a toast. "Another day sober. One at a time seems to work."

The band assembled and Sandy joined them.

When she began to sing again, Kate leaned over to Tony. "She had a drinking problem?"

Tony nodded. "Major. She's had a tough life. Her little boy, Zachary, died in a motel fire. After that she started drinking."

"That's terrible." Kate shuddered. "How old was he?"

"Four. He'd be nine now."

McKensy's age. Eliza's age. Kate understood now why Sandy had sounded brittle. Sympathy welled up inside of her.

They danced again, but he noticed when she yawned, once and then again. "Would you like to go, or just fall asleep here in my arms?"

Oh, the temptation. "I guess we'd better go."

He called a cab, and with a wave to Sandy, they left.

Tony was quiet in the cab, and then he said, "I've always been grateful to Sandy."

"Why's that?"

"It was because of what happened to Zachary that Jessica didn't fight me for custody. Sandy had her son with her, traveling from one gig to the next. He was asleep, and she raced out for milk. The fire was an accident, but she blamed herself. She figured if she'd left him home with her family, the way her mother wanted, he wouldn't have died. She made Jessica see that being on the road was no life for McKensy."

"It must be lonely for her."

"There're a lot of ways to be lonely."

The matter-of-fact way he said it touched a chord deep inside her.

"She said you were there for her when she needed you."

His shoulder moved under her head in a noncommittal shrug.

"She called me once when she was low. I did what I could. What anybody would have done."

He didn't say anything else, and Kate didn't ask. He was a good, kind man, a fine father. And he needed a steady woman, Sandy had said. Someone like Kate—though steady was the exact opposite of the way her body was reacting to him right now.

He sighed and looped his arm tighter around her shoulders, every so often giving her an affectionate squeeze. It felt companionable, but it also felt sexy. She rested her head back against his arm.

At the hotel, Tony paid the cab and the doorman greeted them. As they rode up in the mirrored elevator, it felt to Kate as if days had passed since they'd last looked at themselves in this mirror, but she didn't say anything.

They walked along the corridor in silence, her hand in his, her heart hammering with anticipation.

At her door, Kate had to fumble in her bag for her access card. When she retrieved it, she turned to thank Tony for the evening, and found herself in his arms. She drew in a shaky breath and slid her hands around his back, aware of hard muscles under expensive tailoring, the intoxicating smell of clean man and lemony aftershave and heat and desire. She moved farther into his embrace and tilted her head up to make it easy for him.

Man, was he adept at kissing. She kissed him back and couldn't help wondering if he was just as good at the rest of it. *Better,* her brain suggested. *More room for imagination. More space for invention.*

And as the kiss deepened and her heartbeat increased, she knew she had to make a decision. Should she ask him in? She'd fantasized for so long about making love with him, and now was her chance. But the fantasy had always been raunchy, sexy, fun—and devoid of tomorrows.

Now that the opportunity was here, she found she wasn't at all sure she could do it. He'd become so much more than a gorgeous, unattainable body. He was Tony, father, ex-husband, co-worker, friend to women in need. He was a man who intrigued her, made her laugh, touched her heart with his thoughtfulness. He was a guy she could fall in love with so easily, and he'd made it all too clear that he wasn't looking for a life partner.

Well, neither was she, another part of her brain argued. Why not take pleasure when it was offered?

They were alone together in a hotel far away from Vancouver. They enjoyed each other's company, they laughed at each other's jokes, and if the looks he'd been giving her all evening meant anything at all, he found her appealing and sexy.

What did she have to lose?

Only your heart, idiot. Kate already had feelings for him that went beyond simple lust. She'd have to work with him afterward, probably for a very long time. Neither of them was planning on retiring anytime soon. She'd see him every day, she'd have to hide her feelings from him, she'd have to constantly pretend. She'd have to lie, and she hated lying.

If only he was a stranger. If only he wasn't, technically at least, her boss. She wanted to tell him it wasn't false morality or lack of wanting that made her pull away gently and give her head a negative shake, but she didn't trust her voice.

He got it. He sighed, put his forehead against hers for a moment, and then stepped reluctantly back.

"'Night, Kate."

"'Night, Tony." She felt as if she was choking. "Thank you for a great evening."

"Want to go for a long walk in the morning down by the river?"

"Absolutely." *Not*. She knew exactly what she'd love to do with him in the morning, but it was too late. She'd burned her bridges.

"See you at six, then."

"Six. Right." She gave him a peppy smile, and when the door closed behind her, she slumped to the carpet, beat her fists and wondered if there were rules against screaming after midnight.

What was wrong with her head? Instead of sleeping in his arms, she'd be dragging her backside out of bed before dawn just to go for a walk. Instead of finding out whether or not his kissing ability extended beyond her mouth and neck, she'd be cuddling a lousy pillow that had been sanitized for her protection.

Idiot. She got to her feet and stripped her clothes off. What a waste, the black lace thong and garter belt, the lace-top stockings.

Kate spent the whole restless night wondering

why she'd been such a fool, and vowing that if the opportunity came again, she'd jump his bones.

Anywhere, anytime. Well, maybe not on the walk first thing in the morning. It was already the middle of the night, and she'd probably only get to sleep half an hour before she had to get up. She wouldn't have energy for anything except putting one reluctant foot in front of the other.

Tomorrow night, though. If he didn't make a move on her again, she'd take matters into her own hands tomorrow night. Figuratively speaking, of course. Well, maybe not so figuratively. She thought of his long, lean body and groaned aloud.

TONY KICKED OFF HIS SHOES in disgust. It had been a stupid, idiotic thing to do, taking her to the jazz club. He hadn't thought of Sandy in a long time, hadn't dreamed she'd be singing with that particular band, here in Edmonton, of all places.

He sent his shoes skittering across the rug and tugged off his suit coat and vest. If only he had the evening to do over again, he thought, throwing himself down on the bed. Meeting Sandy had brought up stuff that wasn't exactly romantic. Now all his fantasies about making love to Kate and staying in bed with her all morning and ordering champagne from room service were just that—fantasies.

Lucky thing he'd packed a mystery novel. He dug it out, but soon found that serial murder was cold comfort in the king-size bed.

CHAPTER FOURTEEN

IT WAS BARELY DAWN. The sun was a red bulge on the edge of the prairie.

"*This* is how we get to the walking path?" Kate looked at the wooden steps that led down to the river winding peacefully along the valley floor. Her heart sank, and she couldn't force herself to sound enthusiastic. "Omigod, there must be a hundred of them." She couldn't keep the hopeful note out of her voice. "Are you sure your ankle's strong enough?"

She prayed that he'd say it wasn't. She longed to crawl back into the warmth and comfort of her bed and snooze away the next two hours. And even in its sleep-deprived state, her brain reasoned that what went down would have to come up again. Would her exhausted body survive climbing this stair mountain again? Was there taxi service back up?

"Best thing for my ankle," Tony declared, barely leaning on the railing as he started down. "And just out of curiosity, I asked at the desk—there's a hundred and twenty-four steps down to the water."

He'd already conquered twelve.

"Just going down and then coming back up is great exercise," he declared. "C'mon, that sun's going to be up in a few minutes, we'll get a fantastic view from the rest area down there."

She had a choice, Kate reminded herself. One always had a choice.

She could confess that she'd been lying all along, that she wasn't really a jock at all, and her idea of exercise at this hour involved raising her head from a goose-down pillow to squint at the clock.

If she did that, he'd go walking by himself. She'd miss out on two hours of his company, during which she planned to wangle another dinner invitation, after which she hoped to maneuver him into her room and into a prone position. She had only one night left to do it; they were booked out on a plane early Sunday morning.

There was no way around it. To get to dinner from here she had to go down. Summoning up every reserve in her reluctant body, she put one foot in front of the other.

"YOU SHOULD HAVE TOLD ME you had a trick knee." Tony was puffing hard, and she could feel the sweat dampening the arm he had firmly locked around her waist. They negotiated another step, and another.

Kate leaned on him, heart hammering as they finally reached the top and staggered through the side entrance of the hotel. Was it the painful climb back up the steps, or was it being clamped against his side that made every pulse in her body flutter?

Whatever, she wasn't feeling at all disheartened, even though her right knee was on fire. Truth was, she welcomed the pain. Now she had a legitimate sports injury that was going to necessitate taking it easy for the rest of the day, thanks be to the god of sloth.

"I'd forgotten about that knee. It hasn't bothered me for years." She tried not to sound cheerful. Truth was, she'd avoided anything that might aggravate it, like exercise, ever since the time in high school when that manic phys ed teacher had forced the class to climb rope ladders up to the ceiling of the gym. And there weren't half as many steps on the rope ladder as there were leading down to that cursed river, either.

"I had no idea those steps would irritate it."

"Let's get you up to your room and have a look at it. I'll call housekeeping to bring some ice."

God, he was strong. His arm was like an iron vise around her waist, and even with his weakened ankle he had no problem supporting her.

They got on the elevator, and he kept his arm where it was. She leaned into him and sniffed in the wonderful heady aroma of male sweat. Why hadn't anyone thought to bottle it? Although not just any male sweat would do, she suspected; she'd breathed in plenty during her years as a nurse, and none till now had done the trick.

They looked so good together. The mirror reflected the two of them, both in shorts and tank tops, trainers and sweatbands. Her hair was mussed, his chin had more than a faint shadow of beard.

The bell dinged and she yelped when she tried to step off the elevator. He half carried her down the hall.

"Where's your room card?"

"I put it in my shoe so I wouldn't lose it. Oww." She attempted to bend her knee and reach her foot, but the knee wasn't cooperating.

"I'll get it. Which foot?"

"Right."

"Okay. Just stand on one foot like this." He propped her against the corridor wall and knelt in front of her, undoing her shoe.

She looked down at the top of his head, admiring the way his hair swirled in a double crown. He eased her foot out of her shoe and she prayed that her foot didn't stink. The trainers were the new ones she'd bought to go walking with him, but she'd sweated into them.

He retrieved the key card, picked up her shoe, slid the card into the door and smoothly drew her inside, guiding her over to the unmade bed and easing her down.

"Oww." Her knee hurt like fury when she bent it.

"Slide back on the bed, we'll elevate it."

She did, and he unlaced her other shoe and pulled it off, then stuck several pillows under her leg. Although she'd had her share of fantasies about Tony in her bed, they'd involved areas other than her knee. She was pleased to see that the short peach satin nightgown she'd worn last night had attracted his attention. She'd tossed it onto the end of the bed, and from the long look he was giving it, she hoped he was imagining it on her body.

This was good, Kate mused. It was delicious to lie flat on her back and watch him fantasize.

Clearing his throat, he picked up the phone and asked for ice to be delivered, then hung up and said to Kate in a professional tone, "You should have X rays done when we get back to St. Joe's. It might help to find out exactly what the problem is."

"This from the same man who slipped on a wrapper and ended up on a respirator?" Kate was thoroughly enjoying having him fuss over her.

He gave her a wry look. "I have it on good authority that that fiasco was a series of mistakes and won't happen again. The system is improved."

A knock on the door signaled the ice had arrived. Tony thanked the lady from housekeeping, filled a plastic laundry bag from the closet and put it across her knee.

"Yikes, that's *freezing*." She shivered and grabbed for a blanket, tugging it over her upper body. "How about ordering a pot of coffee from room service? In fact, why not order breakfast?"

"Good idea." He found the room service menu on the dresser and handed it to her. "What would you like?"

You'd do. She gave him what she hoped was a provocative look and then studied the menu. "Hash browns, eggs, fruit. Toast. How about you?"

"The same, with bacon."

She tossed the menu on the bed. Once again, he picked up the phone and placed their order.

"This is dripping." It wasn't, but the ice was creating more pain than the knee injury itself. She reached down and took the bag off.

"Here, let me put it in the sink." He did, and then he said without quite meeting her eyes, "Do you think massage might help?"

She swallowed. Finally, maybe, he was getting the message. "I'm not sure," she said in a breathy tone. "Why not try it and I'll see?" Why hadn't she thought of this before? She tossed the blanket to one side.

Once he'd taken off his shoes, he knelt on the bed beside her. His runner's legs were corded with muscle, and she wondered what he had on under the rugby shorts he wore. Probably nothing. Those things had liners, didn't they? She gulped. His large hands began to rub back and forth across her knee.

"Your skin is freezing."

Maybe outside. Inside, she was burning up.

"Ooh," she moaned. "That feels so good." His hands felt hot. His fingers were strong, and he applied just the right amount of pressure, stroking back and forth gently and rhythmically. "Don't stop."

"Where's it hurting the most?"

Not in her knee anymore, but farther up. And it wasn't exactly a hurt. It was more like a fiery ache.

She managed to croak, "Right there, where you're rubbing, that's perfect."

There was a huge bulge developing at the front of his running shorts that assured her she wasn't alone in what she was feeling. Their eyes locked, and his fingers slowed and became still. Then, tentatively, and lightly, he touched the skin on the inner side of her thigh, and Kate melted. She took his hand, guiding it up to her breast.

"Tony, I'm sorry about last night," she whispered. "I was scared, but I'm not anymore."

The wordless sound he made was one of profound relief. He bent over and kissed her, hard and fast, and then slower, more thoroughly. He stretched out beside her. "I was so hungry for you last night I couldn't sleep."

"Me, neither."

"You're sure you're okay with this now? You won't be sorry afterward?"

How could she know that? All she could think of was how much she wanted him right at this moment. She whipped her head from side to side. "No. At least, I don't think so. No. I'm sure."

He leaned over her, and this time his kiss was slow and deep, his lips learning everything there was to know about her mouth. At the same time, his hand traveled from her throat to her collarbone, over to her shoulders, down her arms, and when she wriggled impatiently, finally he cupped her breast.

"Mmm, I like that." *Like* was such a feeble word for what she was feeling, but vocabulary was the last thing on her mind.

"How about this?" He gently tweaked her nipple, and she moaned. She had far too many clothes on, and so did he. Reaching for the bottom of his shirt, she lifted the garment in one neat motion over his head and off. There were distinct advantages to having been a nurse.

He had a mat of soft brown curls on his chest, and she wanted to bury her nose in them. But first she needed to get her own clothing off as well. She tried to sit up, but her propped knee threw her off balance.

"Let me." In two easy movements, he had her T-shirt off and her bra undone. There were distinct advantages to him being a doctor. He stood up for a moment and she watched him effortlessly slide off his shorts and abbreviated black underwear.

"Wow." His erection was magnificent, and she admired it. "You're impressive."

"And you're beautiful." He was tugging carefully at her shorts and panties, easing them over her sore knee and down her legs, then tossing them to the carpet.

She was going to explode if he didn't hurry.

"Kate, you're a lovely woman." He knelt beside her, his eyes feasting on her naked body.

For a moment, she was self-conscious. She hadn't been naked with many men since her divorce. Even before that, sex had become just a wistful memory as her relationship with Scott deteriorated.

She was glad she was on her back; her rounded tummy didn't show in this position. On the other hand, her breasts were flatter than when she was upright. It was a trade-off.

The rapt expression in his eyes told her it didn't matter in the least to him.

"I've wanted you for so long, Kate. I used to imagine doing this to you during those bloody endless meetings."

"You did? Why didn't you ever say anything?"

His raised eyebrow was answer enough. They giggled, imagining the effect such an announcement would have had on St. Joe's directors.

Bending his head, he took her right nipple into his mouth, and she forgot everything as he suckled first one breast and then the other.

She ran her hands down his chest, loving the feel of his flesh beneath the soft, thick hair, the hardness of the muscles beneath the taut skin. She stroked his abdomen and took his penis in her hand, sliding her palm along the velvety length and then cupping him with her fingers. His reaction sent shivers of pleasure through her.

"Witch." His body bucked and his voice was unsteady, but his fingers were sure as he reached down and touched the throbbing nub between her legs.

She moved against his hand and moaned. She was on the cusp, and she wanted him with her. She looked up into his eyes.

"Now, please, Tony, now."

And then he was inside her, and the waves of pleasure carried her up and up, until she thought she'd die of the sensation. He lowered his head and caught her cries with a kiss that intensified her climax.

The explosion in her body came only a moment before his, and the guttural cry he gave melded with her own ecstatic moans.

They were clasped in a moist, trembling heap when the knock came on the door.

"Room service," a cheerful male voice called.

Tony raised his head and gave Kate a horrified look. "Breakfast," he hissed. "I forgot we'd ordered breakfast."

He scrambled to his feet, snatched his running shorts and tugged them on. With a single expert flip of the duvet, he covered Kate, then went to the door.

"*Good* morning," the waiter chirped as he wheeled in a loaded cart. "Shall I place it here by the window, sir?" He pushed the cart across the room, politely ignoring Kate's underwear, her shorts, their shoes, Tony's shirt and Kate herself. She had the duvet pulled up to her chin and she was trying to stifle her giggles.

Tony shot her quelling looks.

"Such a *fine* morning, sir," the waiter purred, parking the cart with a flourish and fussily removing the lids on several silver servers. "I'll just open these—" He jerked the curtains back so that sunshine filled the room. It was too much. Kate hid her head under the covers, peering out just enough to see what was going on.

"Would you like me to pour your coffee, sir?"

"No, that'll be fine." There was a moment of silence as Tony bent over the cart and signed the bill.

"Thank you so much, Dr. O'Connor, and may I wish you a very pleasant day?"

The waiter left, still without a glance at the mound in the bed that was Kate. As the door closed behind him, she poked her head out and her laughter erupted.

Tony pretended to glower at her. "Okay, funny girl, want to share the joke?"

She pointed at him. "Your underwear. It's hanging out the back of your shorts."

With a horrified expression, he reached behind himself and pulled the pair of abbreviated black jockeys out of the left leg of his shorts. "Damn." He stared at them and then tossed them on a chair. "Do you think he guessed what was going on in here?"

"Oh, heavens no." She shook her head and gave him a wide-eyed look. "It was perfectly obvious that my doctor was simply making a house call."

"Room call," he corrected her, collapsing on the bed and taking her in his arms. "I'd planned this differently," he confessed between kisses. "First of all, I didn't want to be covered in sweat when it happened."

"I like your sweat. Besides, you were sweating because you had to haul me up sixty-seven of those blessed steps. I can't believe your ankle isn't hurting all over again."

"As a matter of fact, it is. I think it's swelling even as we speak."

"Oh, no. Oh, I'm so sorry." She raised her head in an effort to see his leg.

"Or maybe the swelling's higher up." He gave her a wicked grin, took her hand and guided it to his erection. "Worse luck, I do believe we're going to miss the morning seminar, and probably the afternoon one, as well. I need to stay off my ankle. And with that knee you can't possibly attend any lectures, doctor's orders. So I propose we just stay right here where we're comfortable. We can discuss hospital business, and when lunchtime comes, there's always room service. Only next time, you get to answer the door.''

He ducked as she whacked him with a pillow.

CHAPTER FIFTEEN

"TONY?"

The curtains were blowing gently back and forth in the predawn breeze. It was Sunday morning, their last morning in this room, Kate thought, and sadness tugged at her sleepy brain. They'd slept in snatches, greedy for each other.

"Tony?" No answer. He was cuddled close against her back, and Kate moved against him.

"Mmm-hmm?" His arm tightened around her, his hand cupping her breast, automatically stroking.

It was delicious. She snuggled into him. "Are you sleeping?"

"I was." His voice was gravelly. He yawned and stretched. "Now I'm not."

"Tony, I wish we didn't have to go home. I wish we could just stay here forever."

"I was going to talk to you about that."

"About staying here forever? Would we have enough money? I think these rooms cost a bundle when we're not paying conference rates."

"No, about going home tomorrow morning. Is there any reason you can't stay until Monday?"

She thought it over for all of two seconds. Scott

had Eliza. School was done. She couldn't remember when she'd last taken a day off work.

"Not a reason in the world."

"Good. I'll change our reservations and we can fly home Monday."

"Tell them at the desk that we only need one room tonight."

She could sense his smile. "I think the room service waiter has already spread the word."

Grinning Kate moved against him again with her bottom.

"Now, Kate, that's going to lead to consequences that will shock the waiter."

She turned in his arms, nuzzling his chin and his neck, loving the taste of him. "He's a mature adult. I'm sure he'll survive." She took his hand and placed it on her breast again, and shivered. "But I won't unless you do this—" She put his other hand exactly where she wanted it.

"Like that?" He touched her and she caught her breath with delight.

"You're such a quick study, Doctor."

"It's a subject I'm really interested in."

How quickly they'd learned each other's rhythms. How easily they'd come to know each other's bodies.

He kissed her, his tongue slowly dancing in and out of her mouth. She shifted slightly, to accommodate him, and he slid deep inside her, hot and hard. She gave a little moan, and he began to move, slow and teasing, pausing when she wanted more. She smiled against his neck, and tightened muscles she'd almost forgotten she had, reveling in his in- drawn breath, his muffled gasp.

It was a dance, one whose tempo increased until she cried out his name and whirled straight into fire.

Afterward, he slept again, and she lay in his arms, her body boneless and sated. One long day, one short night, before they had to return to the world. What would it be like, going back to work with this new awareness between them? Is that all it was, just awareness?

She listened to his deep, regular breathing, feel- ing tender and protective when he began to snore. She felt totally safe here in his arms, but how would she feel when life got back to normal? Could the magic they'd shared in this room transfer itself to Vancouver? How could they be together this way, with his mother and daughter in his house and Scott and Eliza in hers?

The joy that permeated her faltered a little.

They had to find a way. There had to *be* a way.

She just couldn't think of any right now. And she didn't have to worry about it this instant, either. Right now, this was their world.

Nestling deeper into his embrace, she tugged the sheet up over his shoulder and hers, and slid into sleep.

IT WAS ELEVEN-FORTY-FIVE Monday morning when Tony pulled his car up in front of Kate's house.

There were now two old wrecks in the driveway, and Kate made a disgusted sound in her throat.

"Don't tell me Scott found a second old car to dismantle," she muttered.

Tony carried her suitcase to the door and waited as she unearthed her keys, but the door flew open before she'd found them in her bag. Eliza stood there, wearing dirty shorts and a stained T-shirt. She gave Kate an accusing look.

"Kate, where *were* you? We came home early last night, and I wanted to show you the fish I caught."

"Eliza, it's good manners to say hello before you start asking questions." Kate's first, instinctive reaction was intense disappointment that Eliza was there. She'd been looking forward to a few moments alone with Tony, time to bridge the transition between Edmonton and here. She'd been looking forward to a long, passionate goodbye kiss, and time in which to contemplate the last several incredible days.

Immediately she felt guilty. Of course Eliza would be disappointed that she wasn't here to listen to her camping adventures. But that didn't excuse rudeness.

"Eliza?" Kate's voice was stern. "Would you like to start over again?"

"Hello, Kate."

Kate gave her stepdaughter a knowing look, and

after a moment the girl added in a lackluster tone, "Hello, Dr. O'Connor."

"Hi, Eliza. So you caught a fish, did you?"

Eliza nodded, but Kate noticed she didn't offer to show it off.

"Where do you want this, Kate?" Tony put the suitcase down just inside the front door.

"It's fine right there."

"With that sore knee, you'd better let me take it to your bedroom."

Acutely aware that Eliza was tagging along right beside them, Kate limped into her bedroom. The bed wasn't made, and a bra was lying on the chair. Her pink cotton nightie was tossed on the duvet. It seemed much longer than three nights since she'd last slept here.

Eliza got up on the bed and pulled Kate's white duvet over her knees.

"Eliza, you're not very clean. How about putting those clothes in the hamper and taking a shower?"

She shook her head. "I don't feel like it. Daddy said it was holidays. He said I didn't have to have a bath this morning."

Kate felt the usual hot flash of irritation with Scott, but she told herself it wasn't Eliza's fault.

Tony heaved the suitcase up on the old trunk at the foot of her bed. He gave Kate a meaningful look, and they smiled at each other. He'd teased her about bringing so many clothes and then only wearing one black dress and—for fifteen minutes last night, because he'd asked her to model it—her peach satin nightgown.

"Thanks, Tony." Having Eliza right there made Kate uncomfortable. She longed to throw herself into his arms, but of course she couldn't. "Would you like something to drink?"

He shook his head. "I'd better be getting home. McKensy will be wondering where I am."

"I'll see you to the door." Kate led the way, and Eliza scrambled off the bed and tagged right along at their heels.

Tony reached out a hand, and when he would have pulled Kate into his arms, she resisted with a glance at Eliza. She just didn't feel right about kissing Tony with Eliza looking on.

Immediately he understood, and gave her fingers a warm squeeze instead. "It was an eventful trip, Kate," he said in a low, intimate voice. "I never dreamed Edmonton could be like that."

"Me, neither." She returned the pressure of his fingers.

"Better keep on icing that knee. Bye, Eliza." He smiled, but Kate noticed that Eliza didn't return either the smile or the goodbye.

"I'll call you later. And I'll see you at work tomorrow, Kate."

Kate watched him walk out the door and down the front path to his car, feeling as if a piece of her heart was going with him. How could she be homesick for something she'd only had for three days and three nights? She wanted to run after him, throw herself into his arms. God, she wanted to go back to Edmonton.

"*Now* will you look at my fish, Kate? What happened to your leg? I found a turtle. It was *this* big around."

Kate sighed and shut the door on her dreams.

HE DIDN'T WANT TO DISLIKE a child, but it was hard not to feel resentful of Eliza. Tony slammed the car door hard and pressed his foot against the accelerator with unnecessary force. The wheels laid rubber, and it gave him a perverse sense of satisfaction.

The way that girl looked at him, you'd think he was planning rape and pillage. If she were his, she'd be given a time out and sent to her room in short order for being rude. But she wasn't his, he reminded himself. And it was her attachment to Kate that made her act the way she did, which was a reaction he could well understand. He'd give a guy the evil eye, too, for coming on to Kate.

But Eliza's negative reactions were going to make it difficult to further their relationship. In Edmonton, he'd projected family outings for him and Kate and their girls, trips to the Omnimax, the Space Center, Science World. He'd envisioned them all having burgers together, hanging out in parks, tossing Frisbees.

At the light, he pulled the car to a stop behind a

bus, and like a harsh smack on the back of his head, he realized what he'd been doing.

He was thinking family here. For the first time since his divorce, he was actually considering involvement again. Which was why he was so pissed off at Eliza, because she wasn't fitting into his scenario the way he'd envisioned it.

Certainly the picture didn't include Kate's ex, either, dismantling cars in her driveway, barging into her bedroom. The way Kate had explained her living arrangements had made sense at the time, but now he thought about how possessive Eliza was, how few boundaries there seemed to be between Scott's living space and Kate's, and it bothered him. It bothered him a lot.

How would he fit into that picture? Their kids weren't buddies the way he'd hoped they might be, although with time that could sort itself out.

But a relationship like the one he'd been imagining was pretty unlikely. There was the issue of privacy, for one thing. Eliza had the run of Kate's entire house, which meant it would be difficult for him to spend a night there.

His heart sank when he thought about his own house. Things were even worse at home—he had Dorothy to contend with, as well as McKensy. And he also had the complications of his father's visit, coming up in just four weeks.

He'd been on an emotional high, but now his spirits came crashing down. Unless he planned to rent a hotel room every time he and Kate wanted to make love, which would mean a permanent rental, it looked as if they were in for a long period of abstinence. He couldn't even figure out how they'd manage dating, never mind sex.

And damn it all, he wanted her in his arms. He ached to take her to his bed. They'd made love that morning. It wasn't even afternoon, and already he desired her. He needed her. Maybe he even— A bus pulled out in front of him, and he forced his mind away from what he'd been about to admit.

ONE NIGHT WITHOUT TONY, and Kate already felt deprived. Her knee hurt, and the clutter of decrepit cars, greasy spare parts and discarded beer cans in her front driveway wasn't helping her mood.

"Daddy got the other car from a wrecker," Eliza explained. "He's gonna make ours just like new."

Yeah, Kate thought, *and it's going to rain ten-dollar bills.*

She hadn't had the energy to confront Scott on Monday afternoon, and he and Eliza were still asleep when she went to work Tuesday morning. She left a note on his door asking that he get rid of the mess before she got home that night.

The entire drive to St. Joe's Kate was fuming over the way Scott took advantage of her. She reminded herself that there weren't any victims in relationships, only volunteers, but somehow it didn't help her state of mind one bit. She arrived twenty minutes early and made her way to the ER, hoping Leslie would have time for a cup of tea and a chat. She needed to make sure her friend was doing okay, and she also desperately wanted to confide in Leslie, get some impartial advice on what was happening with her and Tony. Her heart sank when Leslie shook her head.

"Sorry, Kate, I can't this morning." The ER seemed quiet, but Leslie looked weary, Kate noted, the lines in her face more pronounced than she'd ever seen them.

"This afternoon, then?"

Leslie shrugged. "I'll have to see how it goes."

There was a distance between them that hadn't been there before, and Kate struggled to bridge it.

"Les, are you sure you should be back at work? Maybe a few more days off—"

"I'm fine, okay?" The harshness of her tone softened a little. "I'm just tired, that's all. I haven't been sleeping well." She glanced past Kate at an orderly and her voice became shrill. "Elliott, how many times do I have to tell you that the patient in two needs to be taken to radiology?"

Kate was shocked at the venom in Leslie's tone. She'd never heard her friend speak that way to anyone. Leslie was famous for her good nature.

Elliott, too, was shocked. "Hey, keep your shirt on, Les, I'm on my way to get him right now."

"I don't want to have to tell you again," Leslie snapped.

The orderly gave Leslie a hurt, resentful look, then shrugged before he hurried off.

Deeply concerned now, Kate reached out a hand and put it on Leslie's arm. "Les, if you need to talk—"

Leslie shook her head and moved her arm away. "I *don't* need to talk. And I've got to get back to work, Kate."

There was nothing Kate could think of to do or say. She made her way back to her office, feeling forlorn and hurt and terribly worried about her friend.

She checked her messages, thinking that Tony might have called, but he hadn't. Well, she'd call him. She picked up the phone and dialed his number, but his secretary answered. "Sorry, Kate, he was here but now he's up in the OR. One of his patients is having a hysterectomy and the surgeon asked Tony to assist."

Feeling let down all over again, Kate checked her morning schedule. She had a meeting with a disgruntled patient, and she was pleased when he arrived early. She greeted him and introduced herself, making him comfortable and offering him a cup of coffee, which he refused.

Walter Rundle was a tall, emaciated man who looked much older than his forty-three years. He sat slumped in the chair, cradling his right arm.

"Tell me what's bothering you, Mr. Rundle,"

Kate invited. "I understand you had recent surgery on your arm."

Her words unleashed a torrent of emotion and information. Walter had come to St. Joe's for simple surgery, an ulnar nerve transposition to relieve tingling and numbness in his right elbow. He was a house painter, and because of the numbness he was having difficulty doing his job.

"Before the operation, Dr. Snider told me there was nothing to it, he said it was real simple surgery," Walter recounted in a bitter voice. "But now I've got awful pain in my hand and arm. It never quits, and I can't work at all."

"Did you ask the surgeon what might be causing it?"

Walter nodded. "Sure I did. I asked Dr. Snider but all he said was, *There's nothing more I can do for you.*" He shook his head. "That just isn't good enough, Ms. Lewis. I don't even know how the operation went, nobody would explain it to me. And this pain in my hand and arm is so bad I gotta take pills to sleep, and I get so mad I feel like hitting somebody, and that's not my nature. I'm not a fighting sort of man."

Kate thought of Leslie. The pain of her mother's death had made her angry enough to say she wanted to kill the doctor she thought responsible. No doubt about it, pain could bring out depths of anger. The one lecture she'd attended in Edmonton had warned that patients needed explanations when something went awry.

"Would you like me to try and find out exactly what happened during the operation?"

"Yeah, I really would." Walter nodded. "Just knowing would make a difference. Just thinking somebody cared what happened."

Kate talked to him awhile longer. Walter told her that his wife worked as a waitress and they had two teenage sons still in school. He was terribly worried about being able to support his family.

She arranged to meet him again the following day, after she had more information. She told him she'd speak to Dr. Snider and see if he would talk to Walter about the operation.

"Thanks for taking the trouble to listen," Walter said before he left. "Trouble with a hospital this size is nobody takes the time to listen."

Touched by his words, Kate did her best to find out what had gone on in the operating room during Walter's surgery. Dr. Snider didn't return her message, so she made her way to his office just before lunch.

Snider was in his early fifties, distinguished, perfectly groomed and smartly dressed. He was obviously not pleased to have Kate asking questions. When she explained why she was there, he snapped, "Really, I think we're making far too much of this incident."

Kate wondered if Snider would think so if it was

his arm that had been damaged, but of course she didn't say that. Instead, she asked him to describe what had occurred during surgery.

In an impatient tone, he explained, "The patient had a small bleed into his arm following the initial procedure. The problem was recognized immediately and he was taken back into surgery."

"And what exactly was the problem that caused the bleed?" Kate made certain she kept her tone and her questions nonjudgmental, even though she could see by the reddening of Snider's face that he resented her queries. She'd used Walter's name in an effort to force the doctor to see him as a person and not just as a patient.

"A small vessel hadn't been tied off—it's a very common occurrence," he told her. "And now, Ms. Lewis, I have patients waiting, so if you would be so kind…" He held a hand out toward the door, but Kate wasn't quite ready to leave.

"Would you come to a meeting with the Rundles and explain to them exactly what you've told me? I feel it would make a huge difference to them, just to know—"

"Absolutely not." Snider's face went purple and his eyes bugged out. "You know as well as I do what an admission of error would mean in cases like this—there'd be a lawsuit. St. Joseph's can't afford that and neither can I. I'm appalled you'd suggest such a thing."

"I'm not suggesting you say the mistake was

your fault, Doctor.'' Kate recalled the lecturer's words. "Patients most often sue when they suspect a coverup and feel that the problem could happen to someone else. All I'm asking is that you meet with the Rundles, tell them an error was made and apologize for it. I really believe that's all Walter wants here.''

"And why would I do that?'' The surgeon was outraged. "It certainly wasn't *my* fault. I wasn't in that OR all by myself, you know.''

"We're not trying to lay blame here.'' Kate did her best to remain composed, but it was tough. "As I said, this isn't a case of finding fault. It's simply an effort to make the patient understand why he's having pain and to say we're sorry.''

"Well, you can count me out.'' Snider stormed over to the door and held it open. "Goodbye, Ms. Lewis.''

Kate had no choice except to walk out the door. The encounter upset her, and she wished that Tony were available to talk to about it. She called his secretary again and learned that the operation was over, and he'd gone straight from the OR to his office. She didn't bother trying to reach him there. She knew he'd have a full roster of patients waiting to see him.

Feeling off balance and very alone, Kate bought a sandwich from the cafeteria and took it back to her office. She had calls to answer, calls to make, reports to write. Her knee still ached, but in the space of one short day, the rest of Edmonton was becoming little more than a wistful memory.

"DR. O'CONNOR, YOUR MOTHER'S on the phone, line three." Tony's office nurse, Heather, stuck her head in the door just long enough to give him the message.

One patient had left, and Tony knew that another two were waiting in his examining rooms. He picked up the receiver and pushed the button.

"Hello, Mom. What's up? Is McKensy okay?"

Dorothy seldom called him at the office. Her voice was high and strained, and Tony was immediately concerned.

"She's fine. She just got home from her friend's house, and she's in the kitchen having a snack. I just wanted to tell you that I spoke to the RCMP this afternoon. They may call you—I gave them your number there."

Tony frowned. "What would they be calling me about?"

"About my ring." Dorothy's voice was defiant. "I told them your father is coming back into Canada and that I want the ring that he stole from me."

Shutting his eyes, Tony prayed for patience. "He didn't steal the damned thing, Mom. You *gave* it to him. When you give someone a gift, you don't ask for it back or pretend it's been stolen."

Dorothy ignored reason, as she always did. "The ring was mine. It was an heirloom and he didn't return it when I asked him for it," she insisted. "That's theft."

"And what did the cops say about it?"

There was a long pause. "The corporal was young, he was very nice," Dorothy finally said. "He asked if I'd made a complaint to the police when the ring was taken, and of course I hadn't. I was far too upset at the time to think straight, and I had all of you children to support. I told him that."

Tony surmised that the police had politely told her she didn't have a case. One mark for the RCMP.

"He said that one of you should speak to your father about it for me. He said the RCMP is reluctant to become involved in family matters of this kind, and that the best thing would be for one of you kids to ask for the ring back. I talked it over with Wilson, and he said since you're the one who's kept in contact with Ford, you're the one he might listen to."

And Wilson was an expert at passing the buck and stirring the pot, Tony fumed. "Well, Mom, that's not going to happen. I'm not asking Dad for the damned ring, so don't entertain that idea for one moment." Tony couldn't believe Dorothy would go to these lengths. He remembered Kate saying that his mother might benefit from counseling, and now he knew she'd been right. Dorothy was acting deranged.

She was crying by this time. Tony could hear the

sniffles, the nose blowing. "You have no idea what that ring meant to me," Dorothy wailed.

"Grammy? Do you want a tissue?"

In the background, Tony heard McKensy's concerned voice, and his heart sank. He hated having his daughter witness these hysterical scenes.

"Grammy, what's wrong?"

"Mom, let me talk to McKensy." Tony waited, and when his daughter came on the line, he said, "McKensy, Grandma's not feeling too well. Make her a cup of tea and I'll be home in about an hour and a half."

He'd see the patients waiting in the office, but he'd get Heather to cancel the ones who hadn't arrived yet. "You and I'll go out for dinner, duchess—you pick the place."

"Okay, Papa. Is Grammy coming with us?"

Not if he could help it. "Grandma's upset. I'm sure she'd prefer having the evening to herself."

He decided that after McKensy was in bed he'd have a talk with Dorothy and try to convince her that it would be a good idea for her to speak to someone besides her family about her feelings. Not that it was likely to do any good; Dorothy didn't respond well to advice.

But this time he was going to tell her that if she went on with this drama about Ford and the ring, Tony would make other arrangements for McKensy's care. He hadn't a clue what arrangements those would be, but he wouldn't have his daughter exposed to any more of Dorothy's viciousness about Ford.

"Doctor?" Heather tapped on the door. "Mr. Chan is waiting in three."

Tony had hoped to find time to see Kate, but it wasn't going to happen. He'd call her and make a date for tomorrow evening. He wanted to be with her instead of just hearing her voice on the phone. How was it possible to miss someone this much when he'd only spent a couple of days with her?

The idea of renting a hotel room for a few hours was beginning to sound better and better.

CHAPTER SIXTEEN

IT WAS TWILIGHT THE FOLLOWING evening by the time Tony pulled up in front of Kate's house. The two old cars were still there, and even more engine parts were strewn across the overgrown lawn. He walked up the sidewalk and rang the doorbell, and Kate opened it almost immediately. She must have been watching for him. It made him feel good when she took his hand and drew him inside, then wrapped her arms around him.

"I miss you, I miss your smell, I miss room service," she mumbled into the front of his shirt. He bent and kissed her passionately, and just having her in his arms again made up for some of the frustrations of the past two days.

"Let's go." He'd invited her to go out for dinner, but she'd said she was giving Eliza dinner that day. She'd asked him to join them, but he suggested they go out later for dessert and coffee. He wasn't comfortable around Eliza; the kid really knew how to push his buttons.

"Eliza's gone swimming with a friend, and Scott's going to pick her up afterward, so the evening's free. And I so much want to talk to you,

Tony. There's a situation at work I really need your help with.''

He almost suggested just staying here, at her house. He thought of her bedroom, of making love to her on her wide bed, but then he thought of her ex-husband living somewhere behind one of the walls and decided against it. The guy was liable to come thundering in on some pretext or other, and then Tony would have to kill him. It was probably wiser to go out. They'd find a quiet spot with a bench where they could sit, and maybe he could kiss her without worrying about interruptions. Later he'd bring up his suggestion about going to a hotel for a few hours. He had a nice one in mind, down by the ocean.

THEY HAD FROZEN YOGURT, and he drove them to a park. He found the bench, but the kissing wasn't happening the way he'd hoped. Instead, Kate was filling him in on an incident involving a patient and George Snider.

"So let me get this straight." Tony had an arm around her shoulders, and the velvety softness of her skin was distracting him. "This patient had a bleed, which George took care of, and now you think he ought to tell the patient exactly what happened and say he's sorry?"

Kate bobbed her head, and her hair tickled his cheek.

"Yes, I do. Walter is in constant pain. He needs

and deserves an explanation and an apology. I really think it would make a difference if Snider would just tell the poor man exactly what happened.''

''And George refuses?''

''Absolutely. He was angry with me for even suggesting it. Do you think you could speak to Snider, convince him that it's in St. Joe's best interests for him to meet Walter and tell him he's sorry for his pain? Or if Snider refuses, which I'm pretty sure he will, then maybe you could meet with Walter and extend the hospital's sympathy.''

Tony considered it, but the whole idea seemed just as ridiculous as Dorothy's request that he speak to his father about the damned ring. It was the second time he was being asked to do something he didn't want to do, and he was getting damned tired of it.

He kept his voice reasonable. ''Look, Kate, there's no real proof that this guy's pain is because of the bleeding vessel.''

''What?'' He felt her shoulders stiffen, and she moved away so that his arm was no longer around her. ''I can't believe you said that. The pain began directly after the bleed. Of course that's what caused it.''

Annoyance was fast becoming anger, and he didn't want to be angry with her. He wanted this whole conversation to go away. He wanted to draw her into his arms and remind her what it felt like to kiss and be kissed. He held on to his temper and tried reason. ''There's absolutely nothing anyone can do about the pain except prescribe medication. George is right about that. He's a competent and careful surgeon, there's never been a question of negligence, and in my opinion, there isn't now. Kate, all I'm thinking is that there's huge potential here for a costly lawsuit against St. Joe's.''

''Darned right there is. Which is exactly why I think Snider should accept responsibility and tell this poor man he's sorry for what happened. At that session I attended in Edmonton, the lecturer said that one of the big reasons people go ahead with lawsuits is they feel it might stop someone else from going through the same thing. And I can't believe you're suggesting nondisclosure just to avoid a lawsuit, Tony. I think Walter's upset because he feels, and rightly so, that an error was intentionally concealed from him. And not a single person has said they're sorry for what happened to him, either.''

Tony felt his temper begin to simmer. She couldn't be accusing him of unethical behavior, could she? ''I'm not suggesting nondisclosure to avoid a lawsuit,'' he snapped. ''And I resent you even suggesting I am. What I am saying is that you're overstepping hospital boundaries by hinting that Snider did something wrong.''

Her eyes were green ice particles, and her arms were folded protectively across her breasts. ''I'm not trying to lay blame here, Tony, don't you get that? All I'm saying is that when a mistake has been made and the patient is in pain because of it, an apology is in order. Walter's angry and an angry person is a person in need.''

Kate and her damned aphorisms. He blew out an exasperated breath and shot to his feet. ''In this instance, an angry person is just a potential lawsuit, don't *you* get *that?*''

She gave him a pitying look that really got under his skin. ''An apology isn't an admission of guilt or liability. Walter needs to hear that someone's sorry for what happened to him, and it's not enough for me to say it. He needs to hear it from the person who made the mistake in the first place, or from someone in a position of authority.''

The frustration he felt with his mother and the frustration he was feeling at the way the evening was turning out combined and pushed him over the edge—he completely lost his temper.

''For God's sake, Kate, stop being a bleeding heart and get practical about your job, or you'll lose it,'' he thundered.

Her sharply indrawn breath told him he'd gone too far.

She looked up at him with huge, wounded eyes. ''Are you threatening me, Tony?''

He felt like a bastard, but he was too frustrated and angry for apologies. ''Of course I'm not,'' he growled. "We're simply having a discussion, that's all."

"No we aren't." She shook her head. "We're having a fight. You really hurt me Tony, when you called me a bleeding heart."

The pain in her voice made him ashamed of himself, but this had gone way too far for him to back down now. He believed what he said about Snider. "I'm sorry for that, Kate, but the fact is I think you're wrong about this situation."

"Yeah, I can see you do. And it points out the differences between us. I'd have thought you'd have learned during your own hospital stay how important it is for people to be honest and to apologize when something goes wrong. It's too bad you didn't attend some of those lectures in Edmonton on the need to inform."

Her accusation stung, and her words hurt. In the heat of the moment he'd entirely forgotten about his own experience as a patient. And to have her say he should have gone to lectures rather than make love with her really crushed his ego. He clamped his mouth into a tight line.

Kate didn't stop there, either. "You don't understand conflict resolution, Tony. Just because your mother deals with conflict by bullying and accusing doesn't mean there isn't a better way."

She was dead on about Dorothy, and any other time Tony would have been the first to admit it. But right now he wasn't in a mood to admit anything. All Kate was doing was making him feel defensive and hurt—and furious. She was making him say things he wouldn't have said if she hadn't backed him into a corner.

"Well, I don't think letting that ex-husband of yours walk all over you is a particularly good example of conflict resolution." He knew he shouldn't bring her ex into this, but she'd used his mother, hadn't she?

Her face flushed and then went completely white. "I'd like you to drive me home now, Tony."

The realization that they'd wasted precious time fighting when they could have been in each other's arms absolutely galled him. Half of him wanted to grab her and hold her until the anger went away, but there was still the ugly business of Snider and the damned patient. He couldn't compromise on that.

She walked to the car and he silently opened the door for her.

They didn't speak on the drive home, and Kate got out of the car the moment he pulled up in front of her house.

Even then, he would have gotten out and followed her to the door, but three men were lounging against the old wrecks in her driveway. They had cans of beer, and one of them, the fat one with the beard, called out, "Hey, Katie, Eliza's in bed. She wants you to go down and say good-night."

"Did she wash her hair, Scott? The chlorine always discolors it."

The domesticity of the scene revolted him, and Tony drove away before Kate's ex-husband replied.

KATE WAS DEVASTATED by the things she and Tony had said to each other. She kept thinking all evening that he'd come back, or at least call, but he didn't. His harsh words reverberated in her brain, and the depth of the hurt she felt was a direct indication of how deeply she'd come to care for him. That frightened her as much as the quarrel.

At work the following day, she considered going to his office, and by midmorning she managed to screw up the courage to do so, but his secretary said he wasn't in and wasn't expected. She didn't say where Tony was and Kate didn't ask.

Walter and his wife both came for the meeting Kate had set up, and she had to tell them that Dr. Snider refused to attend. She apologized on his behalf, and although Walter and his wife thanked her, they also said they were going to see a lawyer. A friend had advised them they had a good case against the surgeon and the medical center as well.

Kate felt absolutely defeated and on the verge of tears. The feeling intensified when Margot, one of the nurses from the ER, knocked on her door that afternoon.

"I hate to bother you with this, Kate, but everyone in the ER is worried and upset. There's something going on with Leslie. I know her mom just died, but she's hollering at people and she even told off a patient yesterday, an addict we see a lot who's just a sad, harmless person. When I tried to talk to Les about it, she went ballistic, and we got into a big fight.''

Margot had worked in the ER for several years, and now she started to cry. ''She said that I've always been a problem,'' she sobbed. ''She said that I'm hard to get along with and that before now she's covered for me, but she won't anymore. I couldn't sleep all night, thinking about it.''

Kate was appalled. She'd never known Leslie to attack anyone this way. ''That must have been very hurtful, Margot.''

Unable to speak for sobbing, Margot nodded.

''Would it help if I got Leslie to come over, and the three of us talked it through?''

''I don't know.'' Margot hesitated. ''I guess so. I don't see how we can go on working together unless we get it sorted out,'' she said in a choked voice.

''I'll go to the ER right now and see if she can join us,'' Kate said, putting the cup of tea she'd just made and a box of tissues in front of Margot. ''I'll be back in fifteen minutes.''

But Kate came back alone. Leslie had flatly refused to discuss anything with Margot. ''She's deserved a reprimand for a long time,'' Leslie had said in an angry tone. "There's nothing more to talk about as far as I'm concerned."

Margot was more upset than ever when Kate told her that Leslie wouldn't discuss the issue. "I'm going to see if there're any openings in another department," she said. "I can't stand the strain of being around someone who thinks I'm not a good nurse."

Kate did what she could to reassure Margot, but she knew it wasn't effective, and she felt deeply frustrated when the woman finally left her office.

The phone rang and Kate snatched it up, hoping it was Tony.

"Ms. Lewis?" It was a man, but not the right one. "My name is Kent Johns, my firm represents St. Joseph's in legal matters."

Kate's heart sank, and her spirits dropped even lower as she listened. Dr. Snider had contacted the lawyer. In Snider's opinion, Kate had left the hospital wide open to a charge of medical negligence by what she'd said to Walter Rundle. The lawyer wanted to hear from her exactly what had occurred.

She told him, wondering why the surgeon hadn't gone to Tony instead of to the legal firm. Or maybe he had; maybe Tony had told him to call the lawyer. Despair almost overwhelmed her. She had to make an enormous effort to stay calm as she informed Kent Johns that there was no question of blaming Dr. Snider, that all she'd suggested was that he speak to Walter Rundle and explain what had happened during the operation.

The lawyer listened in disapproving silence and then gave Kate what amounted to a reprimand. "Your first responsibility should be to your employer," he concluded in a snotty voice, and by the time he hung up, Kate felt like a child who'd had her knuckles unfairly rapped.

The phone rang again, and this time she was wary as she lifted the receiver.

"Kate, could you come over to my office for a moment?" This time it was Tony, and for an instant her spirits soared, but they plummeted to an all-time low when he added, "Three members of the hospital board are here with me. We've just been notified that a charge of medical negligence is being brought against the hospital. The claimant is Walter Rundle, and he says you supported him."

Kate swallowed hard. "I'll be right there." She'd thought she couldn't feel any worse, but apparently there were depths of misery she'd never explored until now.

AS HE SAW ONE PATIENT after the other late that afternoon, Tony felt worse and worse about the meeting he'd had with Kate and the board members. The disconsolate look she'd given him when she walked in the room had gone straight to his heart. He'd had no choice except to ask her to be present, but he wished now he'd also found a few moments to be alone with her afterward.

He had nothing but admiration for the way she stuck to her beliefs, and also for the dignified manner in which she conducted herself. She didn't defend herself. Instead, she simply repeated quietly what had occurred, explained that she thought a meeting between Snider and Walter Rundle would have made a difference, and then listened as the controversy raged. Tony had been surprised to learn that one of the board members totally agreed with Kate, although the other two were critical of her reasoning.

"In an ideal world," one of them said, "total honesty might work. But as we all know, from a litigation point of view, the less we admit to the better."

Tony thought about that as he drove home after work. There was something wrong with that reasoning. There was also something very wrong with the way he'd been avoiding Kate. He felt horrible about the fight they'd had, the things he'd said. And he hadn't apologized.

He needed to see her—now. He called his mother to tell her he'd be late and then wheeled the car around and headed for Kate's house.

From half a block away he could see that Scott and three of his buddies were still dismantling one of the two old cars in Kate's driveway. Once Tony had parked and gotten out, four pairs of eyes followed him as he made his way between the greasy engine parts littering the sidewalk and up to Kate's front door.

Eliza answered the doorbell. She didn't return Tony's determined smile, but she did say in a polite voice, "Hello, Dr. O'Connor."

"Hi, Eliza. Is Kate at home?"

"She's watering the flowers in the backyard."

"Could you tell her I'm here, please?"

He waited for what seemed a long time.

"Hi, Tony." Kate was wearing denim shorts, her long legs tanned golden. Her hair was pulled back with a clip, she had dirt on her cheek, and she looked so delicious, all Tony wanted to do was take her in his arms. But her wary green eyes and the reserve in her tone told him he had a long way to go before that would be possible.

"Sit down. I made some lemonade. Would you like some?"

"That sounds good." He'd have liked a stiff shot of gin with it, but he didn't say so.

"Eliza, get us some from the pitcher in the fridge, would you, please?"

The girl had followed Kate in, and now she went off to the kitchen.

"Kate, first off, I want to apologize for the things I said the other day. I was way out of line, I didn't mean—"

"Here's your lemonade, Dr. O'Connor." Eliza handed him a brimming glassful that somehow slopped onto his trousers and the rug. Tony leaped up, catching a sly look on Eliza's face that hinted the spill hadn't been accidental.

"Sorry, Tony." Kate frowned at the girl. "Eliza, go get a damp cloth to wipe that up, please."

Tony took a long gulp of the lemonade to prevent it from spilling again, and started to say what needed saying. "I value what we had together, Kate, and I'd like to try—"

Eliza was back with a wet dishrag. Tony took it and blotted at his pants and the rug.

"Can I have some cookies, Kate?"

"Yes, Eliza, go ahead."

She skipped off. He tried again.

"Could we at least talk about this, Kate?"

Eliza was back. "The bag's empty, Kate. Can I open a new one?"

"Yes, of course you can. And please stop interrupting."

Tony took a deep breath. "I know that what you said is true, Kate. We do have differing views on certain things, but surely that's what makes—"

The front door opened and Scott stuck his head in. "Hey, Katie, is Eliza around? I need her to get the keys for me from downstairs."

"Eliza," Kate called. "Your father wants you."

She came running, and Scott repeated his request. Eliza ran off and Scott went back outside. In less than three minutes, Eliza ran through the room again, swinging a set of keys.

"Eliza, use the back door, please."

"Okay, Kate." She went skipping back through the room and a second later the kitchen door slammed behind her.

Tony could feel his temper slipping. "Kate, for God's sake, will you come for a ride with me so we can discuss this in private?"

The front door burst open and Eliza bounded in again. "Daddy says he'll be back in an hour, he's gone to pick up some parts from the wrecker. Are we gonna have dinner soon, Kate? Because I'm starving."

Kate shook her head and gave a hopeless shrug. "I want to come with you, Tony, but I can't very well leave Eliza here by herself."

Eliza shot Tony a triumphant look. "You promised you'd help me with my science experiment, Kate. You said we could use that stuff from your closet. Can I go get it now?"

Tony set the glass down and got to his feet. He started for the door and then whirled around to face Kate. The words boiled out of him. "Don't you put any value at all on your own life? Or are you so satisfied with the status quo that you don't really want any changes? I thought we had a chance for something good together, but I can see there isn't room here for anything except what you already have."

Her eyes went wide, and she got up and took a step toward him. "Oh, Tony, please don't—"

He walked out the door, avoided the mess in the driveway and got in his car. Some part of him had hoped she'd say to hell with everything and run after him, but she didn't.

It hurt more than he'd imagined it could to admit that it was over between them.

CHAPTER SEVENTEEN

KATE SAT FROZEN AS THE DOOR closed behind Tony.

"Can I get the stuff from your closet, Kate? Hey, Kate, are you listening to me?"

She'd known all along it couldn't last, Kate reminded herself. Her life was just too complicated. And it was too difficult with Tony as her boss. They had to work together, yet his way of handling issues was totally different from hers. Besides, it wasn't fair to Eliza. The girl had enough to cope with. Tony was right—there wasn't room for anything except what she already had.

And is that what you want for the rest of your life? That small, snide voice wasn't easy to shut off, but Kate did her best. She worked with Eliza on the science experiment, supervised the girl's bathtime, watched a video with her and tucked her into bed.

And then she was alone. The laundry had been folded and the following day's dinner planned. The plants were watered, the flowers tended. There wasn't another single thing to keep her from thinking.

Tony's words echoed in her ears, and loneliness and confusion filled her heart. If ever she needed a friend, it was now. She thought of Leslie, of how much she missed the long, intimate phone conversations they used to have, the cozy lunches, the uninhibited girl talk.

Kate understood that Leslie was going through terrible trauma surrounding the death of her mother. She had made it clear she didn't need or want Kate calling her, but tonight, Kate was the one in need.

She hesitated, but the emotions roiling inside of her threatened to overwhelm her and she dialed her friend's number. The phone rang and rang, and Kate was on the verge of hanging up when Leslie finally answered.

"Yes? Who is it?" Her voice was thick and choked. It was obvious she'd been crying.

At any other time, Kate would have immediately asked her what was wrong, putting Leslie's need first. This time, she couldn't.

"Les? Leslie, Tony just walked out on me. I care about him a lot and I really need to talk to you."

There was a long, long pause.

"Leslie, please," Kate burst out. "There's nobody else I can talk to."

Kate heard Leslie blow her nose, then she said in a reluctant tone, "I don't think I'm up to driving. Can you come over here?"

Scott was home—Kate had heard the downstairs

door open and close half an hour ago. Relief
flooded her.

"Yeah. Thanks. I'll be there right away."

Fifteen minutes later, Kate knocked at the door
of Leslie's condo. When her friend opened it, Kate
was shocked. Leslie, who'd always been meticulous
about her appearance, wore a tattered old pink bath-
robe. Her hair was lank, she wasn't wearing
makeup, and her eyes were puffy and red from crying.

"C'mon in." Leslie led the way into the living
room and gestured at an easy chair.

Kate sat, already feeling guilty about practically
forcing Leslie to see her.

"I guess there's something to that old saw about
misery loves company, huh?" Leslie said in a bitter
voice.

The smile Kate tried for didn't quite come off.

"So tell me what's happening with you and
Tony. I didn't even know you two were an item."

Leslie's brusque manner wasn't encouraging, but
Kate *had* forced this meeting. She tried to figure
out where to start and finally just said, "I guess I
fell in love with him."

The moment the words were out, Kate knew they
were true. She sketched for Leslie the weekend
they'd spent in Edmonton, adding, "We had a fight
over issues at work, but tonight it was over Scott
and Eliza. He walked out on me." She painted the
scene in words so Leslie would understand. "Eliza

is a total brat when Tony's around, I'll admit that. But he's an adult—he has a daughter of his own. I thought he'd be more understanding.''

But this new Leslie didn't understand, either. In a harsh tone, she said, ''You know, Kate, you're being a sucker and a fool. You have been for quite a while now.''

Shock waves rolled over Kate, and then she felt herself beginning to get mad, even through the pain. ''That really hurts, Leslie.''

Leslie shrugged. ''Yeah, I guess it does. But right now I just don't have the energy to listen and sympathize, not when I've watched you being a martyr for so long. I never said anything before because I didn't want to hurt you.''

''*A martyr?*'' Kate was so shocked she could hardly speak.

''Call it what you want. The way I see it, you put all your own needs last and allow Scott to control your life. And now you're surprised that Eliza's doing it. She's watched you being a doormat, letting Scott use her to control you. Why wouldn't she try the same thing? She's a smart kid.''

Kate was shaking. Waves of heat washed over her, and her breath was coming in short bursts. She felt absolute outrage rising in her. How dare Leslie say something like that? She tried to hold back the anger, to remember all the things she preached, but none of them worked.

''What—what *right* do you have to say such

things to me?'' The words came out hard, like pebbles she'd swallowed and was regurgitating. They hurt her throat. ''How dare you accuse me of being a doormat, just because I don't choose to rage and stomp around? Because I put Eliza's well-being first? All my life, I've tried to—I've tried…'' Her voice trailed off.

What? What had she really spent her life doing? Kate was far too honest to avoid the awful truth. As a child, she'd placated her angry father and listened to her resentful mother tell her things about him that a child shouldn't have to hear. She'd felt responsible—always—for people's feelings. It was up to her to keep peace, to make things right. Worst of all, she'd let her longing for a child trap her into a loveless marriage, and then compounded it by allowing Scott to control her even after their divorce.

When was the last time she'd thought only of herself?

In Edmonton. In Tony's arms, she'd been completely free, completely herself. And the moment she came home, she'd forgotten all over again how to claim her own happiness.

Harsh as it sounded, tough as it was to admit, Leslie was right.

Kate looked over at her friend, intending to tell her so.

''God, oh my God.'' Leslie was bent double, her head on her knees, and the sounds coming from her were beyond sobs. They were the sounds of a person in agony, deep, harsh noises that seemed to tear their way straight from the depths of her being.

Hurrying over to her, Kate knelt down and wrapped her in her arms. She didn't speak. She just held on to her friend until the storm began to pass.

At last, Leslie blew her nose and sat back in the chair. She looked at Kate through bleary eyes. "I'm sorry, Kate, I'm so sorry for saying those things to you. I just can't stand myself. The pain is so bad I can't bear it, and it makes me say and do things I'm sorry for after. I shouldn't have spoken to you that way."

A few moments ago, Kate would have agreed. Now she realized Leslie had done what was necessary. "It's the truth. It's time somebody made me recognize it." She took Leslie's hand and held on to it. "Tell me about this pain you have, Les."

"It's there all the time, it's like a heaviness in my chest. I can't sleep at night, I can't eat." Leslie gave a halfhearted attempt at a smile that tore Kate's heart out, it was so sad. "Wouldn't you think I'd appreciate that? I've lost eight pounds in the last couple of weeks."

"It's the pain of losing your mother," Kate said softly.

"Yeah…that. But what's even worse is knowing it was my fault."

Kate was shocked. "Oh, Les, that's just not true—"

But Leslie held up a hand. "It is, Kate. Don't try

to deny it. I'm an ER nurse, I'm trained to notice symptoms, but with Mom, I missed them. I should never have allowed Hersh to send her home after that first episode. I should have been a lot more aggressive. I just can't forgive myself for taking her home that night when she should have been admitted.''

''Les, you can't be a nurse and a daughter at the same time, you know that. That's why medical people don't treat their family members.''

Leslie's eyes blazed with sudden ferocious anger. ''Yeah, well, Hersh was supposed to be treating her. I was at fault, but *he* made a gigantic mistake, and I want him to pay for what he did. I'm going to sue him. I've seen two lawyers, and it will cost a lot of money, but I'll sell this town house if I have to in order to raise it.''

''Oh, Les.'' Kate was at a loss. How could she convince Leslie that it would be futile to get into a lawsuit? The only thing she could think of to say was ''What do you think Galina would have wanted you to do?''

As if Kate had touched a button, fresh tears filled Leslie's eyes and spilled down her flushed cheeks. ''I dream about her every night,'' she said in a broken voice. ''She sings to me, Kate, this weird death song. It wakes me up and then I can't get to sleep again.''

''What do you think she's trying to tell you?''

Leslie didn't answer right away. Her body rocked

back and forth in agony. Then, as if the words were torn from her, she blurted, "I guess she's telling me to let it go. I know she's singing that song to let me know that it was time for her to die." She drew in a shuddering breath. "But I just can't accept that. I need—I need—"

"What? What do you need?"

"I need that doctor to know how important my mother was to me." Leslie's voice was vehement. "I need him to understand what his carelessness did to her and to me."

Kate nodded. She knew what the next step ought to be, but recent painful experience had taught her to be cautious about asking doctors to say they were sorry. Her track record wasn't great when it came to arranging such meetings, though for Leslie's sake, she'd try once again.

"If I can arrange it, will you tell Hersh what you just told me?"

"I can't," Leslie moaned, shaking her head. "Don't ask me to." Then she thought it over, and finally she sighed and gave a hesitant nod. "Okay, Kate. I'll try, but I can't promise I'll be able to go through with it without screaming at him. I just get so—so emotional, so *mad,* when I even think about him. Facing him will be really tough for me."

"I know. Facing up to things isn't easy—just look at me." Her voice was rueful. "So what am *I* gonna do, Les?"

"Boot Scott out." Leslie's advice was immediate.

"Easy for you to say. What about Eliza?" Kate wrapped her arms around herself, imagining how painful it would be to lose the child she loved.

Leslie thought it over and sighed. "You're right, Kate. It *is* easy for me. It's always easy to see what another person should do. But my honest opinion is that Scott couldn't manage Eliza on his own. He's relied on you for so long, he hasn't a clue about raising a daughter by himself. But the worst could happen. He could take her and walk, and you'd have to be prepared for that."

Kate's stomach contracted at the thought of taking that chance. "Like you said before, I'm not being much of a role model for her this way, letting Scott walk all over me. But I keep thinking how hard it would be for her, too, not having me around at all."

"It's a tough call, Kate. You're the only one who can make the decision." Leslie seemed a little more like her old self. "D'you think you and Tony could patch things up, if Scott wasn't around?"

It was Kate's turn for tears. They welled up in her eyes and her chest hurt trying to hold them back. "I don't think so. There's too much stuff going on between us, too many things we disagree about, both personal and at work. And he's got hard issues going on with his family. There just doesn't seem to be any space for him and me."

"Make space. If you care about him, make room for him in your life." Leslie's voice was vehement. "Love isn't something you put off until it's convenient. The one thing I'm glad about is that Mom knew how much I loved her."

Kate nodded, but Leslie's words had raised still more disturbing issues. Tony had never come out and said that he loved her. He'd said he adored *making* love with her, he'd said he thought they *might* have a future together. But he'd never once put into words what he actually felt about her.

So maybe the loving part was all on her side, which spelled heartbreak in capital letters. But she'd never know for sure unless she tried.

And the first part of trying was just what Leslie said. She had to make room for Tony in her life, and that meant getting rid of Scott once and for all.

CHAPTER EIGHTEEN

IT TOOK EVERY OUNCE of Kate's courage to march downstairs and tell Scott he had two weeks to find another place to live. And that wasn't the toughest part of the encounter.

"I've made an appointment with a lawyer to obtain joint custody of Eliza," she added.

"You *what?* Have you gone nuts or something?" Scott gave her a disbelieving look. "You're not even a blood relative, you haven't got a hope in hell of getting any kind of custody."

Kate wanted to scream at him, remind him that she'd helped raise Eliza since babyhood. She was trembling, but she did her best to hide it. "That's not what the lawyer thinks. Here's her card. You can give her a call if you like." She held it out.

Scott didn't take it. "Well, I guess it's time to move on, anyhow," he blustered. "My cousin down in Nova Scotia has a job for me anytime, I'll just give him a call."

It was the threat he'd always used, and Kate was so terrified her stomach ached. Again, she tried her best to seem accepting and cool.

"That's your choice, Scott."

"You'll never see Eliza again if I move down there," he threatened.

Anger was beginning to take the place of fear, and for the first time in her life, Kate welcomed it. "I will if I have joint custody. She'll stay with me for whatever time the court decides is best for her."

"I could just take her and disappear, y'know. Nothing's stopping me."

"That's right, you could." Kate had spent two sleepless nights imagining just such a scenario. "But you know that would really hurt Eliza, and I don't think you want to do that."

"She's my kid, not yours."

"The lawyer says that because I've been her stepparent since she was a baby, I have a legal right to shared custody." The lawyer had said that, but she'd also said it was important that Kate and Scott agree on the matter.

He made a scoffing sound, but Kate could tell he was disconcerted. He gave her a wary look. "What's gotten into you all of a sudden? I figured we were going along okay, and then you hit me with all this crap. What'sa matter, your fancy boyfriend dump you and you're taking it out on me?"

It hurt, but Kate stared him down and stuck to the matter at hand. "I'll go to court if I have to, Scott, to obtain custody of Eliza."

His face flushed. "You know I don't have money for a big court case."

She couldn't resist. "Then I guess you'll just have to find a job."

He sneered at her. "That's what bugs you, isn't it, Kate? That you're tied to a grindstone and I've found a way to live where I don't have to work."

For a moment, she actually wanted to laugh. He didn't seem to realize that at least part of the reason for that was her generous financial support of Eliza and the minimal rent she charged him. She'd subsidized him for so long he simply took it for granted. He took her for granted, and that wasn't Scott's fault. It was hers. But starting now, she wouldn't take responsibility for him any longer.

With that realization, the last of Kate's fear disappeared, and the anger went with it. Scott was a bully, and she'd called his bluff. Whether or not he did as he threatened, it wouldn't change her decision. It would be a dramatic learning curve for both of them.

"Oh, and another thing," she said in a cool, controlled voice. "I've called a removal company to come and clear the junk out of the driveway and off the front lawn. They'll be here tomorrow morning at nine."

This time her words brought a flood of invective. But she also noticed that he worked for the rest of the evening clearing away the rubble.

EVEN HARDER THAN the showdown with Scott was setting down the ground rules for Eliza over the next few days. No more rude behavior, she stipulated. No more nasty looks. No more endless interruptions when Kate had company. No temper tantrums. And unless she was invited, Kate's bedroom was strictly off limits.

At first Eliza pretended she didn't understand what Kate meant, and it became necessary to use exact examples. Kate cited the scene at the dance studio and the gift, still in her handbag, that Eliza had rejected. She mentioned Tony's visits and the way Eliza had acted to him. She talked about the way Eliza simply assumed she could sleep in Kate's bed. "We all need friends, and we all need privacy, Eliza."

"Daddy says you're making us move out," Eliza accused.

"I've asked your daddy to find another place to live," Kate corrected her.

"Don't you like us living with you in your house?" Eliza's lip quivered, and Kate felt like a rat.

"I love you, and I love having you with me," Kate replied. "But your daddy and I are divorced now. It would be better for both of us if he lived somewhere else. But that doesn't mean you won't spend time with me. I hope you'll come and stay part of each week at my house."

She prayed that part was going to work out.

"But what about what I want?" Fat tears rolled down Eliza's cheeks. "I want to be with you and with my daddy, too. Why can't you love my daddy, Kate? Why can't we just all be together? Like a family?''

This was even harder than Kate had anticipated. She felt terrible, as if she was betraying Eliza.

But she had to stick to what was best for her, she reminded herself.

''I did love him once, Eliza,'' Kate said as gently as she could. ''That's why we got married. But sometimes big people want different things, and that causes problems. That's what happened between your daddy and me.''

''How come it doesn't matter what kids want?'' Eliza's little face was angry and troubled, and Kate felt like weeping for her.

''Oh, sweetie, it does matter. But one of the things everyone has to learn is that we don't always get the things we want.''

In spite of her brave front, Kate was terrified that Scott would carry out his threats and move far away with Eliza. But the little girl came skipping upstairs a few days after Kate's ultimatum and announced that she and Scott were moving to an apartment just two streets over from Kate's house.

One of Scott's buddies had converted the top of a double garage to living space, and when Kate walked by to check it out, she was relieved to see that it looked good. The yard was well kept, and a girl a bit younger than Eliza was playing on a swing set in the backyard.

"She's my friend Amy," Eliza confided. "Her mommy's really nice, and she says you can come and visit anytime you like, Kate. I've got my own room—it's pink. Amy's mom made curtains with ballerinas on them. And Daddy's friend says I can have a dog if I want. Amy has a dog of her own."

Kate was so relieved she could have wept. At the same time, she felt abandoned and lonely. She was going to miss having Eliza living in the same house.

She wasn't going to miss Scott. With the clutter gone from the front yard, Kate bought flowering bushes and planted them. She mowed the lawn and hired a handyman to paint the front steps, chores Scott had continually promised to do and never got around to. It felt wonderful to have her house all to herself. She'd never really had a chance to enjoy her home. Eventually she'd rent the suite again, but this time it would be a business arrangement.

The best news of all came when Kate's lawyer phoned with the news that Scott had agreed to her having joint custody.

"I think he's nervous about parenting all by himself," the lawyer commented. "And of course, having you help with financial support for Eliza is no small thing."

Kate had been both generous and cautious about the support agreement. She'd stipulated that she'd buy all of Eliza's clothing and pay for her extracurricular activities, as well as maintain a fund for her future education, but Kate drew the line at handing over money to Scott. She knew him too well; if it came to a decision between car parts and dancing lessons, his car would win. The only things he could be trusted to do were pay the rent and buy good food. And love his daughter, Kate conceded. She'd never doubted that Scott adored Eliza.

Scott and Eliza moved on Friday. Kate came home and her heart sank. The house felt empty and forlorn. Had she made a terrible mistake? She wandered around, watering plants and turning on music to fill the gaping spaces Eliza's piping voice and rushing footsteps had filled.

The phone rang.

"Hiya, Kate." It was Eliza. "Kate, do you think Amy and I could have a sleepover at your house tomorrow night? I told her about those big cookies you know how to make out of Smarties. Could we make some of those?" Belatedly, but making Kate smile all the same, she added, "That's if you don't need your privacy."

"Sure, Eliza. You and Amy come over tomorrow." It was going to be all right. Eliza was still going to be a big part of her life.

If only she had reason to believe that about her and Tony.

CHAPTER NINETEEN

KATE'S SMALL OFFICE FELT overcrowded and much too warm. The tension reminded her of an overfilled balloon on the verge of exploding. Nathaniel Hersh and Leslie sat across from her. Hersh was a big man, bordering on fat, and he was loud. In a booming voice, he'd just explained why he'd made the diagnosis he had when Leslie brought Galina to Emerg.

He'd been reluctant and defensive when Kate asked him to meet with Leslie, and it had taken all her persuasive powers to convince him to come to her office. It wasn't easy for him, Kate knew that.

"What can I say to Yates?" Hersh had asked her. "What's done is done. Nothing I say will bring her mother back."

"Just tell her the truth," Kate had advised, but from the stubborn set of his mouth, she figured that wasn't going to happen.

Kate could also see how hard this was for Leslie. Her forehead was shiny with sweat, and her trembling hands were knotted into fists on her lap. She sat as far away from Hersh as the small space allowed, her body tensely upright.

For a panicked moment, Kate wondered if doing this would only make the situation worse between these two. Maybe it was a mistake, maybe she should have just stayed out of it.

"My mother died because you misdiagnosed her." Each word Leslie spoke was like a poisoned arrow, aimed straight at Hersh. "How would you feel if you'd come into Emerg with your mother, and a doctor had done that?"

Hersh shifted uncomfortably in his chair, but he didn't reply.

"I asked you to admit her, and you refused," Leslie accused, glaring at him. Her face was flushed, her voice rising. "You as much as told me that I was only a nurse and I didn't have the expertise you did. And because you wouldn't listen, my mother *died*." Her shriek made Hersh cringe.

The raw pain in Leslie's voice tore at Kate's heart. She tensed, waiting for Hersh to holler back, to defend himself and deny responsibility, and she tried to fight off the panic she felt. This idea of hers was going to cause Leslie more pain rather than less. Hersh was going to lose his temper, and then—

"I'm sorry." Hersh's loud voice had sunk to a mumble. He slumped back in his chair and rubbed a hand over his face. "I'm really sorry." He shook his head. "I was rushed that night, and I made a snap decision—the wrong one."

Kate was astonished that he was admitting it. She glanced over at Leslie to see what she'd do.

For a moment, Leslie just stared at the doctor. Then her body relaxed, and she bent her head. Her shoulders shook as the tears came.

Hersh looked miserable. "I feel bad about it. The worst part is there's nothing I can do, I can't go back and change things."

"It was a mistake," Kate said quietly. "We all make mistakes. The only thing we can do is learn from them."

"Yeah. Well, I've got to get back to work and make some more." Hersh got to his feet. "Sorry," he mumbled again as he inched past Leslie. She didn't look up, but Kate saw her nod her head. It was barely discernible, but it signaled an acceptance of his apology.

When he was gone, Kate rubbed Leslie's back and handed her tissues.

"I still don't like him," Leslie sniffed. "But I don't want to kill him anymore." She blew her nose hard. "What you said is right, Kate, about mistakes. All we can do is learn from them. It was a mistake to let Mom's death turn into something ugly. It's a mistake for me to act the way I've been acting. I'm gonna have to do some apologizing down in Emerg. I've been a bitch on wheels this last while."

"People will understand. Just be honest with them," Kate advised.

When Leslie left, Kate thought about the advice

she handed out so freely. Be honest, she'd told Hersh. Be honest, she'd counseled Leslie.

But how honest was she? Kate pondered.

Not very, her conscience chided.

She'd never told Tony she loved him. She'd never honestly told him what she wanted or needed from their relationship. She hadn't even made an effort to tell him about the changes she'd recently effected in her life, or the fact that she'd give anything to try again with him.

She'd been avoiding him.

It was time to take her own advice. Sucking in a deep breath, she picked up the phone, then put it down and made her way down to his office. She needed to do this in person. It took every ounce of courage she had to march in and ask his secretary if she could see him.

And it was a terrible letdown to be told that he'd taken the rest of the week off. Kate was heading back to her office when she spotted Hersh, hurrying along with an envelope of lab results under his arm. She ran to catch up with him.

"Dr. Hersh? Thank you for apologizing to Leslie."

He nodded and shrugged. "Tony and I discussed it. He said he thought it was a good idea."

Kate was dumbfounded. "Tony—Dr. O'Connor said that?"

"Yeah. He said what you said, that we all make mistakes, and admitting to them is better than covering up. And I figured I have to work with Yates, I don't need the grief.''

Hersh's words replayed in Kate's mind all the way back to her office. Tony had changed his thinking. He'd gone out of his way to help her in this situation, and the least she could do was say thank you.

She had his cell number. She'd call him on it.

She was just about to dial when the calendar on her desk caught her eye, and belatedly, she remembered what day it was. She couldn't call him today.

It was August 4. Tony had told her that his father, Ford O'Connor, was arriving from Australia today.

"WHAT WILL MY GRANDPA FORD look like, Papa?" McKensy was practically bouncing off the airport carpet with excitement. It was nine-thirty and Ford and Betsy's flight had landed, according to the information screens. They should be clearing Customs and appearing through the International Arrivals exit at any moment.

"Will you know who Grandpa is when you see him?"

Tony smiled at her and smoothed a lock of her strawberry-blond hair out of her eyes. "Of course I will, duchess. People used to say I looked just like him."

"How about you, Auntie Georgia? Do you remember what he looks like?"

"I've seen the pictures he sent us, squirt. I don't

really remember him that well, though. I was younger than you when he left." Her voice was pitched higher than usual, a sure sign that she was nervous.

Tony felt more than a little nervous himself. He was humbly grateful that Georgia had joined him and McKensy to welcome Ford and Betsy. It had taken courage and fortitude for her to defy Dorothy and stand up to Wilson. Tony's brother had done his best to convince Georgia that coming to the airport to meet her father amounted to treason. Tony shuddered at the memory of the final hysterical scene that had taken place with Dorothy that morning. His mother had pulled out all the stops.

"What should I call Grandpa's friend, Papa?"

Tony had carefully explained that Ford was bringing a lady who'd been his best friend for many years.

"I'm not sure. Maybe you should ask her."

They watched the streams of people coming through the doors at the arrivals level. When a tall, emaciated old man and a short, plump woman pushing a luggage cart hesitated and then hurried toward them, Tony had to hide the terrible sense of shock he felt at his father's appearance.

The strong, handsome man he remembered was stooped, his bony face lined and sunken. He was bald and his skin was yellow, and he had a look about him that Tony had seen numerous times in patients. He didn't want to recognize it in his father's face, but his medical experience left him no option.

Ford was terminally ill.

Tony felt as if he'd been sucker-punched. Emotions coursed through him—anger, frustration, overwhelming sadness. An aching sorrow that so much of their lives had been spent far apart. A feeling of urgency that this short time they had must be spent getting to know each other again.

He struggled for a shaky smile to welcome Ford and his companion.

"Tony?" Ford's voice was not the hearty baritone that Tony remembered. It was weak and trembling with emotion. "Georgia, sweetheart, how lovely you are. And this pretty lady must be McKensy."

He embraced Georgia, and then McKensy. "Ah, it's a rare treat to see all of you. A million thanks for coming to meet us." Ford had dropped the small bag he was carrying and now he held his arms out to Tony.

Tony walked into his father's embrace, and had to struggle to hold back the tears. Ford's body felt fragile in his arms. He was seventy, but he looked a decade older. The only part of him that hadn't seemed to change was his smile. Being in his father's arms unleashed in Tony a deep and abiding love, a love that overwhelmed him with its raw power.

Ford's tears ran freely down his wrinkled cheeks

as he hugged first one of them and then the other again and again. Betsy was introduced, and once more there were warm, welcoming hugs all round. Her liquid dark eyes and beaming smile telegraphed the warmth of her personality, and her love for Ford was evident in the way she held his hand and matched her step to his slower one as they made their way out to the car park.

"Papa said I should ask you what you want me to call you," McKensy said in a shy voice to Betsy. Without waiting for a reply, she burbled on, "I already have one grammy, so maybe I could call you Grandma Betsy, would that be okay?"

Betsy stopped and put an arm around McKensy's shoulders. Her deep, dark eyes glowed with pleasure.

"I would consider that a great honor," she said in her singsong accent. "I don't have grandchildren, so you'll be my very first."

McKensy turned pink with delight.

There wasn't room for all of them in one vehicle. Georgia had brought her car, and after a bit of discussion it was decided the women would go in one car, the men in the other.

The Barclay Hotel, where Ford and Betsy were staying, was on Robson Street, in the heart of downtown Vancouver, an hour's drive from the airport. As he threaded his way through the heavy morning traffic, Tony felt suddenly awkward with his father. It had been so many years since they'd been in each other's company. Tony had been a boy of eleven, Ford a young and vibrant man of thirty-eight. There had been letters, but in spite of them the years were hard to bridge.

"McKensy's a bonny girl," Ford said. "Meeting my grandkid is a dream come true." He paused. "I'd guess that this visit is causing you and Georgia grief with your mother. I'm sorry about that. The last thing I want is to cause you problems."

Caught between loyalties, Tony couldn't think what to say.

"See, I had to come now, Tony." Ford's voice was urgent. "I wanted to come before, but there was never enough money. There isn't now, either, come to that, but time's running out for me."

Though he was a doctor, Tony still didn't want to hear the fateful diagnosis confirmed.

"Astroblastoma, you doctors call it," Ford said. "Fancy name for brain cancer."

"You've seen specialists?" Tony asked, struggling to remain calm.

Ford laughed. "Too bloody many of the bastards, begging your pardon, son. They operated six months ago. Thought they'd got it all, but now the demon's back, headaches again, blurry vision. They suggested radiation, but I said no. Rather see it through my own way this time. I've had a good run, all told. Only thing I regret is leaving all you nippers the way I did." He cleared his throat, and

Tony could hear the anguish underneath the quiet words.

"And Betsy, I'll hate like blue hell leaving my Betsy." Ford's voice had thickened, and he cleared his throat and turned to look out the car window, struggling not to break down.

Tony was having his own difficulties as he fought against the tightness in his chest. "She seems like a fine lady, Dad." They both needed a bridge back to safety. "How did you two meet?"

"I was working on a sheep station, she was cooking. She's a real fine cook, is my Betsy. Anyhow, I got sick, real sick, some kinda tropical fever. She took care of me. We've been together ever since. I don't know how I'd have made it without her." He was quiet for a moment. "I know you went through that divorce, son. It must be hard for you, raising McKensy on your own." His voice was hesitant but determined. "You never say, and I always wonder. Tell me, Tony, is there anybody like Betsy around for you? I don't mean to pry, it's just that there's so much I don't know about you. So much I *want* to know."

Kate's face sprang into Tony's thoughts, and he felt the familiar emptiness. "There's a woman at the hospital. But things didn't work out for us."

"Sorry to hear that, son. Have you tried to fix it up with her?"

"Yeah, I did. I hit a dead end." He'd gone over and over that final meeting with Kate, and he still couldn't see how he could have handled it any differently. He'd seen her at a couple of meetings over the past several weeks, and they'd been polite and distant with each other, which hurt more than if they'd fought.

"Dead ends happen to all of us, son. I know you didn't ask, but I'm handing out advice, anyhow, not that I've got any right to. Just give it another try, why don't you."

Tony nodded, although he knew there wasn't any hope.

Ford took the nod as agreement. "Good lad. It hasn't always been clear sailing for Betsy and me, y'know. We've had our times when it seemed we couldn't go on, too. But when you care enough, your heart has a way of forcing you to do things you wouldn't otherwise. When you love someone, there's always another chance. See, lad, Betsy wanted to get married, wanted it real bad. Her family turned their backs on her—wouldn't countenance her living in what they called sin. Real sticklers for right and proper, they were. And I couldn't get a divorce, though I asked your mother many times."

Ford sound resigned rather than resentful. "I could've fought it out in court, but it would've cost more than I could afford. And I figured you young ones would be the losers, because money that should have come to your mother for your support would be lining the lawyers' pockets. So Betsy and

I never did get married legal. We never had kids, either, another thing she wanted real bad. We didn't want to bring a nipper into the world a bastard, us not being married and all. So a couple times it seemed as if there was nowhere to go except our separate ways.''

''But you worked it out.''

''Yeah, we did. Neither of us could live without the other.'' The admission was matter of fact. ''That's the test, Tony. If life isn't worth living without the other person, then you gotta move heaven and earth to make it work. In the end, love's the only thing that matters.''

Love's the only thing that matters. Ford's words stuck in Tony's mind as he and Georgia made certain their father and Betsy were comfortable at the hotel. Before Tony left, he arranged to pick them up for the family dinner he was hosting at a downtown restaurant at seven that evening—a dinner that, so far, only he and Georgia and McKensy were attending.

Tony was sick to death of the controversy in his family. Trusting in the truth of Ford's words, he phoned first Judy and then Wilson, shamelessly using blunt honesty and heavy doses of guilt to persuade his siblings to come to dinner that evening. He told them both that Ford was dying, and probably didn't have much time left. Their father's single wish was to see his children and grandchildren.

"Let's try to put aside our differences just for this one night," he pleaded again and again.

As he'd suspected she might, Judy changed her mind and agreed to come, bringing her husband, Peter, and their two children, but Wilson refused.

"He's nothing to me," he blustered. "Our mother's the one who raised us. Why make a big fuss over a guy who walked out on his kids and his wife? So he's on his last legs—maybe he's getting what he deserves out of life."

Tony had learned so much from Kate. He remembered her saying, "Don't defend, just stick to your point and reiterate if necessary."

"We'll be at the restaurant at seven," Tony repeated through gritted teeth. "If you and Margaret change your minds, you're most welcome to join us."

"Don't hold your breath."

THE RESTAURANT TONY HAD chosen was Italian, since Ford had said that his favorite food was veal scallopini, and Betsy loved pasta. It was a good choice for a family dinner, because children were warmly welcomed.

Tony had arranged with the manager for a semi-private location in an alcove, and Judy and Peter and their children were already seated when he arrived with Ford and Betsy. Georgia had brought McKensy.

Obviously ill at ease, Judy got to her feet and

went over to Ford, stiff and awkward. He drew her into his embrace, and when he released her, she was crying so hard Tony had to introduce his brother-in-law, Peter, and his niece and nephew.

They were all enjoying a glass of wine when Georgia leaned over to Tony and whispered, "I don't believe it, Wilson and Margaret just walked in, and the kids are with them."

Tony, too, could hardly believe it. His brother, red faced and avoiding Tony's eye, went over to their father and shook his hand.

"I'll bet Margaret made him come," Georgia said in an undertone as her sister-in-law introduced her children to Ford and Betsy, and politely welcomed them to Canada. "Good old Maggie," Georgia gloated. "She's the only one who's ever been able to make old rod-in-the-ass do anything."

Wilson's reasons for coming didn't matter to Tony. All he cared about was the incandescent pleasure on Ford's face as he lifted his wineglass and toasted his family.

The meal took on the atmosphere of a celebration. While they waited for the food to arrive, Betsy opened a large carryall she'd brought and distributed gifts to the grandchildren. She and Ford had obviously given careful thought to each one. No two children received the same gift, and each was age and gender appropriate.

McKensy received a koala bear whose belly contained a tape player.

"This is *way* cool," she enthused. She sprang to her feet and rushed over to hug Betsy. "Thank you, Grandma Betsy," she caroled. She hugged her grandfather as well, and her cousins followed suit.

Betsy and Ford were mobbed by children, and obviously loving every moment. Georgia took out her camera and snapped pictures, and the noise level increased.

So did the laughter. Everyone relaxed, and by the time the salads were eaten and the main course arrived, it seemed that the party was well on its way to being a total success.

Tony looked around the table at each of his siblings and their partners, and then he glanced at his father.

Ford and Betsy were leaning toward each other, and Betsy was saying something into Ford's ear. The two of them looked at each other and laughed with the intimacy only lovers have, and Tony's aloneness suddenly overwhelmed him.

He imagined Kate sitting beside him, sharing in the pleasure he felt, sharing also in his amazement at this unbelievable spectacle of his brother and sisters all getting along for once.

The moment he got home tonight, no matter what time it was, he'd call her. His father was right about trying again.

Making the decision lightened Tony's spirits, and he smiled with anticipation when Ford got to his feet to make a speech.

Ford teetered for a moment, and Betsy reached out an arm to steady him. Alarmed at how pale and drawn Ford looked, Tony decided that the evening should end soon.

"Quiet, everyone," Wilson ordered in an authoritative voice.

"I just want to say how much it means to me to have all of you here," Ford began. "I can't take credit for being around to raise you, but you're a family to be proud of." His breathing was shallow, and he gulped for air before he managed to say, "Thank you for coming tonight, and I hope—" He gasped and leaned a trembling arm on the table, and then tried again. "I—I hope—"

Tony leaped to his feet as Ford staggered and began to fall. Betsy tried to support him.

Georgia grabbed his arm, but Ford was still a large man. He went crashing down, dragging the tablecloth with him. The floor was tile, and the sound of glass shattering brought waiters running.

Judy screamed, kids began crying, and Tony knelt over his father, searching for a pulse and undoing his tie.

"Wilson, call 911," he ordered. "Georgia, go out to my car and get my medical bag." He tossed her his keys.

"Please don't let him die, not now, not yet." Betsy was kneeling beside Ford, her body trembling, her round face ashen. Her dark eyes pleaded with Tony, begging him to perform a miracle.

As much as he longed to, Tony couldn't supply it. But for the next fifteen minutes, until the ambulance arrived, he did everything he knew to keep his father alive. And for the first time in many years, he prayed.

CHAPTER TWENTY

ST. JOE'S EMERG WAS uncharacteristically quiet. Tony briefed the ER doctors on what little he knew of his father's condition, and Dr. Suchanek, the hospital's leading oncologist, was called.

Ford was conscious by this time, but extremely weak and disoriented. It was Betsy who gave Suchanek detailed information about the operation Ford had had in Australia. He'd been on drugs, she said, but he wasn't taking anything at the moment.

Tony's entire family was now at the hospital, and it was obvious that the children were exhausted, the adults weary and anxious. After the initial examination in the ER, Ford was taken to the Intensive Care Unit, and Tony suggested everyone go home.

"Betsy and I'll stay with him tonight. If there's any change, we'll let you know."

Georgia offered to drive McKensy home. "If Mom asks how it went, what should I say?"

"Tell her the truth." Tony sighed and rubbed a hand through his hair. "She knew tonight was the dinner. She was in tears most of the day, and when I left, she was locked in her bedroom. She might as well know what happened."

Georgia shook her head and rolled her eyes. "Think she's ever gonna grow up?"

Tony ruffled his sister's hair and bent to kiss her cheek. "All we can do is hope."

AS THE NIGHT WORE ON, Ford's condition slowly improved. He grew aware of his surroundings and was able to talk a little as the long hours rolled toward morning.

It was evident how worried Betsy was about Ford, and Tony was amazed and humbled by how cheerful and optimistic she stayed. She told Tony a little about the simple life she and Ford led, and she showed him photos of their modest house in a Brisbane suburb.

"See, here on the wall, these are the photos that you sent over the years. He hung them up in the living room," she confided. "He'd show each new one to our friends, he's so very proud of all of you. Leaving his kids behind when he came to Australia left a big hole in his heart."

"Do you have any family you're close to, Betsy?" He remembered Ford saying her immediate family hadn't approved of their relationship, but maybe there was someone.

She shook her head. "My parents died long ago, and my brother and sister live in New South Wales, I don't see them much. Ford's my family, I reckon. We have good friends, but basically there's just the two of us."

Tony thought of how much this woman had given up to be with Ford. When his father died, Betsy would be totally alone, and yet there was no sign of resentment in her. At this moment, Betsy was in a strange country with people she didn't know and a companion who was terminally ill, and still she retained her good nature.

It was hard not to compare Betsy with his mother. Dorothy had the support and love of a large family, but she spent much of her time being miserable. Maybe happiness was a choice made fresh every day. Tony silently vowed to choose more of it.

Toward morning, Ford improved dramatically. When Bob Suchanek arrived at 6:00 a.m., he left orders that Ford be moved out of ICU.

"I'm trying him on Decadron again," he told Betsy and Tony. "From what you've told me, Mrs. O'Connor, he got a significant reprieve the last time he was on it. Maybe we'll be lucky again." He paused, and Tony could tell that what Suchanek was about to say wasn't good news. "He's been having headaches, ataxia, pain in his joints. I've ordered some tests, because I'm afraid the tumor's metastasized into the bone. If it has, we could try radiation—"

Betsy shook her head. "He doesn't want it."

Suchanek nodded. "He told me that. So we'll put all our faith in the Decadron." He took Betsy's hand in both of his. "The very best of luck to you both, Mrs. O'Connor."

Betsy didn't correct him, and Tony certainly wouldn't. As far as he was concerned, Betsy was his father's wife in every way that mattered.

Tony arranged for a private room, and by seven Ford was in it and sleeping comfortably.

"Let's go find some breakfast, Betsy." It had been a long night, and she looked pale and fragile. She sat beside Ford's bed, holding his hand.

"I don't want him to wake up and not find me here," she said doubtfully.

"The cafeteria's just downstairs—you'll be back before he wakes up," Tony promised. He planned to eat, and then shower and shave in the doctor's lounge. He had a meeting at eight-thirty, and he was glad he kept a change of clothes at St. Joe's. He had to phone his sisters and Wilson as well, to update them on Ford's condition. And as soon as he got a moment, he needed to talk to Kate. More than a moment, he corrected. They needed a stretch of uninterrupted time.

The cafeteria was crowded. It was a full forty minutes before Tony escorted Betsy back up to the oncology floor, and the moment they stepped off the elevator, he could hear his mother's raised, angry voice coming from Ford's room just down the hall.

"Don't tell me you don't have it—that's a lie and you know it. You stole that ring from me."

Tony swore under his breath and raced into Ford's room with Betsy right behind him.

Dressed in a pink suit, hair perfectly coiffed, Dorothy was standing at the foot of Ford's bed. Her face was suffused with angry color, and she was shaking a finger at the gaunt figure in the bed.

"Stop that." Betsy flew to Ford's side and put a protective hand on his ear as if to block what Dorothy was saying. "You stop hollering at him and get out of here, right now," she ordered. "You have no right to talk to him that way."

Dorothy stared at Betsy. "I have every right," she spat. "I happen to be his *wife*, not some—some *whore* he picked up on the street."

"Mom, that's enough." Appalled, Tony took Dorothy's arm, intending to bodily remove her if he had to, but she shook him off with surprising strength and grabbed the bottom railing of the bed.

"I—want—that—ring," she shouted. *"I'm not setting foot out of here without it."*

She was totally out of control. Tony put his arms around her, trying to dislodge her grip on the bed, but it was impossible. Her hands were welded to the railing.

Gasping for breath, Ford raised his head and whispered, "I—told you, many times, I—I sold it, Dorothy. I—I had no—no money, and I—I sold the bloody thing—years back—"

But Dorothy wasn't listening. "I suppose he gave it to *you*," she railed at Betsy.

Tony could see Betsy's self-control evaporating. Her entire body trembled and her face was pasty white beneath her tan. "I don't know what you're talking about. The only ring I have is this one. Take it, if it means that much to you." She twisted a small diamond from her left ring finger and offered it to Dorothy.

Dorothy took it, and after one glance, she threw it across the room.

"That's not my ring," she screamed.

Tony had had enough. He gripped his mother's shoulders and tried to lift her, intending to drag her bodily out of the room, but she clung to the bed, and it rolled along with them. Ford's IV tipped and threatened to fall over, and his oxygen mask was pulled forcibly from his face.

Betsy cried out and two nurses came running in, their wide eyes registering their horror and shock when they saw Tony and recognized Dorothy.

"Should we call Security, Tony?"

It would be humiliating for Dorothy to be forcibly removed by security personnel, but Tony knew something had to be done.

"You let me go," Dorothy was shrieking, kicking at Tony. *"I'm his legal wife, you can't force me to leave this room."*

If ever there was a time for defusing hostility, it was now.

"Call Kate Lewis, and be quick about it," Tony ordered, praying that she'd be at work by now, and available. One of the nurses flew out of the room, and the other one readjusted Ford's IV and the oxygen as Tony did his best to restrain his mother. She kept her death grip on the bottom of the bed and went on struggling with him.

Tony could feel her body shaking, smell the dank perspiration that poured from her. He was astounded at her strength. She went on with her tirade, accusing Ford of stealing the ring, calling Betsy a slut and a whore, telling Tony to let go of her. She writhed and squirmed in his grasp, and it was all he could do to hold on to her at all.

Betsy ignored everything but Ford, leaning down to stroke his cheek and murmur into his ear.

Tony's back was to the door, but some extra sense told him the instant Kate walked in the room. He literally felt the calmness of her presence, but he wondered what she could possibly do to help matters. He was going to have to forcibly sedate his mother.

Kate didn't hesitate, and neither did she pay attention to anyone in the room except Ford. She walked to the side of the bed, and she took the trembling hand Betsy wasn't holding.

Calmly and clearly, in a voice that everyone in the room heard, she asked, ''What do you want, Mr. O'Connor?''

Dorothy stopped struggling for a moment.

Ford raised his hand and fumbled at the mask the nurse had put over his nose.

Kate helped him move it aside.

"I—want—her—out—of—here," he gasped, pointing a shaking hand directly at Dorothy.

Kate nodded and turned to Dorothy. In a quiet but firm tone she said, "Will you come with me to my office, Dorothy, or shall I call Security?"

Holding her as he was, Tony could sense his mother's indecision.

The room was deathly quiet, and finally Tony felt the tension in Dorothy's muscles ease.

Kate walked over and took hold of Dorothy's hand. "C'mon, Dorothy," she coaxed. "Come with me now. I'll make us a cup of tea."

Dorothy let go of the bed and turned toward Kate.

For the first time, Kate looked at Tony. Her green eyes registered care and compassion, and she gave him a little nod.

"I'll be down to take her home in a few minutes," Tony promised. He was shaking and needed time to collect himself. He also had to find out where McKensy was. Dorothy wouldn't have left her alone, Tony assured himself. But the state his mother was in—

Dorothy allowed herself to be led out of the room by Kate. Tony could hear her sobbing all the way down the hall, and he could also hear Kate's low, soothing voice comforting her.

TWENTY MINUTES LATER, shaken to the core by what had happened, Tony tapped on Kate's office door. Ford had survived the hideous scene better than he had; his father and Betsy were holding hands and talking quietly when Tony left them.

"Come in." Kate's calm voice was like balm to his frazzled nerves.

"Hi, Kate." He tried to convey what he felt with a smile, but it would take much more than that to show her how grateful he was.

It was much harder for him to greet Dorothy, hard to subdue the sense of shame and outrage he felt toward her. "Hello, Mom."

Dorothy didn't respond. She was sitting in Kate's visitor's chair, a mug of fragrant-smelling tea cradled between her palms. A pile of crumpled tissues, her ravaged face and the tearstains down the front of her pink suit telegraphed the stormy scene that must have taken place before he got there.

Tony's anger faded. He felt sorry for his mother, and sorry that Kate had had to deal with Dorothy alone, but he was also endlessly grateful that she had.

"C'mon, Mom. It's time to go."

Kate got to her feet, and after a moment Dorothy did as well.

"I'd like to talk to you later, Kate, if you're free," Tony said. "I'll be coming back here right after I drive Mom home."

"I have a meeting in a few minutes, but after that the day looks pretty flexible," Kate assured him. Her voice was quiet and confident, but the look she gave him wasn't at all. Her green eyes were troubled and sad.

He longed to wrap his arms around her, tell her how sorry he was for everything that had and hadn't happened between them. He wanted to pick her up and take her somewhere far away, where there was room service and a wide bed and nobody either of them knew. He thought of his patients, the endless tasks that awaited him here at St. Joe's, his father upstairs, McKensy, the rest of his family waiting to hear from him. Frustration threatened to choke him. For a moment he balanced all of that against the feelings he had for Kate.

The scales tipped all the way over.

"Kate, could you finish up in the next hour and take the rest of the afternoon off?"

Her eyes widened and she shook her head. "I don't think—"

She stopped and really looked at him, and he tried to put everything he was feeling into that single moment of eye contact. He must have succeeded a little, because at last she nodded.

"I guess I could, Tony." She sounded uncertain, but at least she'd agreed to try.

Not even daring to hope, he drove his mother home.

He'd called the house, worried that McKensy was alone, and Judy had answered. Dorothy had phoned her early that morning and said she had a toothache and had to go to the dentist, and would Judy come into town and care for McKensy.

"Dental appointment, huh?" Tony told Judy what had occurred in Ford's room. "I honestly feel like admitting her to the psych ward."

Judy let out a horrified gasp, then after a few seconds of silence said, "Maybe you should. Mom needs help."

It had been an enormous relief, knowing that his sister understood and supported his feelings about Dorothy.

"I'm going to give you a sedative when we get home so you can rest awhile, but you do understand that you have to go to counseling," he told Dorothy sternly as he negotiated the morning traffic. "Either that, or I'll admit you to the psych ward at St. Joe's." He hated to threaten her, but he knew his mother well. She'd promise today, and tomorrow she'd find a reason to break that promise. "I'm going to insist you stay with counseling until you've resolved this anger. And until that happens, I'll make other arrangements for McKensy's care, Mother. I will not have my daughter exposed to your irrational emotions any longer."

To his surprise, Dorothy didn't argue. "Kate said she knew somebody I could talk to, a woman at the hospital." Her voice was subdued. She hadn't apologized, but neither had she defended what she'd done. "Please don't get someone else to care for McKensy," she pleaded in a broken voice. "I promise I'll do whatever you say, but don't take McKensy away from me.''

Tony sighed. How many times had she said that in the past?

"Promises aren't enough this time, Mom. Until I'm convinced you've made a real effort, McKensy will be staying with Judy.'' Feeling like a tyrant, but knowing it was the only thing to do, Tony handed his sobbing mother a box of tissues. "And another thing, it's past time you divorced my father. It's one last way of hanging on, and you've got to let go, Mom. For your sake, and for his, too. I know a lawyer—I'll make an appointment for you.''

He should have said that to her a long time ago, Tony admitted. It was partly his fault, this whole fiasco. He probably could have prevented it. He remembered Kate suggesting that Dorothy have counseling in anger management, and how easily he'd dismissed the idea. Now, thinking back on the scene in Ford's room, he shuddered.

Who knew what his mother might have done if he and Betsy hadn't arrived back in Ford's room when they did? Dorothy had been totally out of control. He didn't want to believe that she would have been capable of physical violence, but he couldn't deny the possibility, either. He'd felt the absolute rage vibrating in her body.

Judy was waiting for them at Tony's house. They'd agreed that Dorothy shouldn't be alone, and neither was she in any shape to care for McKensy.

Tony stood by while his mother swallowed the sedatives and then went quietly to her room.

Judy, pale faced and wide eyed, whispered, "How's Dad?"

It was the first time Tony had ever heard his sister call their father Dad. "He seems to be okay, at least for the moment. We'll have to see how the day progresses." He explained about the bone scans and the possibility that the cancer had spread.

"I hope he doesn't— He isn't going to die right away, is he, Tony? I mean, I know he's really sick, and you said it was just a matter of time, but I hope he gets a chance to enjoy the rest of his stay here in Vancouver." She hesitated and then blurted, "He's a good man, isn't he?"

Tony put his arm around her and gave her a reassuring hug. "Yeah, he really is."

Judy hugged him back. "I thought—well, it was really Peter's idea, but I agree with him. We wondered if maybe Betsy and Dad would like to come and stay with us instead of that hotel? It doesn't seem right when we've got plenty of room. When will he get out of the hospital?"

Tony felt a rush of overwhelming affection for his sister. It had bothered him, not being able to ask Ford and Betsy to stay with him.

"That's a great idea, but won't it cause you problems with Mom?" Judy had always needed their mother's approval more than he had.

Judy's chin came up. "Yeah, I suppose it will.

But I can see now that it's wrong to agree with her all the time. I've done way too much of that already."

"Ask them, then. I know they'll be pleased," he told Judy. "And now I've got to get back to St. Joe's."

He knew it was unwise to use his cell phone while he was driving, but he did it, anyway. He had a date with a lady, and he had no intentions of being late.

CHAPTER TWENTY-ONE

"WHERE ARE WE GOING?" Kate slid into the car beside him, and the instant she closed the door and fastened her seat belt, Tony pulled into traffic and sighed with relief. Until this moment, he hadn't been sure he'd be able to pull this off.

There'd been a woman in Kate's office when he got there, and she was crying. Kate shot him a helpless look and motioned him out.

He'd paced the hall for what seemed an hour, trying to avoid making eye contact with anyone who might have something they wanted to discuss with him.

At last, the red-eyed woman had scurried out of Kate's office and he strode in just in time to see her reach for the ringing telephone.

"Don't touch that." His voice was louder than he'd intended, but he was desperate.

She jumped, and then slowly replaced the receiver.

"Tony, what—"

"Sh." With one hand, he snatched her handbag from the top of the file cabinet. With the other he took firm hold of her fingers.

"Don't answer if anyone speaks to you. Don't meet anyone's eyes. Walk as fast as you can," he instructed, leading the way to the elevator.

"Tony, I don't understand."

"Just trust me on this."

Several of the hospital's cleaning staff were on the elevator with floor mops and a bucket on wheels. Kate raised questioning eyebrows at him, but he shook his head and put a quelling finger on her soft lips.

Even with traffic, it only took fifteen minutes to reach the waterfront hotel. He pulled in under the awning and thrust his keys at the parking valet.

"Room 518, O'Connor," he snapped, hauling Kate out of the car before the bellman had even started across the tarmac.

Inside the opulent lobby, he stopped at the desk only long enough to retrieve the room card and, with one sinister glare, wipe the smirk off the face of the youthful clerk who asked about luggage.

He was pleased to see that 518 had a panoramic view of the inlet, a king-size bed and an extensive room service menu. The ice bucket holding the champagne he'd ordered was on the dresser, the vase with the dozen red roses on the coffee table. Tony kicked off his shoes and only then realized that he was wearing the same clothes he'd put on to go to dinner the night before. His feet probably smelled. In fact, all of him likely did.

He shoved his shoes back on and opened the

closet, relieved when he spotted the lush white robes hanging in it. There was a bathroom with a glassed-in shower, which he'd use in a minute. As soon as he talked to Kate.

She was watching him without saying anything, then she dropped her handbag on the floor and walked to the window. Turning back to look at him, she said, "Tony? What's this all about?" She sounded confused and wary.

She had every right to be.

He started feeling nervous. Maybe she was getting the wrong impression. Maybe she thought he'd brought her here just for sex.

"It's not Edmonton, but it's the best I could do on short notice." He hauled in a deep breath. "There're so many things I need to say to you, Kate, and I don't want us to be interrupted. There doesn't seem to be a single damned place we can go to be alone." He motioned to a soft gray armchair. "Just come over here and sit down. Please?"

She hesitated, but she finally sat. When she was settled, he tried to figure out where to begin, and decided that the end would probably be the best. Who knew how much time they'd have before somebody banged at the door for God only knew what reason. And it was getting harder and harder to keep his hands off her.

He dropped to one knee in front of her.

"I love you, Kate, more than I can say. Will you marry me?"

Her mouth dropped open. When she didn't say anything, panic set in.

"I know we've got a million things to settle between us. I acted like an idiot at work, and I'm sorry about that. All I can say is I *am* learning all this stuff about mistakes and admitting to them. I'm trying, Kate. You'd be taking on McKensy as well as me, but she's been in love with you from the beginning. I know your Eliza doesn't much like me, but I promise you, Kate, she will eventually. She's already got a father, but I'll do my best to be her friend."

He rubbed a hand over his chin and realized he hadn't shaved since yesterday. "I can't honestly promise much about your ex, but I will do my best not to murder the guy. We'll put some locks on the bedroom door, maybe. And you're going to have Dorothy to contend with. I know that's asking a lot of you, but it does give both of us a real chance to practice your ideas about dealing with angry people—"

She still wasn't saying anything. The energy that had fueled him through the long, difficult night and this even longer morning was gone all of a sudden, and he deflated like a popped balloon.

"Hell. I guess this is a huge mistake. You're not in love with me."

"Yes, I am." Her voice was soft, and so were her hands. She put them on each side of his whiskery face and looked into his bloodshot eyes. Hers were shimmering. "I have been for a long time, but I'd stopped hoping."

He was starting to again. "I can't figure out where we'll live, Kate. I can't ask Dorothy to move out on top of everything else." Inspiration struck. "Maybe we can sell both houses and buy a triplex. That way everybody'll have their own space."

She nodded. "Okay. But my suite is for rent. Dorothy could live there if she wanted."

It took a moment, but he got it. And grew worried all over again. He knew how much she loved her stepdaughter. "What about Eliza?"

"She's with her dad, but I've got partial custody. She spends half her time with each of us. You were right about me—I needed to take my own life back again. I think it's going to work out fine. For all of us."

His sense of relief was so great he bent his head and rested it on her lap. His knee was aching, and more than anything in the world he wanted to lie down with her in that giant king-size bed. After he had a shower. After she said what she still hadn't said.

"So, Kate?" She smelled so good. He could feel the warmth of her skin through her cotton skirt. "What do you say?"

He knew she was smiling.

"Yes, I say yes. Yes, Tony, I'll marry you." There was fierce joy in her voice. "I love you so very much. We'll be a family, you and I and the girls. But first can we go on a honeymoon? Just the two of us?''

His relief was so great he had to squeeze his eyes tightly shut or embarrass himself totally. He thought of his father, of how precious each moment was.

''Anywhere in the world, my love. Paris, Rome. Anywhere.''

Anywhere was perfect when two people had a lifetime of loving to share.

EPILOGUE

THE CEREMONY WAS HELD in the back garden of the small brick house. Exotic birds twittered, and the heady smell of roses and hibiscus filled the late September afternoon.

Tony held tight to Kate's hand while the majestic words of the marriage service were read, and he winked at her every now and then as she swiped at her brimming eyes with a tissue. All the women were crying, and many of the men's eyes were suspiciously damp, as well.

"In sickness and in health…"

Betsy tipped her head back and with a radiant expression looked up into the eyes of the man she loved as each of them repeated the age-old vows.

Ford was growing thinner by the day. The blue suit Tony had helped buy just a few days ago already hung in loose folds on his father's gaunt frame, but by some miracle Ford's mind remained clear. The Decadron had given him this window of time, he'd assured Tony, to complete the things that mattered to him, and marrying Betsy mattered most of all.

Dorothy had agreed to the divorce, and with the

assistance of a judge who was one of Tony's patients, the decree had been hurried through.

As his father's best man, Tony had Betsy's gold wedding ring looped on his little finger. When the moment came, he pressed it firmly into his father's hand, so Ford could slide it on his bride's finger.

"With this ring, I thee wed..." Ford's voice was weak, but the power of his emotion rang strong and clear. "With my body, I thee worship, and with all my worldly goods I thee endow."

Overcome with feeling, Tony turned his head to look at Kate. They, too, had repeated these holy vows just ten days ago, half a world away, in the Vancouver church his family attended, where first his grandfather and then his mother played the organ. Dorothy had played for their wedding.

In this small garden in Brisbane, there was only birdsong as background music. Just fourteen people were gathered here to witness the ceremony, close friends of Ford and Betsy.

In Vancouver, it had seemed to Tony that half the city was there. Kate had wanted a big wedding, and the females in Tony's family had been overjoyed. The men had given him sage advice.

"Lie low and just agree to everything." He'd found it invaluable.

McKensy and Eliza were flower girls, Leslie was matron of honor, Georgia a bridesmaid. His entire family turned out in force, cousins and aunts and uncles, nieces and nephews. Kate's sister and her family flew in, friends and co-workers from St. Joe's demanded invitations, and patients brought gifts.

The day of his wedding, Tony missed his father more than he'd ever thought possible. Ford and Betsy had flown back to Brisbane two weeks earlier.

"It wouldn't be fair to your mother," Ford had said when Tony pressed him to stay. "Kate's a grand girl, I'm honored I've had a chance to get to know her. And I'll be thinking of you on your wedding day, lad. But the only two people who really matter at a wedding are the bride and groom."

After Ford was released from St. Joe's, he and Betsy stayed with Judy for the remainder of their visit. Dorothy tried her best to change Judy's mind, and when tears and tantrums didn't work, she flew off to Portland in a huff to visit a friend for the duration of Ford and Betsy's visit.

Those few days had been one of the happiest family times Tony could ever remember. Judy organized a picnic to celebrate Kate and Tony's engagement, and Margaret and Georgia followed suit with barbecues and potlucks. The mood of the family changed without Dorothy there to dampen it. Even Wilson managed a joke or two. The entire family gathered at the airport when Ford and Betsy left, and the parting had been emotional on both sides.

It was Kate who insisted on Australia for their

honeymoon. When the telegram arrived announcing that Ford and Betsy were marrying, she'd asked Tony to cancel the Bermuda trip.

"We're flying to Brisbane. Going to a wedding has to be the best way to start a honeymoon," she'd said in a tone that brooked no argument. Tony hadn't thought he could love her more than he already did, but at that moment his heart felt as if it would burst from his body.

It felt the same way now.

"To love and to cherish until death us do part," Ford was repeating, and the poignancy of the moment hung in the air, touching every heart.

"What therefore God hath joined together, let no man put asunder. I now pronounce you husband and wife. Ford, you may kiss the bride."

Incandescent joy radiated from Ford's face and reflected back from Betsy's. He gathered her gently into his arms and lowered his mouth to hers.

Tony put an arm around Kate and gathered her into his embrace, thinking of what his father had once told him.

Ford had been so right.

In the end, love was really all that mattered.

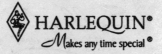

Coming in May 2002

**Three Bravo men marry for convenience—
but will they love in leisure? Find out in
Christine Rimmer's *Bravo Family Ties!***

Cash—for stealing a young woman's innocence, and to
give their baby a name, in *The Nine-Month Marriage*

Nate—for the sake of a codicil in his beloved
grandfather's will, in *Marriage by Necessity*

Zach—for the unlucky-in-love rancher's chance to
have a marriage—even of convenience—
with the woman he *really* loves!

BRAVO
FAMILY TIES

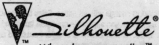

Where love comes alive™

Visit Silhouette at www.eHarlequin.com   BR3BFT

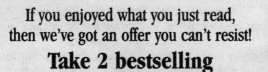

If you enjoyed what you just read,
then we've got an offer you can't resist!

Take 2 bestselling
love stories FREE!
Plus get a FREE surprise gift!

Clip this page and mail it to Harlequin Reader Service®

IN U.S.A.	IN CANADA
3010 Walden Ave.	P.O. Box 609
P.O. Box 1867	Fort Erie, Ontario
Buffalo, N.Y. 14240-1867	L2A 5X3

YES! Please send me 2 free Harlequin Superromance® novels and my free surprise gift. After receiving them, if I don't wish to receive anymore, I can return the shipping statement marked cancel. If I don't cancel, I will receive 6 brand-new novels every month, before they're available in stores. In the U.S.A., bill me at the bargain price of $4.05 plus 25¢ shipping and handling per book and applicable sales tax, if any*. In Canada, bill me at the bargain price of $4.46 plus 25¢ shipping and handling per book and applicable taxes**. That's the complete price, and a saving of at least 10% off the cover prices—what a great deal! I understand that accepting the 2 free books and gift places me under no obligation ever to buy any books. I can always return a shipment and cancel at any time. Even if I never buy another book from Harlequin, the 2 free books and gift are mine to keep forever.

135 HEN DFNA
336 HEN DFNC

Name	(PLEASE PRINT)	
Address	Apt.#	
City	State/Prov.	Zip/Postal Code

* Terms and prices subject to change without notice. Sales tax applicable in N.Y.
** Canadian residents will be charged applicable provincial taxes and GST.
  All orders subject to approval. Offer limited to one per household and not valid to
  current Harlequin Superromance® subscribers.
® is a registered trademark of Harlequin Enterprises Limited.

SUP01   ©1998 Harlequin Enterprises Limited

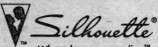